Miranda

BOOKS BY DIANN SHADDOX

A Faded Cottage

Whispering Fog

Miranda

Miranda

DIANN SHADDOX

Graphic Designs by Exousia Marketing Group

MIRANDA

By Diann Shaddox

This is a work of fiction. All characters, places, businesses, and incidents are from the author's imagination. Any resemblance to actual places, people, or events is purely coincidental. Any trademarks mentioned herein are not authorized by the trademark owners and do not in any way mean the work is sponsored by or associated with the trademark owners. Any trademarks used are specifically in a descriptive capacity.

The unauthorized reproduction or distribution of this work is illegal. Criminal copyright infringement is investigated by the FBI and is punishable by up to 5 years in federal prison and a fine of $250,000.

ALL RIGHTS RESERVED: No part of this book may be reproduced, stored in a retrieval system, or transmitted, in any form or by any means, without the prior permission in writing of the publisher, nor be otherwise circulated in any form of binding or cover other than that in which it is published and without a similar condition including this condition being imposed on the subsequent purchaser. You do not have resell or distribution rights without the prior written permission of both the publisher and copyright owner of this book. This book cannot be copied in any format, sold, or otherwise transferred from your computer to another through upload, or for a fee.

Eagle Quill Publishing
www.eaglequillpublishing.com

First print Edition July, 2015
Printed in the United States of American

ISBN 978-0-9912805-6-8 (pbk.)

ISBN 978-0-9912805-7-5 (Hardback)

ISBN 978-0-9912805-8-2 (eBook)

Miranda Copyright © 2009, Diann Shaddox

This book is dedicated with love to Randy, my husband.

Acknowledgment

To Kim Poovey. Thank you for allowing me to use your photo on the front cover to bring Miranda to life.

Mary Hill "Hilly" Dewey, Karen Oates, Marsha Tolleson Rhodes, my editors. Thank you for your encouragement, kindness, your patience, and the many hours you have spent working with me. I will be forever grateful for everything you've done.

Miranda

Miranda

Prologue

Going Home

April 19th, 1955

The gray haired woman, Emily Grace Sims, stepped from her car. The car door closed; however, she didn't move; a lone tear escaped and ran down her face.

"Now, Emily Grace you stop that! There will be no more tears," a caring voice sang into the morning air bringing a smile to her face.

Her intense blue eyes stared at the stately house remembering that day in April when the ground shook with enormous power leaving death and destruction all around, but this house was a survivor standing tall for over a hundred years. The weeds now had taken over the once manicured gardens, but the heads of a few roses were poking through the mangled mess showing their magnificent colors of pink and red. The only thing missing from the home was the dark haired, hazel-eyed woman who had lived here for over fifty years.

Emily Grace's hand turned the doorknob as she pushed the wooden front door open. The only sound in the quiet home was the clicking of her shoes on the marble floor in the vestibule. A cobweb swayed from the ceiling in the slight breeze of the open door.

She made her way into the parlor. A layer of dust blanketed the furniture looking like ghosts covered in white cloths draped to the floor in the once spotless room. Stopping next to the massive bay window tears glistened in her eyes as she remembered times when this house was full of laughter and joy and she stared at the beautiful blue water surrounding the Golden Gate Bridge.

As she stepped one slow step at a time up the long staircase, her hand gripped the mahogany railing. Opening the bedroom door, her eyes panned the room. The dust-laden drapes hung elegantly framing the windows. The grandmother clock stood silent in the corner of the bedroom. The top of the bureau was covered with different sized pictures. Crossing the room, she lifted a picture frame and softly blew the dust from the glass revealing the faces of a petite woman holding a small girl with curly hair. The child's face, her face when she was three, peered up at the woman in the faded black and white photo.

Emily Grace set the picture frame down on the bureau and opened the top drawer. There, lying worn, was the soft leather journal that she'd come for. Her fingers tenderly caressed it as she moved to the chair next to the window. Lifting the white sheet from the flowery chair, she gently laid the cloth on the floor. Getting comfortable, Emily Grace snuggled against the curved back of the chair. Her eyes were drawn to the leather bound book opening it to the first page.

Lying between the first and second pages, broken and worn, was the symbol of love that had lasted a lifetime. The once light pink rose, so velvety and smooth with its long green stem, was now a brittle flower pressed between the pages, but its everlasting love would never die. The story of this pink rose, given to a young woman by a handsome gentleman, would live on, just as the words written in the journal.

Lying with the dried flower was this note:

My dear Emily Grace, don't shed any tears for me. The tragedies of my life have been indescribable. I have had tears of joy and tears of sorrow; the loss of my family, husband, and child, but the love I've known will hold in my heart and never fade. Always remember, one single rose means…I love you." With all my love forever, Miranda

In the quiet of the room, Emily Grace laid the note in the journal and slowly turned the tear-stained page and the words began to flow as she read the tender, sweet story. The words were written by a beautiful woman in an era when women were proper and men were genteel.

Miranda Cathleen Curry's Journal

My name is Miranda Cathleen Curry and I was born in the year 1870 in Boston, Massachusetts, to proud parents Daniel and Cathleen Curry. Today January 8th, 1882, is my 12th birthday and this journal, a gift from my momma, is for me to write all my dreams in of traveling and seeing this great country.

***

Friday morning January 13th, 1882, I woke early, dressed and was ready for school.

Reluctantly, I walked down the towering stairs to the dining room for breakfast. The room was ominously quiet—too quiet with only the sound of the crackle of the flames eating the logs in the fireplace. I called for Momma, but there was no answer. I yelled louder.

Marion, a plump, gray haired colored woman, our compassionate housekeeper of many years, came swishing into the room with her large brown dress swaying from side to side. I saw a look in the woman's dark squinty eyes that I'd never seen before, terrifying me.

"Lordy mercy…hush Miss Miranda…stop ya yelling. Ya need ta be quiet, 'cause yer mother 'n brother are sleeping 'n they need rest." Marion quickly silenced me, with the wave of her large hand.

"It's morning, why do they need to rest and why isn't Jonathon ready for school?" I insisted getting agitated wiggling my hands on the back of the chair.

"Never, ya mind, they're both ill 'n the doctor is upstairs with `em. Miss Miranda, jus' sit `n be quiet." Marion walked over to me and motioned for me to sit. "Mr. Curry will be down in a little while ta explain what's wrong with yer mother `n Jonathon. I'll go fix yer breakfast. Now do as I say, child," Marion said in a firm voice.

I couldn't sit in the dining room waiting for Poppa to come downstairs. I didn't have the patience and never did like to follow orders. Silently, I climbed the long staircase up to Momma's bedroom and peered through the partially opened door.

I could see Poppa sitting in a chair near Momma's bed. Momma lay on the large feather bed and the dim lamp glowed on her motionless face.

A short chubby man, Dr. Berry, spoke in a soft voice to Poppa.

"Daniel," said Dr. Berry with a long sigh as his shoulders drooped, "there's no easy way to say this. Cathleen has typhoid fever."

Poppa's body shivered as his head gradually turned from Momma and peered up at the doctor.

"I'm sorry Daniel, she and Jonathon probably became infected while helping the poor."

Poppa moaned.

"Cathleen's fever won't go down." The doctor shifted his feet nervously. "It has been staying around 104 and won't let up." The man's head shook. "I'm sorry. We'll make her as comfortable as possible, but there isn't very much I can do for her or Jonathon."

Poppa's eyes studied the doctor.

Dr. Berry leaned near Poppa. "I'll send a special nurse. She'll see to them, and she'll know how to keep them comfortable. Daniel, this is a very contagious and deadly disease. You and Miranda need to stay away from Cathleen and Jonathon so that you won't get infected," he said in a low warning voice. Dr. Berry's hand gripped Poppa's trembling shoulder

I felt my heart race as I stood by the bedroom door in the dark morning. How could the doctor consider that I couldn't see Momma or Jonathon? How dare he! Poppa would set him straight. My fists clamped tighter and tighter.

"Sorry Dr. Berry, but I'm not leaving Cathleen. She's my life and I'm staying right here with her. She'll be just fine," Poppa declared, his tear-filled eyes looked up at the doctor.

"I understand how you feel, but you have Miranda to think about. Cathleen wouldn't want her to get infected, and you certainly can't help them if you get infected. Now please, let my nurse see to them." The doctor pleaded. "I promise I'll not let you down."

The doctor moved close to the bed. "Daniel, see the flat, rose colored rash on Cathleen? She's been infected for a few weeks." His head shook. "I just hope no one else gets this or we could have an epidemic on our hands like Chicago did."

Poppa stood next to the doctor.

Dr. Berry squeezed his lips making a puckered face. "This is a very dangerous disease that could spread uncontrollably and many people could become sick."

With his eyes on Momma, Poppa's body slumped. His trembling hand held onto the back of the chair.

"Daniel," Dr. Berry's voice cracked, "You also need to be prepared. She'll become delirious in a week or two and won't remember you. You need to prepare yourself and Miranda."

The doctor paced the room. "I'm sorry that I have to tell you all of this. It's the hardest thing for me to do as a doctor," his head shook back and forth and he sighed, "not to be able to help a patient."

Poppa sat back down in the flowery chair with his body slumped over and his fingers laced as he opened and closed them. His head moved slowly up and down as he muttered he understood.

I began to sob.

Poppa hurried to the door. "Miranda Cathleen, what are you doing here?" He called out in his strong authoritative voice. "Honey, what did you hear?"

"Poppa," I sniffed, "I heard that Momma is very sick, and the doctor said I can't go see her. What does he mean, Momma won't know me?"

"Yes, your momma is very sick and Jonathon is too. You have to stay away from both of them." His lips quivered. "Will you promise me Miranda that you won't go near them? Your momma wouldn't want you to get sick."

"Poppa, do I really have to stay away from them?" I sobbed. "I don't know if I can." I wiped tears from my eyes on the sleeve of my dress.

"Yes, you heard Dr. Berry. We don't want to get sick, and they'll be better soon. Now, you need to go to school. Your momma would be upset if she knew you were missing school today. You be a good girl, hurry, get your things." He put his hands on my shoulders and looked me in the eyes. "You'll have to do as Marion says for a while, until your momma gets better."

"I promise to listen to Marion. Are you all right Poppa, you look very sad? Are you sure Momma will be better soon?"

"Yes, Miranda, Momma will be better soon and everything will be back to normal. Momma will be singing and busy in the house before you know it, and Jonathon will be playing ball and wanting to go with me to work. Everything will be fine. Now, please, you need to get ready for school," he said scooting me down the hallway.

"Okay Poppa." I turned around and grabbed him. Tears built in his eyes, and I knew he was trying to be strong for me. This wasn't right for me to leave, but I had to go to school, just as he'd asked. I'd see Momma when I got home in the afternoon. I'd promised to help, but didn't promise that I wouldn't go near them.

I made my way down the stairs. Marion stood at the bottom looking up, a frown covering her face. I'd disobeyed her. She handed me a piece of warm bread to eat and tenderly wiped my face with her apron.

"James," Marion called out, "ya bring the carriage around ta the front of the house. Ya see ta Miss Miranda 'n ya be sure she gets ta school," Marion insisted.

I saw in Marion's eyes with the same worry Poppa had but I was terrified and powerless until after school. I unwillingly slid onto the seat of the carriage. The clip-clop of the horse's hooves made time move slowly.

When I arrived at school, the Sisters stared with keen eyes. I could hear their whispers. Gossip had spread like wild fire about Momma's sickness.

Impatiently I went through the day without thinking about my schoolwork, only about Momma. It was the hardest day of my life. I watched the hands on the clock tick meticulously slow eventually nearing three o'clock. The bell rang and quickly I ran to my carriage.

Finally, James pulled on the reins letting the horse and carriage stop in front of the large front doors of my beloved home. I ran into the house, but my feet slid to an abrupt stop on the marble floor. Standing with her arms spread out wide in front of the mahogany stairs, Marion had intercepted me.

"Miss Miranda," Marion began with her stern eyes staring down on me, "ya know ya can't go upstairs ta see yer mother. Yer father said ya promise ta do as I say."

"Yes ma'am, but how are they doing?"

"They both are doing the same 'n they ain't gonna change soon. The doctor 'n nurse won't even allow me in the room ta see 'em. Ya have ta have patience child. Now eat yer apple pastries 'n do yer homework. Then ya can go play outback fer a while. The weather's nice." The old woman's shoulders hunched as she turned going into the kitchen.

I did as Marion asked, but my mind swirled as I ate the pastry. Jonathon was my world. I liked to hide from the real world in my books and dreams of traveling, but my brother always jarred me back to reality and kept me focused.

I had to talk to him. I listened. The house was silent. I scooted the dining room chair back and quietly left the room. Carefully, I walked up the stairs to Jonathon's room not making a sound. I'd promised Marion to do what she said, but I hadn't promised not to visit Jon. I was on a mission and nothing was going to stop me.

I grabbed my dress tightly so the petticoat wouldn't rustle as I crept down the long hallway. At the end, I could see the nurse in

Momma's bedroom sitting by the door reading a book. As I slowly opened Jonathon's bedroom door, it squeaked. I held my breath and didn't move. The nurse flinched but didn't notice me.

The bedroom was quiet and dark with only a low-lit lamp on the nightstand. The curtains had been pulled tight. I saw a motionless mound covered in colorful quilts in the center of the bed.

My eyes stayed fixed on the bed as I silently moved further into the room. Jonathon was a strapping boy full of energy, standing tall next to Poppa, but now he looked weak. The sight of him, his pale face as white as the sheet, lying so motionless was frightening.

I crept closer to his bed and squatted down next to him. "Jon, are you awake?" He didn't move.

"Jon, wake up," I begged.

His eyes slowly opened. Jonathon had light brownish-red hair with the bluest Irish eyes like Momma's, and the warmest smile that was all his. But today, his eyes were red and swollen and his ashen face was covered with red blotches.

"Miranda, what are you doing here?" Jonathon frantically asked. "You're not supposed to be in this room with me, you could get sick! You need to leave!"

"I'm not leaving until I talk to you." Tears grew in my eyes, but I wasn't going to cry. "What's going on?" I sniffed. "Why can't I talk to you and Momma?"

The look in Jonathon's once strong eyes was of fear. Tears flowed down his face. This wasn't right because Jon never cried. He always told me no more tears, that tears were a sign of weakness.

My voice quivered as I choked back tears, "Jon, what's this all about?"

"Miranda, you need to leave or you'll get sick too," he said with his voice quivering. "You can't be around Momma and me. We have a disease, called typhoid fever. It is very contagious, and you could get infected. Please, leave and go back downstairs with Marion," he begged.

My head shook no.

"You'll be able to talk to us later when we're feeling better," he said trying to catch his breath. Tears rushed down his flushed face. "Miranda, please leave."

"No! I heard the doctor say you aren't getting better. I'm not leaving you!" I moved closer to Jon. "I can't be without you and Momma," I pleaded. "I'm staying right here until you get well!

"Please…Miranda, do as I ask. Go downstairs. I don't want you to get sick."

"Jon, you have to help me with my schoolwork. What am I supposed to do?"

"Miranda," he sighed, lying back on his pillow, "what is the problem?"

Jonathon began to work on my arithmetic homework. A smile came over his drained face.

When my schoolwork was finished, he laid his head back on the feather pillow. I stood by the door and jokingly called out in a whisper, "I'll see you tomorrow, and you can't stop me."

A grin spread across his face as I quietly closed the bedroom door.

Days went by and I wasn't able to sneak into Momma's bedroom very often, but each day I visited Jonathon after school. Time after time, I gently wiped his heated face with the cool rag from the water bowl by the bed.

I asked him why he became sick and I didn't.

He laughed. "Miranda Cathleen, you're too stubborn and typhoid fever isn't coming near you."

Each day, I sat next to my brother's bed. We laughed and told stories just as we always had.

Wednesday, February 8, 1882, was a freezing dreary day. I came home from school, finished my snack in the dining room, and quietly slipped up the stairs to Jonathon's room. Hearing strange voices coming from his bedroom, I stopped at the door.

"Daniel, he lasted longer than I ever thought he could. He sure was a fighter," Dr. Berry said in a somber voice.

I froze in my spot and began to sob.

"Miranda Cathleen, what are you doing here?" questioned Poppa stepping out from Jonathon's bedroom into the hallway.

"I came to see Jon," I answered. "Poppa…what's going on? What was the doctor talking about? What did he mean that Jon had lasted longer than he thought?" My head swayed to the side. "I don't understand."

"Whoa! First, what do you mean? You came to see Jonathon; you weren't supposed to be visiting him."

"I've been here every day since he got sick," I said twisting my fingers together. "Poppa, can I see him? He was fine yesterday," I sniffed.

Poppa wiped my tears with his large fingers, and his caring arms enveloped me bringing me close.

I looked up at his quivering chin.

"Miranda…Jonathon died a little while ago and he isn't coming back. I'm…sorry, he was too sick," Poppa paused. "You shouldn't have been visiting him."

"No!" I yelled, "He's alright! You just don't want me to see him! He's fine. I talked to him yesterday and he was okay! He'll wake up! You'll see. He's sleeping! He's just joking with you!"

"No, Miranda, he won't wake up. I'm so sorry," said Poppa, his fingers wiping more tears from his eyes. "Very well, I'll let you in the room so you'll understand that he's gone," he said sadly. "This will prove to you that he's in Heaven."

I stayed in the doorway watching the expression on the doctor's face when Poppa told him that I'd been spending time with Jonathon. Poppa's hand motioned for me to come into the room.

The doctor and nurse stood near the window. Dr. Berry's eyes stayed fixed on my every move. His face stayed taut, not happy.

As I neared Jonathon's bed, I could see his stilled body and enclosed eyes. The redness that'd stayed on his face for weeks was gone. He looked restful, just as he did the first day I'd visited him.

I leaned over. "Jon, it's Miranda, wake up. Stop playing games. Do you hear me?" The young boy didn't move. "Jon, it's Miranda, please wake up. This isn't a game," I shouted. "I need to talk to you, and you need to tell everyone you're going to be alright."

Jonathon still didn't move.

Poppa slowly crossed the room. His arms wrapped around me. "Jonathon can't talk to you anymore," he said in a soft voice. "Miranda, I told you Jonathon is gone to Heaven, and he's at peace now."

"No!" I yelled pushing away from Poppa. "But Poppa, Jon is right here! He's only sleeping," I cried gasping for air.

Poppa's grip continued to hold me tight. "Jonathon is gone, Miranda," he said in a soft voice, "Please, tell him goodbye."

"Oh…I can't, Poppa. Please bring him back," I begged. "I don't want him to leave. What will I do without him?"

"We will make it together Miranda. Say goodbye," Poppa pleaded.

As I leaned near my brother, my falling tears dropped onto him. "Goodbye Jon, I love you. Please, please, don't leave me."

My throat tightened, choking me.

"Jon, please," I begged, "come back," my voice trailed off into the quiet, cold room.

Poppa pulled me away from Jonathon, and we walked out of the room. My body quivered. Jonathon couldn't be gone.

"Why, Poppa? Why did he have to get sick?"

"Miranda, life is full of things that we don't have a say in," Poppa said, staring at me with red puffy eyes. "You and I will make it; you'll see."

"Why didn't we get sick, Poppa? Why did Momma and Jon get sick?"

"Miranda," Poppa's voice trembled. He squatted. His short round fingers softly moved my wild hair from my face and he looked me straight in the eyes. "I don't know the answer, but God must have a purpose for us."

He became quiet as we made our way down the long staircase.

Marion stood at the bottom of the steps, her hands grabbed me, and she wiped my tears as she led me into the library.

Poppa turned around, his trembling hand gripping the stairs' railing. He was going back upstairs to be with Momma.

The grandfather clock ticked in the silent room. My eyes were pulled to the window as I stared into the darkness.

My chest was so tight with grief that it was difficult to breathe. Grief squeezed my throat and tried to suffocate me. This was my first meeting with loneliness, and I despised it from the start. From that moment on, I learned how to fight it and vowed it'd never win.

I sat by the window listening to the tick of the clock as the evening moved on, my mind not able to think.

"Miranda, it's time to eat," Poppa called from the dining room.

I sat down and lifted a piece of bread to my lips, but I couldn't take a bite. My soul had died just as Jon's person had.

Poppa stared at his food. We sat quietly, each lost in our own thoughts, and the only sound came from the crackling fire on that cold winter night.

"Miranda," Poppa's voice trembled. "You don't have to go to school for a few days. We need to plan Jonathon's funeral, and I'd like you to be a part of it. You knew what he liked best, and I'd like you to help me." His head dipped, and the back of his hand wiped the wetness from his face.

"I'll help you, Poppa," I promised. "What do you want me to do?"

"Tomorrow, we will go to the mortuary. I hope this isn't too hard on you. Are you alright?" he asked.

"Poppa, I'll do what you want me to," I said, tears racing down my face. I knew I had to be strong for Jonathon because he wouldn't want me to be a scaredy-cat or coward. *Miranda you need to be uncompromising*, he would say. I'd do what Jonathon wanted and make him proud of me; he had taught me well. I also knew Poppa needed me, and my life would never be the same after today.

The next few days seemed like a blur to me, but I did as I promised, helping Poppa. We planned the most amazing funeral for Jonathon.

Poppa placed Jonathon's casket in the large parlor of our home. People arrived continuously throughout the day. The sound of shoes drumming on the wood floors was tortuous, making me believe I'd surely go insane.

The day arrived for Jonathon's funeral. The crowds of people were amazing standing at the gravesite. The sun shone so brightly in the deep blue sky with soft cotton clouds floating overhead. I believed Jonathon was looking down on us. Momma hadn't improved any in the last few weeks, and worry was on Poppa's face when anyone would mention her name.

Days and weeks slowly crept by, and Momma's fever continued. I visited her after school just as I'd done with Jon, and I would sit and talk to her, but Momma only lay there with an empty gaze. Poppa had not told her about Jonathon, and I believed Momma would've died right then if she'd known the truth.

I remembered the doctor telling Poppa how Momma would get to the point of not knowing who we were, that the fever would take over, but I believed Momma did know us.

I stood each afternoon wiping her burning face with a cool rag, and I'd tell her about my day at school. Those blue eyes would peer up, so intensely, saying she understood. Taking care of Momma and losing Jonathon had taken a toll on Poppa, physically and mentally.

I woke early Monday morning March 6, 1882. I climbed from my bed and shivered to shake off the strangeness in the air. The house was quiet, even quieter than normal as I entered the dining room. My breakfast was missing from my plate. Sounds of sobbing were coming from the kitchen. I push the door open seeing Marion standing by the sink with her shoulders hunched. She heaved up great wails and cupped her face in her hands.

I knew what had come to pass and quickly ran panic-stricken up the stairs.

Momma's bedroom door stood open wide and the room was dark and cold. Poppa sat next to the bed leaning over with his head in his hands and his body quivering.

I became paralyzed knowing Momma was gone, just like Jonathon. She would never again sit and sing to me at night or tuck me into bed. How would Poppa and I make it without my momma and brother? They were the ones who made this house a home.

I unwillingly walked into the dimly lit bedroom and moved near the bed.

Poppa looked up with eyes glazed over. His trembling hand reached out to me.

"Miranda, your momma died in her sleep, and she is at peace now. Please come say goodbye to her, and remember she is with your brother."

Anger grew as I stood with my hands clutched into fists. I knew my momma had become sick because she took care of others. I stared at her velvety face, and my anger melted away. She had so much love for everyone, and she'd be upset with me for being so selfish.

My momma was a frisky woman, Irish through and through. She was born Cathleen Erin Brennan. Her family, potato farmers, had come to America from Ireland during the great famine of the 1840's to start a new life when she was a baby. Life had not been easy on her growing up with immigrant parents who worked hard to support her along with her three brothers and two sisters, but she wouldn't let that get her spirit down.

Naturally, she had the beautiful long wavy red hair and those amazing blue eyes. I had always wished I'd looked like my momma, but my father, who was half-Irish and half-Spanish, thought I was beautiful. I had the look of the Spanish, with my dark hazel eyes and darker hair, but I did inherit her white ivory face and the Irish temper. She taught me to be strong and never give up believing in myself.

I reluctantly leaned over near the bed. "Momma, I love you," I whispered. "I miss you so much. Please tell Jon I miss him, but Poppa and I'll make it, just as the two of you would want."

I fixed Momma's gorgeous wavy hair letting it curl by her ivory face. I knew she wasn't going to wake up, just like Jonathon, and I'd never see her beautiful eyes. I couldn't believe once again I was saying goodbye to someone I loved. How could I have lost my momma and brother so quickly? Our lives had been perfect.

I understood what I had to do—take care of Poppa. The one thing my momma had asked me to do, when she first became sick, was to see to Poppa. I turned and looked at him. He still had his head in his hands. I knew at that moment this was going to be a big job for me, and I was going to take it seriously.

I bent down giving him a hug. He grabbed me tightly as if to cling to life itself.

"What do I do now, Miranda? I can't go on without your mother; she's my life."

I learned at that moment that my poppa wasn't as strong as I'd once believed. He was a great and kind man, but without Momma, he was lost. Cathleen was the strength behind him.

"We'll be alright," I assured. My eyes turned to Momma lying so peacefully and beautiful. I know that she had taught me well on how to be resilient.

I squatted down by Poppa. "I promised Momma we would be fine. She wasn't a quitter and neither are you. Now, we need to make plans for her funeral. Poppa, I'll help you get through this."

I knew I was only twelve, but I'd grown up a lot in the past few weeks. My life as an innocent child was in the past, and I had responsibilities now. I'd see to Poppa and help with the funeral arrangements. I stopped in the bedroom doorway and looked back at Poppa. I would always remember what Jonathon had said. Wiping the tears from my eyes I heard, *there will be no more tears*.

I left Poppa sitting next to Momma's bed and went downstairs. I called for Dr. Berry and asked him to come to the house to help Poppa.

After the funeral, the house became quiet; there wasn't any laughter or singing anymore. Poppa went to work every day and I went to school. I spent all my extra time reading and hiding away in my dreams of traveling across this great country. I didn't want to be lonely.

A Single Tulip

T ime has gone by since I was a young girl of twelve. I am now a young woman of twenty. I've finished my schooling and learned to run this home and help Papa with his work. My days stay busy and my evenings are full of reading and planning. I'd never given up my dream to travel the world.

My life did change the spring of 1890.

It was cold and drizzly Saturday, the 19th of April, a fitting day that reflected my feelings. I stepped out of my nice dry carriage at the cemetery. I stood alone. The mud oozed covering my shoes. I reluctantly began to walk through the slush on the path I'd taken eight years before. The bottom of my dress was wet becoming heavy with mud. The skies were ready to open up and drench me with a flood of cold rain.

Even as the 19th century was nearing its end, I continued the charade of protocol of wearing my long flowing, deep black mourning dress. I loathed the crepe dress with a vengeance. Everything was black—my shoes, cape, nothing had color—a sign of loneliness. It was a punishment, and I was wearing it like a big banner for all to see. My life was being smothered by the conventions of society.

I leaned on my parasol. My black bonnet's veil with silky ribbons covered my long dark hair that was pulled up on top of my head. Its veil hung over my face so I was able to hide from everyone.

Miranda, you can do this, I kept hearing the words repeatedly in my mind.

The sadness of my heart ripped my insides apart. My hands curled, tightening as they clenched into fists. I would not cry. The tears I had for my Poppa would not be shown to all of these people. I'd been taught well. My teeth bit into my lips. I'd never let my quivering lips show.

The cemetery was full of many people hoping to pay their respect for my poppa. This was the largest funeral in Boston in many years. Poppa owned one of the most successful companies in the city, Curry Distributors.

I stood straight and tall as my eyes scoured the crowd in the gray gloominess, seeing scores of carriages with their drivers as they waited at the cemetery's edge. My head was held high while I listened to Father Mulligan speak his words about my father.

"Daniel Curry, a nobleman, has been very generous to this great city and to all the people who helped him when he began his company so many years ago. We are paying our respects to an amazing man on this day of our Lord, April 19th, 1890. Daniel has been very benevolent to our church, and we will never forget how compassionate he was."

Father Mulligan turned toward me. "Miranda, I want you to know how much we appreciated your father and how he will be dearly missed by many." Father Mulligan lowered his head and his prayer began.

I bent my head down seeing the lone red tulip with white stripes, my Poppa's favorite flower, the Semper Augustus known as the "broken" tulip from Holland, in my hands. I placed the flower on Poppa's casket. He had always wanted to visit Holland, but wouldn't take the time off from work to travel.

The red and white tulip lay on the mahogany casket so beautifully, so softly. I squatted near the casket letting my fingers gently touch it.

"Poppa," I whispered, fighting back tears. "I love you and I'll miss you so much, but I have to leave this town." My throat tightened. "I have dreams like you did, and I have to follow them. I hope you understand and aren't disappointed in me." My eyes looked at the single tulip lying so lonely. No, I couldn't end up like that tulip, all alone. I whispered, "I trust you have found the peace and happiness you deserve." I drew in a breath of air, fighting back tears.

Before I stood, my eyes fixed upon the other two mounds next to Poppa's casket. "Momma, Jon," I whispered, "I love you both. I miss you dreadfully." I wiped a wild tear from the corner of my eye. "The three of you will be forever in my heart…" I didn't want to move, staring at the three graves. I wanted to scream. This was all my family. Could I follow my dreams, leaving my family behind?

I stood from the graves, straightened my dress getting my composure back, and slipped my gloves off. I searched the crowd looking out at all the people standing and waiting to come near to say their last good wishes for Poppa. I scooted back, making room for them to tell Poppa goodbye.

One by one, they came near and each shook my hand. The first were the executives of Curry Distributors, who were not sorry Poppa was gone. Their pretentiousness was evident as I remembered many of them trying to take over the company from Poppa.

Then the workers of the company and local storeowners came by. They shook hands with their rough, calloused hands. Many of the men stood with tears in their eyes and their voices cracked holding back their feelings. The line of people saying good-bye kept going and going.

But, the exhausting day finally did end. Alone now, wet and muddy,

I looked at the one single tulip and said a prayer. Sadly, I said goodbye to Poppa. I turned and made my way back to the carriage.

I saw a few people standing and talking on the hillside. Mr. Simon, one of the company executives walked up. "Miss Miranda, if I could speak to you for just a minute. I don't want to interfere with your grief, but I'd like a word with you."

I stopped and turned toward him giving him a hard glare. "Yes, what can I do for you?" I said with a stern voice, clenching my jaw.

"We really need to have a meeting to discuss Curry Distributors. Would Monday at eight thirty be too soon for you?" he inquired.

"I'm busy Monday, but Tuesday morning at eight thirty would be fine. You need to keep the company running the way my father had wanted," I snapped. "We will discuss its future at that time."

I turned and left the man standing alone. As I walked to the carriage, my shoes squished in the mud.

"That will be just fine, Miss Miranda." Mr. Simon called back.

James opened the door of the carriage, and I slid into the old leather seat.

"Thank you, James," I said, looking at Mr. Simon who was talking to the other men.

I couldn't believe the men had already come to me about the company. Poppa wasn't even in the ground. I knew I had a challenge, and I was going to learn fast why Poppa felt like he did about those men.

The carriage began gradually to roll. Tears finally streamed down my face. I was leaving all my family behind on that cold gray day. I looked out the carriage window. The sky was full of clouds that were heavy with rain, just like my heart.

My Safe Haven

Holding the ends of my dress that were sagging with drying mud, I entered into the unbearably quiet home. A dark grayness had come over Poppa's library and the once warm inviting room was cold, even with the fire in the fireplace radiating heat. Only the light of a lone lamp sitting on Poppa's huge mahogany desk glowed in the darkened room. I drew the velvet blue drapes from the window and stood watching the rain gush from the sky and dance on the ground.

An avalanche of feelings consumed me and memories cascaded into my mind about our home.

It was a beautiful sunny day in May 1875 when my father, brother, momma and I first saw this huge house. I was only a young girl of five, but I remember the look on Momma's soft creamy face.

"Well, Cathleen, what do you think of this house?" Poppa proudly asked, a huge grin on his face.

"Oh, Daniel, the home is perfect," she answered with tears of joy building in her eyes.

"Well then, Jonathon, what do you and Miranda Cathleen think of the house?"

My tiny head peered out the carriage window staring at the soaring brick home in front of me. A tall, brick, ivy consumed wall, matching the house, surrounded the sides and back yard. A black, wrought iron fence with massive gates sat as a guard across the front.

"It's wonderful, Dad," Jonathon chimed in. "Can we go in?"

"Of course, are you ready, Cathleen?"

"I'm as ready as I'll ever be," my momma answered breathing in a big drink of air.

My father reached up and took my momma's hand helping her out of the carriage.

He turned to me and a huge smile crossed his face almost touching each of his ears. Poppa wasn't a large man, but he picked me up and swirled me around in a circle. At that moment, he was the happiest man in the world.

Poppa had grown up very poor; his father had died when he was a baby. He had started working at the age of five to help his mamma, but now his life had changed, and it couldn't be any more perfect.

He was short in stature with dark, wavy hair and brown eyes. He was handsome, at least in my mind. He called himself a mutt, but was proud of both heritages of his father, an Irishman, and his mother, Castilian Spanish.

Poppa gently put me down and proudly led us up the steps to two large wooden doors. Flinging them open wide, he welcomed us in. Our footsteps echoed on the marble floors as we marched inside. The sunshine followed us in and flowed throughout the main hall.

In front of us was a large vestibule and to the right was a curved, wooden mahogany staircase that seemed to go on forever. On the other side of the front doors, to the left, was a huge magnificent library. It had massive French doors and wooden, hand carved bookshelves that reached to the ceiling.

Poppa proudly led us up the splendid staircase. Jonathon and I ran ahead of our parents, and I darted past Jonathon finding the most fantastic bedroom that overlooked the backyard. Outside the room was an enchanting old twisted tree that had limbs coming right up to the window. The limbs were like outstretched arms, ready to encompass me with warmth. My bedroom was my new hideaway.

My head shook. "No," I whispered wanting to scream into the darkness as my thoughts from the past faded away leaving reality in its place. "This can't be true. I can't be alone."

Tears ran from my eyes and my body shuttered with realism. It was true. I was on my own as I stared out the window of Poppa's library into the late afternoon, not wanting my memories to vanish. I didn't want to remember that Poppa was gone, and the house was lonely.

Being lonely was the hardest thing for me, my albatross. I could deal with anything thrown at me in life. I was resilient, but loneliness was the most difficult. The solitude of the house was closing in, bleeding my soul. I believed that it could take the life right out of me, and I'd surely die along with the rest of my family.

The day was overwhelming as I made my way to the kitchen.

"Marion," I called out, pushing the kitchen door open. "I'm ready to eat."

"Yes, Miss Miranda." Marion's face tightened as tears brimmed in her compassionate eyes.

I held onto a kitchen chair's back steadying myself. "I'm not very hungry, and I can't go into the dining room, not tonight. Can you serve me here in the kitchen, please?"

"Yes child, that won't be a problem," Marion assured. "Sit down 'n stop worrying so."

The warmth of the kitchen hugged me. I'd always felt so protected here, able to breathe. Loneliness wouldn't venture into this room. I smiled to myself; Marion wouldn't allow Loneliness in this room and, if it tried to enter in, she would swish it away with her big apron.

"Here's yer bread, Miss Miranda. I'll be right back with yer stew," she said placing a basket on the small table.

"Thank you, Marion," I said gratefully.

I sat there staring at the bread.

"Please, Miss Miranda, ya need ta eat 'n keep yer strength. Yer father wouldn't want ya ta sit around 'n be sad. He always wanted the best fer ya."

"I know Marion, but today," My head ducked. "Saying goodbye was difficult. I just don't know what I'm going to do," I whispered as I tried to keep the tears from flowing.

"Ya're going ta do what yer father did. He took one day at a time. Yer father didn't over think a problem. Give yourself time, child."

I picked up one of the warm biscuits with melted butter oozing out and took a bite. Before I finished the biscuit, Marion brought a bowl of her glorious Irish stew, one of my favorites. The steam from the warm bowl gave off an aroma transporting me back to times long ago. The stew was a reality that life would go on, without my poppa, but I didn't know if I wanted to believe that, not yet. The last drop of stew was just as good as the first.

I scooted the kitchen chair back under the table. "Thank you, Marion, for the stew. Goodnight."

"Goodnight, child," said Marion. Her large arms wrapped around my body. "Hope ya sleep well."

I knew each step, as if they were my friends, as I made my way up the long staircase to my bedroom, my sanctuary from the world.

I turned the knob pushing the door wide. I stopped moving.

My voice screamed out into the darkness. "No! I can't have black!" My nightgown lay on the bed. It was black. Even my books had black leather. I couldn't tolerate the thought of wearing black. I began ripping off every thread of black and threw it in a pile on the floor.

"I won't have any more black," I demanded.

The dim light of the lamp flickered in the safe haven. I cuddled my cream-colored sleeping gown in my arms slipping it over my head as the black disappeared from the room. I realize that I had to wear black as the façade of grief when I was out in public but I didn't want to.

I wrung out a soft cloth from the bowl of water that was sitting on my bureau and gently lay it on my face. I held it there for a few seconds feeling the refreshing cool liquid. The cloth slipped down from my face. I glared in the mirror at my puffy eyes and swollen red nose dotting the center of my almond-shape face.

I took in a deep breath. How could I really think of moving away from Boston? I had lived such a sheltered life growing up with everything taken care of right here in this home, never having to work at anything. My momma taught me to sew and crochet, but I wasn't good at either sewing or crocheting.

I sat in my comfortable chair looking out the window at the old giant tree in the backyard as its limbs gently swayed in the moonlight. The limbs put off shadows that danced across the window like lovers at a cotillion. The rain clouds raced by in the sky and left twinkling stars in their path.

Just as I'd done as a child, I picked up one of my books, *Stories of California,* and began to read. Reading had always helped me to escape.

My eyes tired. I gently placed the book on the bureau. I turned the key on the oil lamp letting the flame disappeared and climbed into my clean soft bed. My head dug deep into the feather pillow knowing I could hide from the world in this bed. My eyes closed with thoughts spinning in my head. Could I possibly leave my safe life and travel out West?

The next morning I woke early hearing the sweet singing of a cardinal outside the bedroom window. I felt at peace. The storm had vanished leaving a beautiful day. The drapes swung to each side of the window showcasing a crisp day. Serenading me, the cardinal in his coat of red was in his glory sitting in the old sprawled tree. I did as Marion said, *"When a cardinal sings to you, throw him a kiss for good luck."* I knew the tale when a cardinal visits, it's a loved one from Heaven.

The sun was exploding with splashes of light making the leaves of the tree glisten with the dampness of the rain. I reluctantly picked out a dismal black dress from the wardrobe and began the charade of wearing black. I slipped on my black shoes and draped my black shawl around my shoulders.

Reluctantly, I walked from my hiding place and descended unhurriedly down the stairs. I stopped at the bottom of the stairs and peered into the dining room. Pain came at me and landed a punch in my stomach. It took my breath away. Breakfast sat on the massive dining room table, just as it had each morning since we'd moved into the house.

Nothing had changed, except there was only one place sitting on the huge table. My hands covered my ears. *No, I can't stay in this house any longer and live with the silence.*

I sat in my chair just as I had each morning watching the flickering of the flames from the fireplace as they danced on the wall making unique shadows. Tears streamed from my eyes.

Dreams of the Future

Later that afternoon as I sat in the library, the sun began to sink into the evening sky. The reflection in the oversized plate glass window was one of a young woman draped in a crepe dress. The large chair engulfed her small frame with a childlike essence, and the outline of her well-formed body was easily distinguishable. The young girl's silhouette was rigid like a figurine, no emotion, as she sat so still.

I moaned. *Could that reflection possibly be me? I saw a proper young woman sitting so stiff that it appeared she never had a thought of her own and had done what she was told, young woman groomed her entire life to fit into the correct social order.*

I laughed. I knew the image was a fraud, not the real Miranda Cathleen Curry, a hardheaded, strong willed young woman, showing her quick Irish temper way too many times in public. I had grown up a mollycoddled, pampered child and had even been able to outsmart typhoid fever, an oddity in itself.

Now, I was going to cause a stir in the Boston society, a young girl traveling to the West, to San Francisco, California, without a chaperon. This would push the limits of decency; I would be the talk of the town for many months. I could see all the women sitting around in their little groups, gossiping about me and raising their eyebrows.

Old Miss Martindale would be the leader, her dress covering every inch of her body with the neck of her dress swallowing her head only showing her tiny beady eyes. "Did you hear about that poor little Curry girl losing her mind, traveling out West with the heathens? She'll surely never be heard of again. Such a shame!" Their heads would nod yes in agreement.

A lone tear gently slipped down my face. Maybe Miss Martindale was correct and I had gone mad. My eyes turned to the window seeing the reflection of the young girl softly fade leaving only darkness in its place.

A loud knocking at the front door startled me. I stood from the worn leather wingchair in the study. I straightened my dress and wiped the wetness from my face. I would not let anyone see me cry. My eyes peered through the tiny window of the door.

Standing on the front porch was Carlton Lambert II, a classmate of Jonathon's and a childhood friend.

I gradually opened the large wooden door and shuffled backwards allowing enough room for the young man to step inside the foyer. The tantalizing smell of fresh, sweet apple blossoms drifted into the house along with the soft cool breeze of Spring breathing new life into the room.

"Miranda," Carlton said firmly, standing erect with shoulders squared. "I hope I'm not intruding." He proceeded into the vestibule taking his white hat off, cupping it in his hands with confidence about him. "I arrived home and I heard the news of your father's death. My apologies that I couldn't be at the funeral." His head slightly tilted downwards. "I wanted to stop by to see if you needed anything, and to tell you how sorry I am for your loss."

"Thank you, Carlton," I said, wondering why after all these years he was here.

Marion walked up. "Miss Miranda, don't jus' stand there, invite the young gentleman into the parlor," she said in a firm voice, giving a sharp glance. She held out her hand and Carlton placed his hat on top. Marion maneuvered her body to the side toward the parlor, but stopped quickly. Her dark eyes glared back at the young man standing in front of her. "Lordy mercy, ya wouldn't be little Carlton Lambert?" she declared with a nervous chuckle.

"Yes ma'am, how have you been, Marion?" Carlton said laughing at her excitement. "It has been awhile," he answered, as he followed her into the parlor.

"I've been doing fine, Mr. Lambert. Please, have a seat," Marion said. "Miss Miranda," she whispered, "where is…yer manners?" She glared at me with one of her chastising looks and swished her large skirt as she turned around and walked out of the room. She huffed and puffed a muttered all the way down the great hall.

"Marion hasn't changed a bit, has she?" Carlton added shaking his head slowly back and forth. He straightened his jacket and sat down in a chair by the window.

"No, she's the same Marion, just like when we were kids," I assured.

I settled into the settee across from him. My eyes studied Carlton; he had grown up handsomely. He was taller than I'd remembered and had more composure and self-assurance, and in some ways was more brazen. He'd been easy to manipulate when we were children, but he was somehow different. He still had those greenish-brown eyes with the longest lashes and the sandy, wavy hair, just as he did as a child.

"It has been too long Miranda, hasn't it?" he offered, noticing my stares. His eyes roamed from my head to my toes and he took note that my once straight body had become curvy and shapely. "I've been away at school, and I've just passed the bar exam." His eyes squinted. "I plan to start working with my father at his law firm in a few weeks." Carlton let his words fade away, tilting his head with those eyes observing my every move.

I stood. "Would you like a drink?" I asked, finally remembering my manners. The rustle of my dress was the only sound in the quiet parlor as I made my way over to the sideboard in the corner of the room.

Carlton moved near me. His eyes scanned my body. I tensed, feeling his breathing so close.

"A bourbon and branch does sound nice," he declared, picking up the decanter of liquor pouring his own drink. "Would you like a nice cool drink, Miranda, maybe some sassafras tea?" he asked.

His body brushed up next to me. He gazed into my eyes with such self-confidence, not like the young boy that I used to intimidate.

"No, thank you…I'm fine," I assured, quickly scooting away from him, and slipping down onto the settee.

I took a deep breath, stunned. Instead of sitting in the chair, he scooted in beside me on the settee. I smelled the scent of the spirits he held in his hand and leaned my body away from his.

"Life had a strange twist with my coming home last night," Carlton said, slowly sipping his bourbon. "Miranda," he softly began, staring into my eyes. "I have thought about you often while I was away at school." He paused, taking a soft breath. "I've wondered how you were doing."

"You could have written," I replied, irritably.

He laughed, tilting his head back. "Still the feisty girl I remember; you haven't changed."

"Alright, Carlton, what is it you want?" I asked, straightening my shoulders, not shrinking away.

He grinned. Tenderly Carlton placed his hand on mine. "I would like to be able to come and visit you, to help you get through this trying time. I understand this has to be very difficult on you, losing your father so suddenly and now living in this huge home all alone," he assured as he softly caressed my hand.

My body steamed and my face became warm. I had just become the poor little rich girl who would need to be taken care of. This was more pathetic than I could imagine. This was only the beginning of men wanting to court me.

It would be socially correct for the Lamberts and Currys to marry and to breed like purebred animals, somehow making their children upper class. I laughed to myself, thinking that my parents grew up as the lower working class, thus making me a mutt with the window dressing of upper class. The estate had become my calling card, my dowry, it seemed. How could my life have changed so dramatically?

"Carlton," I said earnestly, "that is nice of you to think about me, but I'll be just fine. I have plans of my own."

He leaned against the settee with the same grin on his face. "The weather sure is nice this time of year," he added. "The daffodils are in full bloom with their yellow dotting the countryside. We should take a ride out into the country to Miller's Lake and have a picnic like we used to do when we were kids." He paused again, rotating his glass of bourbon in his hands. His eyes took in my expression. He wasn't backing down. "Remember those times when our group of the Franklin twins and Bennett's crew of five, along with Jonathon, would all go for a swim in Miller's Lake on those sultry summer days. It seemed when you were in the water that Jonathon was the only one who you'd allow to come near you. Of course, most of the time you and Mae sat on the bank watching the group as we played in the lake."

"I wasn't a strong swimmer when I was a child," I replied, trying to justify my actions. "It seemed the others liked dipping me under the water," I answered giving him a look, remembering he was one of the first to try and dunk me. "I did enjoy sitting on the cool grass by the lake more than playing in the water." My mind wandered with flashes of memories of those days sitting by the lake in the warm sun with my hair dripping water onto my skin keeping me cool. A simpler time.

He grinned. "I think I enjoyed the picnics as much as swimming in the lake. Especially, Mrs. Bennett's fried apple pies. Remember the fresh aroma of the apples and that crispy crust," he said, hesitating for a moment. Slowly he sipped his bourbon with a distressed look overtaking his face. "We had some great times back then," he added somberly, getting quiet.

"Yes, we did," I responded trying not to fall into his trap of relieving the past with all of the emotion it held. "Carlton, I miss Jonathon, too," I assured in a quiet voice.

"It's strange to be here in this house without him running down the stairs with Marion yelling at him," said Carlton as one eyebrow rose. "I haven't been back here in many years," he added, pressing his lips together.

I remembered the last time he was here in this home was to say goodbye to Jon, back when I was twelve and he was a boy of seventeen.

"Well," Carlton said with his composure coming back, gently sipping his bourbon very slowly. "Jon would be the first to tell us to move on."

"Yes," I agreed, "you're right. He did love the summer and going to Miller's Lake."

"Miranda, I treasure all of those past summers," Carlton said softly. "I see Caleb has your garden, prepared for the summer. It seems the buds on the bushes are ready to explode with color." A grin emerged on his face. "I've always loved the backyard of this estate, and I'm quite sure the gardens will be coming alive soon."

I finally laughed. I leaned back in the settee. He wasn't easily defeated and was very resourceful. I did like that about him.

Carlton kept grinning, not deterred with his plan of marrying me and moving into my home. I could see the determination in his eyes and knew he wasn't backing down. I understood his meaning; the garden in the backyard would be a beautiful place to hold an early summer wedding.

He gently patted my hand and gazed into my eyes. "I'll let you get some rest. I see how tired you are." He stood, moved to the sideboard, and set his glass down. "I'll call on you in a few days to see how you're doing. I have to go to New York tomorrow, but I'll be back in Boston the first of the next week."

I hurried ahead of him to the door. "I am tired," I admitted. "The days have been strenuous to me."

"It was nice to see you again. If you need anything, I'll be staying at my parents' home." His hand reached over and pulled open the door. He stopped and leaned down near me.

I stepped away. "Thank you, Carlton, for stopping by, but I'm doing just fine," I said handing him his hat. I held open the door, but he didn't move. He just stared at me for a few seconds before he casually stepped out onto the porch.

"Goodbye."

The door closed and I heaved a sigh of relief. I didn't move. I quietly watched as he walked off the porch and leisurely strolled down the steps with his hat twirling in his hands.

I turned around made my way to the kitchen, but I kept thinking about Carlton. I knew Marion would be all for me staying here in this home and marrying him.

"Miss Miranda…where's Mr. Lambert?" Marion asked. "Ya could have invited him ta have dinner with ya."

"He had to leave, Marion," I answered feeling overwhelmed with my new found state of affairs.

"Miss Miranda, he shor' is a nice young man 'n he comes from a good family." A smile grew on Marion's old face with those dark eyes peering into my soul. "He'd make a good husband fer ya. Ya know he's only a few years older and ya might not get more chances."

"I'm ready to eat, if dinner is prepared," I said quickly not wanting to discuss Carlton with her anymore.

With her infamous smile on her face, Marion turned and headed to the stove. She, too, had daunting ideas of a glorious wedding.

But I had different plans.

The Little Brass Lady

The next morning, I stared into the bureau's mirror in my bedroom. I shook my head from side to side and sighed. This was my new life. I had become the most eligible, wealthy, young woman in Boston. Men would be coming from all over the state trying to win my hand in marriage, along with this estate. Maybe I was as pathetic as others perceived, just as Carlton had said, a young woman living in this huge home all alone.

"Oh, this can't be real," I whispered. I shuddered, but not from the coolness of the room. The pain of loneliness had overcome my mind. Death had reared its head and ghosts of the past were reaching out to me and not letting go. My heart beat faster. The air dissipated from my lungs as I tried to catch my breath. Death was toying with me just as it had since I was a child. It was trying to break me, I dealt with it by getting angry, my Irish temper flared.

"You aren't winning," I yelled thrusting my fist in the air. "I, Miranda Cathleen Curry, will be victorious."

Sadness was consuming my mind. I clasped my hands together remembering long ago. The black of the house had closed in on me after losing Momma and Jon, and it continued for a year. Each day we added a little color that brought me back. I believed the black drove Poppa insane with the house so depressing and lonely. My poppa's soul, I was certain, died the day Momma died.

I couldn't live another year in black, and I couldn't let loneliness win. I had to leave this home and find my own dreams, my own life, as Jon would say throwing his hands in the air laughing. "Hell or high water, Miranda Cathleen, you will always survive." I was a survivor, but at the moment, my heart was breaking.

After breakfast I rose from the chair, scooted it back under the dining room table, and unhurriedly walked to Poppa's library with my head held high.

I sat in the desk chair. My eyes were pulled to the worn pipe lying on the massive mahogany desk, its home for many years. Carefully, I caressed it in my hands as the scent of pipe smoke lingered in the air. I placed it next to the little brass-lady tamper, knowing it would soon become tarnished without the caring touch the tamper was accustomed to. Tears grew in my eyes as the aroma of Poppa's pipe teased my senses. I didn't want my life to turn into a tarnished old gossip sitting around this house with the loneliness I despised consuming me.

I pulled out paper and a list began. First, I needed to go to the Boston and Albany Railroad Train Stations to find the train schedule and buy a ticket. I leaned back in the chair spinning it around. My excitement grew as I added to the list. I'd be riding the Union Pacific Railroad, the first Transcontinental Railroad, on my trip to California.

The desk chair crackled when I stood. I walked to the foyer and my eyes peered up at the huge staircase leading to my bedroom, my hideaway. My hand grasped the smooth wooden rail as I made my way up the stairs.

I studied my reflection in the mirror over the bureau. Could I really leave? Well, I sure wasn't going to sit around this huge house alone and was by no means going to look for a husband to take care of me. I'd never backed down from a donnybrook, and I sure wasn't going to start now. I laid the cool, wet cloth from the water bowl sitting on the bureau on my flushed face and eased my worries.

I smoothed my dress, pulled my shoulders tight, and slowly made my way down the stairs, as lady-like as my momma had taught me.

My head was held high as I walked into the dining room. Marion came out of the kitchen to greet me, just as she'd done when I was a child.

"Miss Miranda, yer lunch is ready. Where would ya like ta eat today?"

"I think I'll eat in the dining room if you don't mind, Marion."

"That's fines, I'm glad y're feeling better."

Marion placed a plate of boxty in front of me. "Here, Miss Miranda, I hope ya enjoy yer meal," she offered hurrying to the kitchen.

"Thank you, Marion."

I took a bite of the round, Irish potato pancake, Momma's favorite lunch, but I couldn't swallow. Choking, I tried to hold back tears, my strength wavering. What would I do without Marion? I knew she wasn't able to travel at her age, but she was all the family I had.

"Miss Miranda," Marion called out coming back into the room. "What's wrong?"

I finally swallowed the bite of food and raced to Marion. "I'm leaving this house and this town, but I don't know if I can leave you," I proclaimed, tears flooding from my eyes.

"Oh, I see," said Marion affectingly giving me a hug with her large, dark arms wrapped securely around me. "Is that what's bothering ya child?" She moved my long hair from my face. "It's every woman's problem letting go of a child. I ain't surprised ya want ta leave this house. Ya're not like others 'n I understand. I'll be fine 'n so will ya. I raised ya right. I'm proud of ya." Marion wiped the tears from my face with her apron. "I knew someday y'd be leaving me," she continued, "Now, where ya going child?"

"I'm going to California."

"California! That's some trip!" she exclaimed with a wide-eyed look. "But, I've listened ta yer dreams yer whole life 'n I taught ya ta stand up fer what ya believe in. I know ya better than anyone does. If anyone can make a dream come true, ya can, my sweet little Miranda," she whispered squeezing me tighter. "I jus' want ya ta know ya will always have someone that loves ya here in Boston, 'n y'll never be alone."

I wasn't alone.

"Thank you, Marion," I said sniffling, holding onto the woman tightly. "I needed someone to tell me I wasn't crazy, and I love you, too."

"Well, I can't say ya ain't crazy, Miss Miranda," Marion chuckled, "but I have faith in ya, 'n y'll make it. Now, eat yer lunch 'n then after ya finishes ya go straighten up. Ya have a meeting with the banker this afternoon."

"Yes, Ma'am," I answered as I wiped the tears from my face.

Don't Let Them See Fear

After lunch, I lingeringly walked up the stairs to my bedroom and opened the door. I smiled. Marion had brought up a bouquet of daffodils in a beautiful crystal vase that brought color into the room.

I undid my hair, twisted strands from my face, and secured them with hair pens leaving the rest of the curls to flow down my back. I studied my refection. I smiled knowing I wasn't alone. I had Marion and knew I'd always have Jon.

I did what Jon used to do before he went to work with Poppa. He'd stand in front of his mirror watching every twitch his face made. "Stand up tall Jonathon. Look the men in the eyes and don't let them see any fear," he'd say in a deep voice. I'd stand at his bedroom door and giggle, but he didn't pay any attention to me.

My eyes squinted tight together to look more forceful. "Miranda, stand up tall and don't let Mr. Mills see your fear. Don't let him talk you out of your journey." I couldn't hold back my laughter. Yes, I'd make it. A smile came on my face, and it was nice to laugh.

"Marion, wish me luck," I called out walking down the stairs.

"Luck's not what ya need, Miss Miranda," added Marion with her big smile which made her cheeks puff up. "Ya need ta remember what ya want ta do `n not let `em tell ya any different."

I ran to Marion throwing my arms around the old woman.

"It's time, my child," Marion said smoothing stray hairs from my face.

I flung the front door open. My black dress swished as I walked down the massive gray stone steps. I slid onto the seat of the carriage, and my mind spun. I had to remember to stay focused.

The carriage jerked to a stop in front of the huge, brick bank. James hopped down from the driver's seat and held out his large calloused hand. I laid my small hand in his as he smiled wrinkling his old face.

I pulled my shoulders back and stepped into the cold, stark bank. To the right side of the lobby was Mr. Mills' office, the bank president. I gently knocked on his door, which eased open engulfing me with the smell of cigar smoke making me cough.

"Come in, Miss Curry; have a seat," Mr. Mills said smirking closing the door. "Now, what can I do for you today?"

Mr. Mills was short and stout with a tiny bit of gray hair that lay curled on top of his head, making him look like a fat, pink-cheeked baby. His appearance took my apprehension away, as I held back my laughter.

I sat in a very nice leather, wing chair facing the man's desk. "Mr. Mills," I began, nervously slipping my black gloves from my hands. "First, I'd like to know my father's net worth, before we begin our meeting."

"Oh! That isn't a problem," Mr. Mills assured, as he slide a small stack of papers across the top of the desk. "Here is all the information you will need."

Shockingly, I read the papers and then I slipped them in my satchel. I had to smile. Now I understood Carlton's visit Sunday and knew he was a smart man. I also knew Carlton's father's law firm handled Poppa's will and, of course, gossip among men swirls just as fast as old Miss Martindale and her busybodies.

"Mr. Mills." I sat up straight in the chair, lacing my hands together in my lap. "I would like to sell the manor and my father's business. Can you help me with each of them?"

His squatty body became restless as he twisted his cigar in his puckered little mouth. He lay his cigar down on a silver tray, then placed his elbows on the desk, and leaned over toward me.

"Wow! That is a surprise, Miss Curry, of course, I'd be glad to help, but you have inherited a small fortune, and there isn't any need to sell neither your home nor your father's business."

"I've made up my mind, and that is what I want to do," I quickly responded, clutching my hands tightly and letting my nails bite into my fingers. "I'll be leaving Boston soon, so I'll need the money to be kept here in this bank until I wire you."

"That will be fine, Miss Curry. I'll talk to some of the businessmen around town and see if they are interested in buying Curry Distributors; it is a very thriving and prosperous company," he added. His head shook slowly. "You sure you don't want to stay? I could help find someone to run the company," he questioned lifting his cigar from the silver tray.

"I'm leaving, Sir," I persisted in a strong voice, "as soon as possible."

"Miss Curry," Mr. Mills probed, leaning back in his chair, "if you don't mind my asking, where are you going in such a hurry?"

I squeezed my hands tighter, taking in a sharp breath of air. "I'm going to California Mr. Mills and start a new life." My eyes peered down at my white knuckles.

The fat man coughed, choking on his cigar. He leaned forward in his chair. "Miss Curry, did you say California?"

"Yes," I offered with confidence, "I've always wanted to go out West, and my father approved."

"That will be some trip for a young woman, and it could be treacherous. Are you feeling alright, Miss Curry?" Mr. Mills continued to question. "Maybe, you need to take a little while and talk to someone. I'd be happy to call a doctor for you."

"I'm fine, Mr. Mills," I assured. "I've thought about my decision, and I appreciate your concern," I took in another breath, "and I know my father would appreciate your helping me in any way you can."

"That I'll do, and I'll let you know as soon as I can what I find out. I'll send the realtor over to the house tomorrow, if that is alright?"

"Tomorrow afternoon will be fine. Thank you very much for your time."

I slipped my black gloves on and stood from the chair. I felt weak in the knees now that my plans had been laid out and a course of action had been taken.

Mr. Mills scooted his chair back against the wall and walked around the desk. He placed my hand in his. "If you need anything, please, let me know, Miss Curry." His eyes searched my eyes and expression, trying to see if I'd gone mad. "Your father was a great and thoughtful man," Mr. Mills paused, "and I'll miss him stopping by to visit."

I walked to the door with confidence. "Thank you for your kindness, and I know my father would be grateful that you are helping me. I'll keep in touch, Mr. Mills."

My dress swished back and forth and my footsteps tapped on the marble floor as I walked out of the building.

I did it. I wanted to shout. I really wished I had Jon to talk to, but I believed he was with me. I was so proud. I'd stayed on course and was going to California. Nothing would stop me now.

When I arrived home, Marion was waiting in the vestibule for me.

"How did ya meeting go?" Marion inquired following me to the library.

I sat at Poppa's desk. "My meeting went well, even though Mr. Mills thinks I've gone insane," I said laughing. "Marion, he is going to send a realtor over tomorrow afternoon to talk to me about selling the house. I hope this isn't too hard on you."

"No child, but ya still seem worried."

"I have so much to think about. I will need to buy a business when I get to California."

"A business! I raised ya ta find a good husband! Miss Miranda, ya're getting old, 'n ya need ta settle down child. Buying a business, Lordy mercy, child! Ya need ta be like yer cousin, Becky. She up 'n got married when she was seventeen. What about Mr. Lambert? He shor' is a fine young gentleman. I taught ya well ta find a husband, not ta be a spinster."

Marion left the room shaking her head muttering the entire way, flapping her arms in the air as if she was going to take off flying. "A business, a business, Lordy mercy."

I knew Marion wouldn't let Carlton's visit die easy, and he wouldn't give up either. I smiled thinking about Carlton showing up at the front door, and Marion telling him that I'd moved to California. He'd stand there and laugh knowing once more I'd gotten the best of him.

I leaned over Poppa's desk and placed my elbows on top with my hands under my chin. I had to prepare for my meeting early in the morning with the company executives. I knew they were very shrewd businessmen and would try to convince me to keep the company to let them run it. I couldn't let them see a glimmer of doubt, or they'd have me.

The darkness of night crept into the room as I finished my notes. I slid my papers into my satchel and leaned back in the chair. The amber glow of the fireplace produced shadows on the walls and books. The old grandfather clock in the foyer chimed patiently announcing it was time for bed.

Saying Goodbye to Poppa and Jon

The stairs creaked in the quiet with each step. I entered my bedroom and the moonlight coming in from the window was flickering images across the walls. I settled into my favorite overstuffed chair next to the window, my journal caressed in my arms. I wanted to savor every memory of my home. A new page fell open, and I began to write narratives of times long ago, tales from my heart of each of my family who I'd be leaving behind in Boston.

The next morning I woke refreshed ready to face the men at Curry Distributors. I dressed in the black tailor suit with large puffy sleeves and a waist jacket. I knew that I was pushing the indecent button by wearing the dress. Marion was scurrying around downstairs, and I realized I was going to rile her yet again.

I walked into the dining room.

"Miss Miranda, what in tar nation, are ya wearing?" she shouted.

"Marion, I can't keep wearing those plain crepe dresses; this is still black," I answered.

Marion's head shook, mumbling to herself, but a smile was emerging on her old face as she brought me my breakfast.

When I finished my meal, I went upstairs and prepared to leave. Once I was ready, I was down the stairs and out the door. I slid onto the seat of the carriage understanding my journey to Poppa's work had begun, but my mind wandered to a few nights ago.

Poppa wasn't feeling well, so I called for Dr. Berry. When he arrived, we entered Poppa's dark bedroom. He stepped next to Poppa's bed while I lit a lamp. As I turned around, my heart sank upon seeing the apprehensive expression on the doctor's face—the identical one I'd seen years before in the same room.

His voice quivered, "Miranda, I'm so sorry, but your father has passed away. His heart couldn't take any more worry. He's at peace now with Cathleen. I'll help with anything you need."

I became petrified, frozen in my spot. Poppa couldn't be gone, and I couldn't be alone. I believed he was going to be with me forever. I stood there and couldn't cry; I was emotionless just as the day Momma had died.

"I'll go and see to things. I'll be back in a while," Dr. Berry mumbled. "Miranda, will you be alright?" He walked over laying his hand on my shoulder just as he had done with Poppa, so long ago.

"Yes, Dr. Berry, I'll be fine," I answered numbly.

He turned leaving the room, and I realized what I had to do. I had to say goodbye again to someone I loved.

Trembling, I scooted close to Poppa and loneliness was already encompassing me, but I wouldn't let loneliness win and let Poppa down.

"Poppa, I love you." I sucked in air. "I do understand you're at peace now, and you're with Momma and Jon. I'll make it, just as you said in this bedroom so long ago, and God does have a purpose for me. I'll miss you dearly, and it'll be lonely without you. Poppa." I tightly gripped the tall bedpost. "I love you, and you'll be in my heart forever."

I stared at Poppa. I believed a smile was on his face, the peace of being with Momma.

The clip clopping of the horse's hooves brought my thoughts back from that night. I wiped the tears from my eyes.

Buildings swished by outside the carriage window. I needed to stay focused so that there would be no more tears, at least until I was done with business today.

The carriage turned onto Oak Street, and I could see the tall stone building Poppa had built in the distance. Curry Distributors was one of the largest buildings in this area. The horse pulled to a stop in front of the massive building.

James climbed down from his seat and opened the carriage door. I stepped from the carriage straightening my dress. James pulled open the beautiful wooden doors to Curry Distributors. I sighed, hearing my shoes echoing as they tapped on the beautiful brown marble floor.

A man dressed in a blue uniform who was sitting in the center of the foyer at a large circular mahogany desk rushed over. "Miss Curry," his head nodded, "it is nice to see you. I'm so sorry about your father. I already miss his coming to work every morning. Mr. Curry was always so happy and energetic." The man's head ducked and tears welled in his eyes. "It is a great loss for us all."

"Thank you, Mr. Bartolomei. My poppa really enjoyed talking to you each morning. He would comment at dinner how you made his day begin with a smile. Poppa loved to hear the stories of your children, and you, sir, were very important to him."

"Thank you so much for telling me, Miss Curry," Mr. Bartolomei assured with a glimmer of a smile on his face. "Your father was a special man," he added, trying inconspicuously to wipe away a lone tear.

"Yes, he was and it was men like you that made him that way. Good day, Mr. Bartolomei."

"Have an enjoyable day, Miss Curry," Mr. Bartolomei offered, moving back to his desk chair.

I turned to the elevator, which was one of the first elevators in Boston. Poppa always loved new inventions, and he was so impressed with this particular one. A small man wearing the same blue uniform as Mr. Bartolomei opened the metal-gated door. I stepped inside the dim box and the man closed the sliding, rattling metal door. The elevator clanged to a stop on the top floor. The gated door opened to a long hallway leading to Poppa's office.

I tugged on the door and walked in. The room hadn't been touched. Papers lay on Poppa's mahogany desk where he'd left them when his life had stopped abruptly.

I strolled over to the window. Staring outside reminded me of times I'd visited this office when I was young and of how happy Poppa was here. I began to remember how happy Jonathon had been coming here, as well. I felt guilty that he wasn't here instead of me. He'd loved to have taken over Poppa's job, and he'd have been great at it. Why wasn't he here, why was I all alone?

A whisper of cool air and a chill circled around the room, as if someone was telling me to stop. I understood Jonathon wouldn't want me to be thinking this way. "Life happens and we can't change it," he had said right before he died. He wouldn't want me to be sad and he'd be proud of what I wanted to do. He would be telling me to be strong. I smiled; Poppa wouldn't have wanted me to let those men tell me how to live my life. He fought them and I would too. He also believed everything happened for a purpose. I smoothed my stray hairs from my face and wiped the wetness from my eyes. I was ready for the board meeting.

I made my way down the long hall to the huge meeting room. The large door stood open and the enormous room was full of men sitting around a hefty granit-topped table. A hush fell over the room when the men saw me.

"Good morning, gentlemen," I said with an air of confidence. "I hope you are all doing well."

"Yes, Miss Curry, we are," answered Mr. Thomas, his hands nervously posed in front of him.

"Please have a seat," I said.

Mr. Thomas and the other men sat.

"Thank you, Mr. Thomas," I replied sitting down in Poppa's chair at the head of the table. "*Stay strong Mirand;, you can do this*," came a sweet whisper. I looked around the room and felt confident that Poppa and Jonathon were with me.

"Miss Curry," Mr. Gasper began, "we would like you to know how sorry we are at your father's passing."

"Thank you, Mr. Gasper, I do appreciate that," I said in a strong voice. My eyes scanned all of the men, their eyes glued on me.

"We also want you to know we are here to help you in any way," Mr. Gasper continued.

"Miss Curry, we have a few good ideas for the company," Mr. Clark, interjected as he stood.

Being interrupted by Mr. Clark, Mr. Gasper irritably became quiet and the muscles in his throat moved when he sat back down.

"We would like to discuss some new ideas for the company, if that is alright," Mr. Clark continued.

"Gentleman, I first have some news for you," I stated interrupting as I stood from the chair. Mr. Clark sat down. I gripped the table's edge to steady myself and began what I'd replayed repeatedly in my mind. "Gentleman, I have made up my mind." I looked into the faces of the men sitting around the table. Some of them had been kind to Poppa, and others had not. "I have decided to sell Curry Distributors as soon as possible."

A silence fell over the men, but only for a moment. Each of them had the same expression of shock as Mr. Mills—that I'd gone insane.

"Miss Curry, why would you do such a thing? We can run the company without any problems, and you would not have to worry about it at all," Mr. Simon said in a loud voice trying to stay calm. "You need to let us help you. Your father wouldn't want you to sell the business so soon. He loved Curry Distributors."

I glared at him knowing he was playing on my feelings, but I wasn't letting him get to me. I remembered thinking at Poppa's funeral that he was one of the men Poppa hadn't trusted.

"Mr. Simon, I appreciate the confidence on your part, but I have made up my mind. I have already put the idea into motion. I should have bids for the company coming in very soon. I want to thank you for your support, and I will inform the new owner that you are all qualified to help run the company."

I slid my chair under the table. The men didn't move. They were speechless for the first time in their lives.

"Well, I guess this is goodbye. I wish the best for each and every one of you." I lifted my papers into my arms and spun around leaving the men stunned.

I rushed into Poppa's office quickly closing the door. Sitting at Poppa's desk, I began to pull out the drawers and found pictures of Momma, Jonathon, and myself with him—four happy faces.

I packed his things in boxes and would have them delivered to my home. I then put all of the special keepsakes in one box. Poppa's memories were now my memories.

It was heartbreaking as I looked around the room. The scent of pipe smoke still lingered in the air from Poppa's pipe that was sitting in its special spot along with another little brass-lady tamper. Poppa cherished his pipes. My eyes closed seeing him distinguishedly standing by the window holding his pipe with his right hand, as he pondered the day's thoughts. Poppa and Jonathon had loved this company. Again, I felt guilty that I was selling the company and leaving their dream. That was it—this was their dream, not mine. Poppa did what he dreamed of, and I had to do the same.

I couldn't leave. I sat and stared out the window looking across the great city of Boston.

An hour later, I rose from my chair with the box of keepsakes clutched in my arms.

"Good bye…Poppa and Jon," I whispered. "I hope you both approve of my decision to sell the company and move to California."

The door closed behind me for the last time.

"Mr. Bartolomei," I began walking into the lobby, "I'm selling the company, and I wanted you to know. I'll put in a good word to the buyers that you are a great asset for the company. I wish you the best."

"Thank you, Miss Curry." Mr. Bartolomei stood. "This is painful for me to think about your selling the company, but it's not the same without your father. He was the company. I do appreciate the good word, and God bless you."

"Goodbye. All the best is wished for you and your family." I hugged the box of keepsakes and turned for one more look at the building Poppa had built from the ground up, the one he had loved so dearly. I had to smile. Mr. Bartolomei was correct; the company was Poppa, the heart and soul behind it. His love was what made the company a success. I'd never thought how a company could be like a person, but even if I had stayed to run it, nothing would have been the same without him.

The carriage came to a stop at the front of my home. I rushed through the doors. Marion walked up to me.

"Marion," I gasped. "I had to say goodbye to Poppa and Jon all over again."

"Yes'm, Miss Miranda," she said, "but now it's time fer ya ta prepare ta leave. Ya have ta say goodbye ta the ones you love sometimes. Y'll be fine. Go 'n wash yer face 'n I'll help ya pack. Ya also have the realtor coming this afternoon. Ya can do this, remembers," Marion reminded, "we will have no more tears."

"Thank you, Marion," I said gratefully. "I don't know what I'm going to do without you."

"Honey, y'll never be without me, yer father, mother, or Jonathon. We'll always be with ya, don't ya know?"

"I'm beginning to."

The library gave off the smell of old leather from all the books, along with the hint of pipe smoke making my memories of good times flow in my mind. Marion would see to the packing of the rest of my family's things and store them until I was settled into my new home.

I sat at the desk and began to clean out the drawers, surprised by how much Poppa had kept over the years. With great care I dropped love notes that Momma had written him into my special box of keepsakes.

Goodbye Boston

week had passed since my poppa had died, and I'd made the decision to move. Again, I knew I had to keep moving forward and not let the past interfere with my plans.

Sunday morning arrived very early; my eyes opened with the sweet singing of the cardinal sitting in the snarled tree outside my window. I finished dressing into my new blue tailor suit with a matching bonnet with its light silk ribbons. There would be no more wearing black. I picked up the matching parasol and satchel but didn't move for a few minutes while searching the bedroom to be sure I had everything. I swung the satchel nervously in my hand as I made my way down the stairs for my last time.

At the bottom of the staircase, I stopped wanting to remember everything about this house. My hand tenderly stroked the smooth, cool, wood railing.

Breakfast sat on the huge dining table, just as it had all of my life, but I couldn't swallow the food because a huge lump was rising in my throat. The words, "No more tears," paced through my mind. I rose from the table and walked to the kitchen.

I pushed open the kitchen door. It was quiet. Marion was busy by the sink just as she'd done the day Momma had passed away. I walked up to her and put my arms around her.

She turned and gently wiped the tears from my face with her apron. She smiled, looking at the blue dress, knowing even traveling I should be wearing black; blue wasn't proper, but she wasn't chastising me, not today.

"Miss Miranda, I see y're ready ta leave. Ya know how much I love ya 'n I'll miss seeing ya every day. Ya better write me all the time. God bless 'n keep ya safe my child," Marion sniffed, hugging me tightly.

"Marion, I love you, too," I said softly. "I'll write often," I grinned. "You know I love to write, so you may be sorry. Goodbye," I whispered with the words choking me, "if you need anything, please let me know."

I turned to walk out of the kitchen, but stopped to take one more look at the room—the kitchen where I'd grown up.

I stood in the doorway and whispered, "Goodbye." I slowly walked to the large, mahogany, front doors and tugged them both wide open, just as Poppa had done that wonderful day in May when I first saw this amazing home.

Marion stood in the doorway waving goodbye. My eyes stayed fixed on the house as the carriage moved away. I told myself that Poppa, Momma, Jonathon, and Marion would always be in my heart forever. I turned around in the carriage seat and wiped the tears from my eyes. My journey was beginning and there'd be no more tears.

My Journey

This early morning, the carriage wobbled along the streets nearing the Boston and Albany Railroad. I listened to the horse's hooves clacking on the cobblestone road and remembered that day so long ago when Momma and Jonathon became ill. With each click of a hoof, I had a memory flash through my mind. How life twists and turns!

I looked down the long unending railroad tracks glistening in the morning sun that was peeking on the horizon. The tracks were going everywhere like arms of an octopus. My heart started pumping hard hearing the screech of trains pulling to a stop. Off in the distance, a train whistle blew. My dream was becoming a reality.

The horse pulled to a stop in front of the train depot. People were busily scurrying everywhere. James jumped from his seat to help me out of the carriage. I shivered, not sure if it was from the coolness of the morning or the apprehension of beginning my journey, but I wasn't backing down. *"Miranda, you're going to California; don't let anyone stop you or see fear.* Tales of the old West that people had told me about the dangers of buffaloes, train robberies, and Indians were only energizing me.

A colored porter, a short older man, picked up my small bag and satchel. "Miss Curry, please comes with me. My name is George, 'n I'll be yer porter fer yer trip ta Omaha. This superb train is called the *Overland Limited."*

"It's nice to meet you, George. Please give me one minute."

I turned around and reached out my hand. "Goodbye, James. Thank you for everything you have done for me. God bless you and your family."

"Thanks ya, Miss Miranda, 'n God keep ya safe in all of yer journeys," James said, with tears growing in his old dark eyes.

I followed George, walking past train cars to a wide vestibule car. The train waiting to leave was making hissing noises, as if it were breathing. My trip would take four days or more to reach the West Coast. I knew I'd soon feel the power and hear the bellow of the locomotive. My journey to California and my new life were beginning.

George held my hand helping me to climb up the wrought iron steps onto the platform and into the parlor compartment. My body tingled with excitement.

The compartment's side-arched, stain glass windows were letting the morning sun flicker inside, making designs on the seats flowing across lacquered walnut trim walls.

George stopped. He placed my bags in a slot next to two chairs with a small table in front and two more chairs on the other side. An elderly woman sat in one of the chairs.

"Mrs. Scott," George began. "I'd like ta introduce Miss Curry. I thoughts that the two of ya might enjoy sitting together."

"That's a nice idea, George," Mrs. Scott said kindly looking up at me. "Please sit Miss Curry, and you may call me Dorothy."

"Thank you, Dorothy," I offered. "My name is Miranda."

"Now, is there anything I can get ya ladies before we departs?" asked George.

"Nothing for me right now, thank you George," assured Dorothy.

"I'm fine, too," I added, settling into a chair.

"Alright, Miranda, now where is a young girl like you headed all alone without a chaperone?" Dorothy asked curiously.

"Ma'am, I'm moving to San Francisco."

"That is some trip for a young girl," added Dorothy looking at me inquisitively.

"I'm not that young. I'll be twenty-one this winter," I replied.

Dorothy smiled.

The woman had to be just a few years younger than Marion. She was a short, heavyset woman with big blue eyes and a pointed little nose. Her curly, gray hair was pulled up on top of her head with long curls hanging down each side of her pure white face. She was wearing a dark green dress and a beautiful navy, silk shawl.

"Dorothy, where are you traveling?"

"Oh, I'm going to a small town outside of Chicago. My husband died last year, and it has been very lonesome for me, so I decided to move closer to my daughter Claire, her husband Bob, and her children. The oldest child is Byron, who is nine, Ruby, is five, and the baby Henry will be two this month. Miranda, what do your parents think about your traveling to California? That is some journey for a young woman," she became quieter, "all alone."

"My mother and brother died about eight years ago, and my father just died," I explained. It was hard to hear those words that I was now alone. "I don't have any other family."

"Oh, I'm sorry to hear about your father, but what made you pick up and want to move to California?"

"It has always been my dream to go to California."

"My gracious," said Dorothy shrugging her shoulders, "that is some undertaking. I wish you the best."

"Thank you, Dorothy."

I looked around the compartment car. Dorothy and I were sitting at the back left corner. Across from us on the right side was a family with a baby dressed in blue. Grandma and grandpa were sitting across from the young family. At the front left side by the compartment entrance was a family with two children; a boy with red hair and freckles, who looked about ten, and a girl with blonde, curly hair, who might be eight years old.

To the far right front corner, a very distinguish man in his early thirties sat alone. He was facing the front of the car looking out the window; his wavy hair was light brown with streaks of blond sparkling in the morning sun. He was dressed very nicely in a black, wool, frock coat, silk, puff tie, and a copper basin vest. While I was looking around, two young men came to sit in the seats across from Dorothy and me.

The first man spoke. "Good morning, ladies. May we have the pleasure of joining you?" He was dressed in a gray, tweed suit and had a straw, boater hat on, with a black bow tie. He had short, dark hair and small, dark brown eyes and was about my age.

"Yes," Dorothy offered anxiously, looking at the two young men.

"Thank you," he added. "I am Edwin Holt, and this is Grady Wilkins."

"Nice to meet both of you," Dorothy said softly. "This is Miss Miranda Curry, and I'm Dorothy Scott. Please, sit down gentlemen."

Grady Wilkins was wearing a brown, tattered, rumpled coat and a linen sporting cap, braces on his pants, and he, just as the first young man, had on a black bow tie. He had the most unusual green eyes, and sugar freckles across his nose that made him look even younger. His long, reddish brown hair proved to be messy when he pulled off his worn cap.

Dorothy began to question the men, and I was glad she had someone else to focus on. "Mr. Holt, where are you traveling?"

"Ma'am, I am going to San Francisco to open a new jewelry store. I have been working with my father in his jewelry store since I was a small boy. When we have a chance, I hope you'll let me show you some of the pieces that I have brought with me on my trip."

"That would be very nice," Dorothy added. "And, Mr. Wilkins, where are you headed?"

"Please, call me Grady, Miss Dorothy. I'm traveling with Edwin to help him open his store," Grady concluded with an energetic smile.

"Yes," Edwin assured. "And you may also call me Edwin, Miss Dorothy."

"Why, thank you gentlemen. Grady, are you a jeweler too?" Dorothy questioned.

"Oh, my no, Miss Dorothy, I'm a wanderer. I want to travel all around this magnificent country. I grew up in the northern part of New York on a farm, and I've always believed it would be great to go out West."

At that moment, Edwin whispered in a low and thrilled voice, "Look, who's coming aboard?"

They became silent. Both men turned around in their seats with their eyes glued to the entrance. My eyes, along with theirs, peered at the entrance to the parlor compartment.

A silhouette of a man stood in the doorway next to the porter. The man stood tall, broad shoulders, thin hips, and dark, thick, wavy hair. The robust man turned around in the passageway of the compartment. He stood with shoulders erect. He was wearing a black, frock, wool coat with a Western bow tie and a forty-niner vest and a black, gambler, Stetson hat. He was a very strikingly handsome man with a strong jaw and russet, sun-drenched face. He pulled out a gold pocket watch with a chain connected to his vest and glanced at the time. Snapping the watch shut, he slid it back into his pocket.

I kept staring even though I knew it wasn't polite. He looked up showing the most enticing blue eyes that sparkled like blue topaz from the mines of Russia. His baby blue eyes became fixed on me with an alluring, amused grin. He studied me as I watched him; quickly, I turned my eyes away.

"Who is that man?" inquired Dorothy sitting up in her chair.

"That man is Vaughn Ellsworth, and he's a well-known gambler. He is a legend in the West," said Grady delightedly sinking deep into his chair.

My eyes stayed on the handsome man who sat at the front of the car. Facing me, he removed his hat and combed his wild, wavy hair with his fingers letting his blue eyes peer back at me. His mouth curled into a light smirk and then slowly, he placed his hat over his face and leaned back in the seat.

"Oh! Miranda!" Dorothy said quickly raising her hand as if to signal hault. "Don't look at that man. He's not a gentleman. He is scandalous, and you shouldn't be encouraging him," she snapped, panting as if this were more than her heart could take as she lightly slapped me on the back of my hand.

"I'm not encouraging him, Dorothy, but he's fascinating," I protested still staring, thinking of those blue eyes.

The train swayed back and forth moving slowly and then began to pick up speed. The whistle blew. We were on our way, and later, I'd write in my journal every detail of my journey.

Nicholas Vaughn Ellsworth

About thirty minutes later, George came into the parlor car. "Mrs. Scott 'n Miss Curry would ya like ta have breakfast?" he offered kindly.

"Yes, George, that sounds just fine." Dorothy rose from the chair to fix her shawl.

"That would be fine with me, too," I assured, standing by Dorothy.

George graciously led us to the dining compartment to an elegant table covered with a white linen tablecloth next to the window. A beautiful pink rosebud in a small silver vase was placed in the center of the table.

Edwin and Grady stopped at our table. "Ladies, have an enjoyable breakfast," Edwin said kindly walking to the table next to us.

The two men who had been sitting at the front of the car followed Edwin and Grady. The one Edwin called Vaughn Ellsworth brazenly walked up and stopped next to our table.

"Good morning ladies, a beautiful morning for a train ride," he said full of self-assurance. He leaned over near me to see outside. He smelled earthy. Peering out the compartment's window at the sun rising, he continued, "Not a cloud in the sky."

Dorothy, a frown on her face, scooted her chair away from him moving closer to the window.

My body tingled excitedly. I wasn't going to let Dorothy discourage me from talking.

"Yes, it is a gorgeous morning, Mr. …" I stopped short to see what he'd do, not wanting him to know I already knew his name.

"Nicholas Vaughn Ellsworth Ma'am, from San Francisco, California." He offered with a smile and a half bow. He was very attractive, and his words flowed elegantly as he spoke. I stared into his enchanting blue eyes alive with enthusiasm. I thought about Dorothy calling him scandalous, making him even more appealing.

"Mr. Ellsworth, I am Miranda Curry and this is Dorothy Scott," I offered. "I'm also traveling to San Francisco," I declared.

I could see Dorothy puckering her face as she quickly turned her head from me. She wasn't pleased that I was having a discussion with Mr. Ellsworth. I'd even told him where I was traveling. He wasn't a decent man to be having a conversation with, and I was acting scandalously. I also saw Edwin looking my way. Mr. Ellsworth's face showed he was enjoying every minute.

"Well, Miss Curry and Mrs. Scott, I do hope you have an enjoyable meal," Mr. Ellsworth added with confidence. He had an aura, a mysticism about him that attracted and scared me at the same time.

"Thank you, Mr. Ellsworth." I answered back, wondering if he was toying with me, and knowing we didn't fit into the same social circles.

"Please, Miss Curry, you may call me, Vaughn," he answered staring down at me as if he could see into my soul. I felt warmth surging through my body. I'd never met a man like Vaughn before… so intriguing.

"Vaughn, it is, and I'm Miranda," I said, never letting anyone get the best of me, especially if he was playing with my feelings. He may be a gambler, but I could read his face, and I could see he had more on his mind than social niceties. This time I was having fun. He was so different from predictable Carlton.

"Enjoy your meal, Miranda," he said grinning, tipping his hat, and walking to the table behind us.

Vaughn sat in the chair behind me facing Grady and Edwin. I knew they were in awe of him—probably terrified to talk.

I waited for Dorothy to chastise me like Marion would, but she was quiet. I knew I'd been shocking many people since Poppa died. I wasn't following society's traditions, and I wasn't being respectable talking to a known gambler, but I had never met anyone like Vaughn.

She finally spoke, "The rose is beautiful in the vase. My late husband Edgar used to grow roses. He had some of the most gorgeous red roses in his garden."

"I have always loved light pink roses, just like this one. It is perfect," I said, looking at the beautiful flower, touching the soft delicate petals. "Pink roses have always been my favorite flower. When I was young, my mother would let me pick them from her garden to put in the most exquisite vase on the dining room table."

"A light pink rose means joy and happiness, which fits you Miranda. I believe each person should have their own flower, and the pink rose is ideal for you."

"Dorothy, I never knew roses had meanings."

"Yes, of course, a red rose is love and a yellow rose is friendship, white is purity and innocence. Giving one rose means love at first sight, six roses means I'm yours. I like thirteen roses, which means secret admirer, and fifteen roses means I'm sorry; the best is two roses entwined which means marry me. That is how my husband proposed to me on that special evening, one I shall never forget," she said softly becoming quiet. Her sad eyes focused out the window. It was as if she were seeing her late husband. "When he proposed, he brought me two beautiful, long-stemmed, red roses entwined, and for forty-five years on each anniversary, he gave me one rose."

I was in awe thinking about a beautiful rose given to Dorothy each year. I could see the affection in Dorothy's eyes that she had for her husband and how much she missed him.

"That is amazing. I hope someday to meet and fall in love with someone like him. You're a very lucky woman, and your husband was even luckier," I assured, placing my hand on hers as she finally smiled.

George interrupted my thoughts setting our plates on the table and adding something new called orange juice. I'd never tasted anything so sweet. The delicious breakfast consisted of eggs, bacon, biscuits, butter, and jam.

The morning was pleasant as the countryside swished by while we ate our meal. The dining car was slowly emptying. Dorothy stood and I leisurely followed her to the parlor.

"Thank you, George. My breakfast was delicious, and I enjoyed the orange juice." I graciously said to him.

He bowed and his face lit with delight. "Yes'm, I's glad ya enjoyed yer breakfast, Miss Curry," he answered.

I did notice Vaughn was close behind me. Dorothy hurriedly sat down to avoid him.

"I hope you had a lovely breakfast, Miranda," Vaughn offered. I turned around and peered up at him standing only inches from me. Dorothy shook her head, not approving. Vaughn seemed to know what I was thinking. His head titled to the side, and then he grinned a playful grin.

"Yes, thank you, Vaughn. I did enjoy my meal." I smiled and sat in my chair next to Dorothy.

Vaughn slightly bowed, turned, and walked to the front of the compartment. As he sat in his seat, his dark eyebrows lifted, and the grin stayed on his face. He looked at me with those piercing blue eyes, just keeping a watchful eye.

Following Vaughn into the compartment, the other man who had been sitting at the breakfast table with Vaughn walked up. "Ladies, I would like to introduce myself; I'm Braxton Sims. I'm a banker from San Francisco."

Of course, that was who Dorothy wanted me to talk to, so she quickly perked up leaning over near me. "Nice to meet you, Mr. Sims. I am Dorothy Scott, and this is Miranda Curry. Miranda is traveling to San Francisco, and she is planning on buying a business after she gets settled. I think you should talk," Dorothy said with glee in her voice.

"That sounds very nice, Miss Curry. I hope we have the opportunity to do just that, and please, ladies, call me Braxton."

"I look forward to talking to you too, Braxton, and I am Miranda."

"Thank you, Miranda," he said bowing. "Ladies, have a nice day."

Braxton, who was also very attractive and charming, was very different from Vaughn. Braxton was highly educated and very sophisticated. Vaughn, not missing anything going on, peered out from under his hat. He understood what Dorothy was up to trying to keep him away from me. He grinned and leaned back in his seat and lay his hat back over his face. Women like Dorothy didn't bother him.

I studied Braxton. He was very handsome and engaging with his kind bluish-green eyes and freckles across his nose. He tipped his hat and sat in the seat across from Vaughn. But, Braxton didn't have the mystic that Vaughn had; however, he'd be someone I would need to know in San Francisco.

I could see buildings flashing by and knew we were coming to our first stop in Buffalo. The family sitting across from us stood and prepared to leave.

The train pulled to a stop and sat idling at the station for about forty minutes. Then its whistle blew, and we were on our way to Cleveland.

I lifted out my journal from my satchel. Dorothy had dozed off, and it was a perfect time to catch up on my writing. I watched the landscape passing by and started to recall each step of my journey as I began to write.

About an hour later, the train whistle blasted four times to let us know we were coming into Erie, a short stop. The family with the baby, who was sitting across from us, stood, and gathered their things, ready to disembark.

I closed my journal, and my attention quickly was pulled to the entrance of the car. A nun busily came aboard. She smiled, nodded her head in a polite manner, and sat in the seat across the aisle from Dorothy and me.

A few minutes later, the train shook and the wheels began to roll along the tracks. The late afternoon light was filtering through the windows. It was quiet; the men, including Vaughn, had left for the smoking compartment, so I sat letting my thoughts appear on page after page.

That afternoon the sun began to set painting red streaks cutting the evening sky. I watched the sky change colors, as it added shades of blue and purple across the landscape. I thought to myself, "What a splendid ending of a perfect day."

Before George led us to the sleeping car, Edwin sat down in front of us holding a dark blue case in his arms. "Miss Dorothy, before you retire for the night, I would like to show you some of my jewelry, if that is alright."

"Yes, Edwin, that sounds very nice," assured Dorothy, pulling out her reading spectacles from her woven bag.

Beautiful jewelry poured from the small case onto a dark, maroon, velvet tray. Dorothy sat quietly studying the pieces.

I examined a fabulous golden locket, a pendant from Belgium. It was about an inch around made with Orient, half-seed pearls that were placed precisely on the front of the locket in a rose design. I'd have given anything to own something so beautiful, but I wasn't prepared to spend my money, not yet.

Dorothy, on the other hand, found a heart-shaped pendent, necklace and bought it. Her fingers caressed it, and her eyes stared off into a world of her own.

The two young men stood. They excused themselves leaving to go to the smoking car.

George walked up to our chairs. "Ladies, if ya'd like, I will show ya ta the sleeping compartment."

"Yes, George, that would very nice. I am tired. This has been a long day," Dorothy replied holding onto the necklace with twinkle in her eyes.

"Miss Curry?" George questioned with his head bowed.

I nodded my head yes and stood to leave.

George led us to our sleeping quarters. I slipped into my small bed, but my mind churned over the day's events and questions about what would unfold as I continued my journey. However, my body was tired, and I gradually fell asleep. The train would be dashing down the tracks throughout the night while we slept, and we'd awake in the morning in Chicago.

Sarah Reed

I woke refreshed. I'd slept superbly with the sound of the train singing me to sleep and its wavelike motions keeping me asleep. I climbed from my berth and hastily prepared myself for the day. I noticed Dorothy had already left the sleeping compartment, so I hurried to find her before she disembarked.

The train sat hissing at the station in Chicago. I rushed into the parlor compartment; Dorothy was standing by her chair gathering her things.

"Oh, Dorothy, I'm glad I didn't miss you," I called out trying to catch my breath.

"Miranda, I'm glad you made it," she said in a kind voice. "I was a little worried that I might not be able to say goodbye."

"I've enjoyed spending time with you," I said watching as she straightened her small bag.

Dorothy turned to face me. "Miranda, I wish you the best of luck in San Francisco, but, young lady, please don't let just any handsome man sweep you away," she said firmly, giving me a stern look. Then she patted my hand and gave me a warm smile.

I smiled back. "Dorothy, I do hope to see you again someday," I said.

"I, too, hope we will meet again, but you write and let me know how you are doing. Please tell Grady and Edwin goodbye and that I love my necklace," she said touching it. She picked up her small satchel and turned to leave.

"I will keep in touch, and if you are ever in San Francisco, please come by and visit," I called back to her.

George gently took Dorothy's arm and helped her off the train. A woman and three children ran to her, but before she left, she looked up at me and smiled.

I proceeded down the train steps onto the platform and scanned the area. It was April 27th and I was in Chicago, Illinois. A light drizzle touched my face, along with the smell of the damp earth mixing with the steam of the engine. Pulling my shawl around my shoulders, I shivered in the coolness of the morning. The city in the distance was one of the largest I had seen on my journey. I had read the account of the fire of 1871 and how it had devastated the large city, but I could see it was being rebuilt.

I strolled around the General Union Passenger Depot. The whistle blew and slowly I made my way back to the train. When I walked up to the train steps, George leaned down from the car reaching out his hand, but Vaughn stepped up from behind me. He didn't say anything just held out his hand. I slowly placed my hand in his looking into those blue eyes. Not moving for a fleeting moment, I could feel his eyes upon me as I moved forward to my seat. I couldn't resist and glanced back at him. How dashing he was! Vaughn's head rested on the back of his seat with that mischievous grin covering his face. He was always in control.

The train car was quiet. Vaughn and I were the first to arrive back on the train. The nun, who had stayed in her seat, was reading, but her eagle eyes peered up with a disapproving glance when Vaughn and I came into the car together.

Others began to arrive. Braxton walked into the car, tipped his hat at me, and then sat across from Vaughn.

At that moment, another woman stepped into view trying to balance the bags that she held in her hands. She was tall, very voluminous, and wearing a white, frilly, low-cut blouse with a dark, greenish blue silk skirt. She had red rouge on her smooth white cheeks and dark red lips. She also had a feather in her hair. Vaughn and Braxton both took interest in her as she walked towards me.

"I think that is my seat. I hope you don't mind?" She asked with a glee in her voice.

I looked at Vaughn who was grinning from ear to ear like a Cheshire cat.

"Please, sit. I'm Miranda Curry," I said.

"Thank you, Miranda, I am Sarah Reed from San Francisco," she answered in a sweet voice.

"Sarah, I'm happy to meet you. What do you do in San Francisco?"

"Oh, I'm a singer and dancer at one of the nicest establishments downtown," she offered. Her eyes turned to look at me. She was waiting for my reaction.

"Then you know a lot about San Francisco," I said not judging her. "I hope you don't mind my asking you some questions about the city after you get settled in."

"That would be just fine," Sarah replied with a smile accentuating her beauty.

Sarah was busy straightening her bags and setting them on the floor when a scruffy, bearded man in his late forties dressed in dirty dingy clothes walked up to the compartment's entrance. The man noticed

Sarah. He stopped at the door watching her every move and then sat in the seat next to Vaughn, but the man's attention turned to Sarah. He gave her a distasteful look. He leaned back in his seat, lifted his hat over his eyes, and quickly fell asleep.

The train's whistle blared, and the train began to rumble and shake rolling down the tracks.

I had not seen Grady and Edwin all morning. That meant they were up late, and I was sure they had been drinking and playing poker with Vaughn in the smoking car, not a good sign.

George walked up. "Miss Curry 'n Miss Reed would ya like ta have breakfast nows?"

I stood. "Yes, George, I would love to have some of the orange juice again."

He smiled, ducked his head downward in a slight bow, and led us to the same table that Dorothy and I had sat at yesterday.

"Ladies, is it alright for us to join you?" asked Braxton with his stately smile and proper manners.

I saw the look on the nun's disapproving face from across the room.

"Yes," Sarah quickly answered, "that is fine, gentlemen."

"I'm Braxton Sims and this is Vaughn Ellsworth," Braxton proclaimed scooting in beside me.

"This," I offered upon seeing Sarah had become overwhelmed for a moment, "is Sarah Reed from San Francisco.

Vaughn grinned his mischievous grin as he sat in the chair next to Sarah. "Another beautiful morning, isn't it Miranda?" Braxton announced.

"Yes, it is Braxton," I added staring out the window.

"I see Mrs. Dorothy has left the train," Vaughn chimed in, squinting his eyes making a playful look.

"Yes," I answered, my eyes turned to him knowing what he was up to. He felt as if I'd lost my protection. "Dorothy is moving to Chicago to be with her daughter."

At that minute, Grady and Edwin walked into the dining car looking like whipped puppies.

Vaughn grinned.

"Good morning, Miranda," Edwin said. "Sorry we missed Mrs. Scott's leaving this morning."

"She wanted me to tell you goodbye and that she loved her necklace."

"I do hope she enjoys it. Have a good breakfast," Grady said giving Vaughn a hard stare.

"Alright, what went on last night?" I asked leaning over the table looking at Vaughn.

"I don't know what you mean," he answered with the grin still on his face.

"You know perfectly well what I mean," I said getting agitated, my Irish temper flaring. "How much money did those young men lose last night in your poker game?"

"What poker game?" Vaughn replied, crossing his arms and leaning back against the chair.

"Don't play games with me; just answer my question," I declared in a strong voice giving Vaughn a steady gaze.

"They didn't lose much money, Miranda, but we did try to teach them a lesson," Braxton assured. "They need to know what they are getting into when drinking and gambling. Most men would have taken advantage of them, but Vaughn didn't. They will be fine. Their pride is hurt, but at least they still have their money—or most of it."

"I hope that is the truth Braxton. They seem like such nice, young men."

"That's the problem, Miranda, they are," Braxton added. "They're the ones who will be taken advantage of in this world. We can only try to teach them a lesson about playing cards; we can't stop them."

My head nodded yes. George brought our breakfast with the amazing orange juice.

"Now Miranda," Braxton began, "Yesterday, Mrs. Scott said that you are moving to San Francisco to start a business. What kind of business are you thinking about?" he sighed. "Maybe a dress shop?"

"My owning a dress shop? Oh, that wouldn't work! I haven't really thought much about what I should buy. I'm planning on looking around at what is available."

"When we arrive if you will give me your address and how to get in touch with you, I will check into businesses for sale," Braxton assured.

Vaughn lit up and was all ears. He knew that was one way to find out where I was going to be staying.

"How do you plan to buy a business, if I may ask?" Braxton said ignoring Vaughn.

"I am in the process of selling a business in Boston, and then I will decide on a new business." My eyes glanced at Vaughn, "I will be staying for a while at the Old Grand Hotel downtown until I get settled."

"That is a perfect place for you," Vaughn intervened leaning over the table. "I will be staying at the hotel while I'm in San Francisco, too. It is one of the most popular places in town."

"Yes, I have been to the Old Grand Hotel before," added Sarah. "It is a lovely place suited just for you, Miranda."

"Miranda," Braxton added, "I will check on businesses for sale and get back with you. I'm sure we can find the right one."

"That would be very helpful, Braxton. Thank you," I added sipping my orange juice.

Breakfast ended with normal conversation, and Braxton was able to keep Vaughn in check.

Vaughn and Braxton left for the smoking compartment, and I pulled out my journal and began to write. The rhythm of the wheels on the train had a calming sensation and Sarah fell asleep.

The morning went by quietly, and I even rested for a while. At lunch, Sarah and I sat at our same table in the dining car.

The nun walked up and introduced herself. "Ladies, I am Sister Margret Mary. I hope you don't mind my joining you," she asked kindly.

"Oh no, please sit down," I said happily, introducing both of us. "How far are you traveling?"

She had dark brown very intense eyes that you would think could see into your soul and a very soothing voice. "I am from San Francisco, but I'm now on my way to St. Mary Magdalene in Salt Lake City," she added very compassionately. "I travel from church to church helping out.

"How long will you be in Salt Lake City?" I asked curiously.

"I'm not sure, but I do hope I will be able to return to San Francisco soon to Old St. Mary's on O'Farrell Street," Sister Margret Mary announce proudly.

"For now, I'm staying at the Old Grand Hotel. When you come back to town, please look me up."

"That would be very nice, thank you. The Old Grand Hotel isn't far from Old St. Mary's, so you should come by and visit. It is a very special place," she added smiling.

Sarah didn't talk. She quietly ate her lunch with her eyes fixed on her plate.

Our next stop would be Omaha. The train ride was going by fast—almost too fast.

Fool's Gold

Sarah's head faced the window and her reflection in the glass showed sorrow.

"Have you lived in San Francisco all of your life?" I questioned. Sarah's shoulders slumped and she bit her lip. Her sad eyes looked back at me.

"Most of my life," Sarah began. "I was born in Sacramento, California, but my family moved to Coloma, at Sutter's Mill, close to where the Gold Rush started years ago. My parents dreamed and believed that they could find gold. It was the year I turned eleven years old, and my sister Annie seven, both innocent children.

My memories are very clear of all the 49'ers panning for gold on the American River. There were high hopes of becoming rich overnight. People were everywhere. It was like an ant colony. We lived in a tiny tent my father bought; water would drip on us at night through the many holes in the top. Even though we didn't have food or a home, my father determinedly kept searching for gold. He got what they called back then," she took a deep breath; "gold rush fever, and he continued to believe each day that he would find gold. Nothing could discourage him. Only a few men discovered it; more of the men found fool's gold, a fitting name for the gold *and* the men.

Days and long nights were unrelenting and there wasn't any schooling for my sister and myself. To help us survive, my mother, along with many other women, began to work by cooking and cleaning for the men.

The small town was disgustingly filthy; it held untamed men." Sarah's hands gripped the arms of the chair, her knuckles turning white. "It was a repulsive place, horrible, just horrible." She shuttered as fear grew in her eyes.

"Those men…they would," her head bent down, "Touch you with their disgusting hands," her entire body breathed in a heavy sigh. "I did what I had to do to stop them." Sarah's face became stark white.

"Why didn't your father leave?" I asked.

"He believed he was going to find gold, and we would be rich. He didn't think of anything else except that gold.

My sister became sick not long after we moved to the horrible place. The cold, damp weather was too hard on her; she wasn't as strong-hearted as I was."

Sarah's head wiggled, she sniffed, "Annie was a delicate thing so beautiful with her long, red hair, soft little hands to match her petite body, and it sure wasn't a place for her. There just weren't any doctors available; of course, we couldn't have paid them even if they were near. My sister didn't have the heart or the soul to live in that place."

Sarah's fingers continued to grip the chair's arms tighter making her knuckles turn white. "Right after her eighth birthday in January, Annie died of pneumonia. My mother and sister were the only thread of innocence left in my life. My father buried my sweet sister in a small pine box in a shallow grave. My mother, a few of the women, and I stood saying a prayer, leaving my baby sister on that atrocious day in the cold, wet muddy ground."

Sarah's head dropped down. "My sister escaped the only way she could. Since I was a fighter I wasn't gonna let the place take my soul.

I promised myself I would never live like that again.

At night, I would lie awake. I couldn't sleep for the yelling and screaming coming from the other tents. I used to hear my mother crying begging my father to leave that disgusting place, but he wouldn't. I will never forget the nauseating stench of cigars, sweat, urine, and garbage. How I hated every minute living in that hellhole! The only way I was able to stay sane was in my dreams. I dreamt of a prince coming to save me and take me far away from the filth, but that never happened." She sighed.

"The year I turned thirteen, my life once more changed, but not for the better." Sarah's face flushed with anger in her eyes. "My mother knew what she had to do. We packed what we had, not much, and the two of us left without my father for San Francisco. My father just wouldn't leave. I have not seen or heard from him since.

My mother was a very pretty woman. Even living such a very hard life had not taken her beauty away. She found a job at a hotel serving drinks in a saloon. The owner, Arthur, was a kind older man that needed help running the place so he allowed us to live in one of the rooms above the saloon.

I grew up singing in the saloon and helping my mother wait tables, but she died when I was seventeen. Her life had been hard leaving Annie's final resting place and my father in...that abode of the damned. Arthur allowed me to stay on and live in the same room my mother and I shared for as long as I needed.

When I was nineteen, I decided to leave. I have been traveling since. I have lived in many towns, Boston, and of course, Chicago, but my love is San Francisco. That is where I want to stay, and I hope to get my old job back," she sighed with tears still in her eyes.

"I'm sorry to hear about your mother and sister," I said sympathetically. "I understand how you feel because all of my family is gone, too. It has been lonely and that is the hardest part for me."

"I'm sorry, Miranda, about your family. Thank you," Sarah added still overwhelmed, "for taking the time to listen to my story."

"Look, any time you want to talk, just let me know."

I leaned back in my seat and could see so much pain in Sarah's eyes. She was a kind person and just had a hard life. I knew there was more to Sarah's story that she wasn't sharing. I couldn't conceive what Sarah had lived through at the camp. My body flinched at the thought. What had happened to her at the age of thirteen? I noticed the scruffy man leering at us. He gave me a creepy feeling. Was he was one of those men that Sarah had described at that awful camp?

Christening Gowns

The train neared Omaha. It was the end of my ride on the *Overland Limited,* and now I would be riding the *Overland Flyer* to California, known as the Transcontinental Express. It was official. I was going to board on the Transcontinental Railroad.

The train shook coming to a stop. I gathered my things and disembarked onto the depot's platform.

"Miss Curry, it's been my pleasure serving ya. Ya haves an enjoyable ride ta San Francisco," said George. "I wills be headed back east."

"Thank you, George." I nodded my head. "I hope someday to see you again in my travels."

A smiled lit up his dark face. "Thank ya, Ma'am `n enjoy yer ride on the *Overland Flyer.* "

Excitement grew as I walked around the huge depot. Then I noticed Sarah was following me.

"Miranda, do you mind my walking around with you?" Sarah asked shyly.

"That would be nice; I would enjoy the company."

We strolled along the streets of Omaha. It was lovely and seemed quite civilized. I sighed.

"Miranda, what's wrong?" Sarah stopped and turned to face me.

"We are in the Wild West, right?" I said as my eyes panned the buildings along with all the people. "Where are the Indians?"

Sarah laughed kindly. "Yes, we are in the Wild West, and you do need to be careful. You will probably get to see some Indians and some ruthless men, especially in bordertowns. I have seen shootings and street brawls, but we're fine. Don't worry."

I nodded my head; my eyes searched the quiet street. It wasn't worry, but curiosity getting to me as I remembered all the stories I had read and the ones told to me about the dangers of the Wild West.

"Miranda," Sarah began talking in a soft excited voice, "there was one man known as Texas John Reed, not related to me," she said giggling. "They say he's a tall, wild-looking man with dark hair and a scar on the right side of his face. He is known to live in this area—Indian Territory. He is a notorious outlaw responsible for many stagecoach, bank, and train robberies. He has killed many men, but doesn't hurt women. He thinks he is a modern day Robin Hood and goes after gold shipments on trains. He is a legend out here, and I do believe he really exists," Sarah concluded. I must have looked wide-eyed because Sarah went on to say. "I haven't heard of any gold on this train, so we should be safe. We also have Vaughn and Braxton, so we will be fine. Miranda, don't look worried."

"I'm not worried, just enthralled by your account of Texas John Reed. I was just wondering if he was real or just a legend."

I recoiled. Standing next to one of the buildings was the scruffy man watching Sarah and me. He was way too near for my liking, and I knew he was real and as dangerous as Texas John, maybe even more, since Texas John didn't harm women. He grinned, chewing on a cigar and spat tobacco on the ground in our direction. His nasty body leaned against the post of the building, and he squinted at us with a drunken smirk on his scarred face.

Sarah noticed the scruffy man. "Miranda," she grabbed her arm. "Just ignore that hideous man. Don't acknowledge him, and then he will leave us alone," Sarah assured letting go of my arm.

"All aboard," yelled the new porter, Jefferson, a tall thin colored man.

We made our way to the train's steps. Vaughn walked up and held out his hand to me and then to Sarah helping us board the train. He grinned. I turned my face from him trying to hide my smile.

An elderly man with long, gray sideburns had boarded our train car while we were on our walk and was sitting across from Sister Margret Mary. He dressed exceptionally well and wore a nice dark suit with a black, silk, puff tie.

"Hello, young ladies," the man spoke in a British accent. "My name is Hirum Freeman, and I am a tailor from Salt Lake City."

"Nice to meet you, Mr. Freeman. I am Miranda Curry and this is Sarah Reed. We are both traveling to San Francisco."

"San Francisco is very nice. I have traveled to that great city many times," Mr. Freeman offered, his hands rubbed together. "I do ride this train more than I should," he said with a smile.

"Then you have seen the spectacular scenery many times?"

"Yes, Miss Curry."

Our journey continued, and the train stopped at many small towns along the way. At each stop, Sarah and I walked around for a few minutes; however, we still had that scruffy man near, watching our every move.

It was interesting watching people come and go at each of the small town's depots. Our group of Sister Margret Mary, Braxton,

Vaughn, Edwin, Grady, and Sarah didn't change, except we added Hirum Freeman and an elderly couple, Mr. and Mrs. Burkhart, joined us at Plum Creek.

After dinner, the men left for the smoking compartment and all of the women, except Sarah, sat and talked. I felt badly Sarah wouldn't join us, but she knew she wasn't welcome with Mrs. Burkhart sitting with us, a snooty woman so like old Miss Martindale.

Sarah sat absorbed sewing the most elegant baby gowns in pure white, soft pink, and lullaby blue.

"The baby gowns are beautiful," I said overwhelmed. "What are you going to do with them?"

"Oh," Sarah blushed speaking softly, "I have been making christening gowns for newborns since my mother and I moved back to San Francisco. I take them to the churches and hospitals for poor women having babies."

"May I look at some of them?"

"Sure, maybe someday I will make you one," Sarah said with a smile lighting up her face making her emerald eyes sparkle.

Sister Margret Mary was listening to our conversation. She moved next to our chairs and squatted by Sarah and caressed one of the soft gowns in her hands. "These are wonderful, Sarah." The nun's eyes turned to her. The Sister's judgmental attitude toward Sarah melted into a smile of admiration. Sister Margret Mary stood with her hands cradling the delicate baby gowns. "Sarah, this is one of the kindest gestures I have observed in a long time, and I hope to get to know you better when I'm back in San Francisco."

"Thank you, that means a lot to me," Sarah assured, with great humility as her cheeks radiated a red glow.

"May I have a few of these gowns to take with me to my new parish? I will tell everyone how generous you were to give these precious gowns to new mothers."

"Yes, please take as many as you would like." Sarah beamed.

I sat holding one of the soft gowns. "Maybe you will be able to use one of these someday, too."

I saw in Sarah's face that it wasn't going to happen. I knew something awful had taken place in that terrible camp, and she would never be having a child. Her story from earlier played havoc in my mind, and even I wasn't ready to hear her story of what really happened to her at the age of thirteen. I didn't push for an answer knowing her life had been filled with wretchedness and violence. Even with all of the sickness and loss in my family I felt fortunate to have lived a safe life.

The day wore on, and I became tired, so I decided to retire for the night. I tossed and turned in bed mulling over Sarah's likely dilemmas during her deleterious childhood. Tears clouded my eyes and my heart broke, not for myself, but for Sarah. Although I wanted "no more tears," I realized this was the first time in a long time that I was not focused purely on my grief, my needs, my desires. Although I was sad, perhaps this was a step in the right direction.

My reverie was broken by a short whistle stop at an Army fort to unload medical supplies. It was getting late, and I needed to get some rest. As I drifted off, my last thought was that I would awake in Cheyenne, Wyoming.

The First Transcontinental Railroad

I woke early and hurriedly dressed thrilled to see Cheyenne. The train rumbled along the tracks as Sarah and I sat eating breakfast at our table next to the window. Sarah smiled the most beautiful smile that accentuated her kind eyes. She was stunning with her light reddish-brown hair, similar to my mothers.

Vaughn and Braxton sat at the table behind us. My eyes drew to the door when the wretched man entered the dining car. I shuddered. I turned toward the window, but I could see his reflection in the glass. Scraping his boots on the floor he shuffled by our table. He reeked of old tobacco, sweat, and liquor, and had an untamed expression on his face. Vaughn scooted his chair letting the back of our chairs touch. His head leaned back next to mine and his hand rested on his vest. I sat paralyzed watching each man's reflection in the window. The horrid man's head peered down near Vaughn. He made a low, snarling noise like a mountain lion making ready to pounce on its prey, but continued walking past cautiously.

Anger built inside me as my hands gripped into fists. I wasn't letting that man ruin my day, so I turned my attention to Sarah.

Ignoring the horrible man, Sarah sat peering down at the table. "Oh Miranda," Sarah whispered in a soft voice, her long fingers touching the velvety flower in the silver vase. "Look, the red carnation is beautiful. It has such a dark crimson color; it's my favorite flower.

This trip has been wonderful; even my adored flower is on the table. Everything has been perfect," Sarah announced excitedly.

"I agree, the dark red carnation is gorgeous and fits you as well as the pink rose fits me. Everyone should have their own favorite flower," I added kindly.

Sarah cupped the flower in her creamy, smooth hand as if it were a tiny delicate bird. I enjoyed watching Sarah's face beam with delight.

The morning light flooded through the window as shadows flashed against the windowpanes. The hilly landscape zoomed by. Yelping and yowling men sitting tall on horseback waved their hats as they raced the iron horse. I smiled to myself thinking, "Could Texas John be one of these cowboys or was he hiding and plotting his next robbery?"

"That was a dandy breakfast," Sarah said settling into her seat in the compartment car.

"Yes, it was," I said pulling my journal from my satchel. I knew I had time to write since Rawlings and Green River were the next short stops, and we wouldn't be getting off the train to look around.

Later that afternoon Sister Margret Mary and Hirum Freeman stood gathering their things. They were to get off at the stop near Salt Lake City. The large train blew its whistle and slowed to a stop.

Sister Margret Mary leaned over. "Miranda, Sarah, I hope to see you when I'm back in San Francisco. God bless and keep you both, and Sarah, thank you again for the christening gowns. They are lovely. You are truly using your God-given talents to advance the cause of Christ. Sarah blushed at the praise she had been given.

"Oh, I too hope to see you in San Francisco," I replied looking into Sister Margret Mary's kind eyes.

I watched Sister Margret Mary and Hirum as they made their way into the depot and disappeared. When the train pulled out, I began to write about my new friends and got lost in my task as the train trekked mile after mile. All of a sudden, brakes were applied and all the passengers heard the shrieking wheels agonizing against the rails as the train pulled to a stop at Promontory Summit.

This was the place where the railroads had been joined together in 1869 as *The First Transcontinental Railroad* in North America.

My hands gripped the worn railing as I descended the wrought iron steps. Scanning the area, I couldn't move for a few seconds. I was on a mission to find out all the information that I could about the railroad. It was such a controversy in the lyceums across the country.

One man noticed my enthusiastic reading of the plaques. He pulled his shoulders back as he began to recollect his story of the Transcontinental Railroad:

"The crowds of people were crammed together on both sides of the train tracks. People stood along the track as far as your eyes could see. I had never seen that many people together in one place in my entire lifetime. My wife and kids had come days before to be ready for the striking of the golden spike into the tie plat.

You see, I was one of the workers for the Union Pacific Railroad. I wanted my children to be a part of history and see the end of the hard work. I wanted them to know how many workers had given their lives that this might happen. That was what this stood for—the hard work of so many men.

It was a glorious Monday that May 10th, as we all listened to the sound of the joining of the two great railroads. The striking of the golden spike driven into the last tie plat will forever be echoed in my mind. It symbolized the unity of the nation after the War of the Southern Rebellion. Our great country was now joined with 3,500 miles of Transcontinental Railroad. I have stayed on with the Union Pacific Railroad and worked here in Promontory Summit and Ogden since that day. I love the railroad and will live my life, I hope, alongside the large locomotives." The man ducked his head with a bow. "Ladies, I hope you enjoy this magnificent railroad and always remember how it began."

"Thank you very much for taking the time to tell us your story," I said kindly, as the man lifted his hat onto his head and turned to leave.

Sarah gripped my arm and leaned near. "Miranda, Vaughn has been watching you," she beamed.

"How do you know he isn't watching you?"

"I see the look in his eyes. Oh, Miranda, I wish and dream that he had that look for me."

"Sarah, I think you are imagining things. You have all of your fantasies about a prince riding up on a stallion and stealing you away. That's not going to happen to me."

"No, I'm not imagining things. You just wait and see," she added. "Time to board."

We strolled to the train. Vaughn stepped up and as usual with his hand reached out. Sarah giggled. I was glad Vaughn had been watching since he wasn't the only one following us. That despicable man was watching, too.

The train ride was peaceful for most of an hour, but then the barbarian began boisterously remarking to Vaughn and Braxton.

Obnoxious words flowed, his eyes narrowed, and he sneered at Sarah making detestable remarks about what he could do with her. The pain and embarrassment was very clear in Sarah's eyes. She turned her head to the window with tears streaming down her shamed face.

I had enough of his talk, and my temper flared. My eyes burned with wrath. I stood. My small feet stomped making my way toward the man, but Vaughn stood and stepped in front of me blocking my path. He looked down at me with intense eyes and nodded his head for me to sit back down. He turned back to the horrible man, and I took my place next to Sarah.

"Mister, you keep your mouth shut in the presence of these ladies," Vaughn stated in an authoritative voice. With the veins in his neck showing, he continued. "If you can't sit quietly in your seat, you are welcome to get off the train right now," His shoulders tightened, "and I will be glad to assist you."

The man, who wasn't quite as tall as Vaughn, stood. He pulled a long knife from the side of his boot. His glazed, evil eyes glared at Vaughn.

Knowing the man wouldn't hesitate to stab Vaughn, I felt my heart pounded in my ears.

Vaughn stood his ground, a small derringer slipped from his vest, and his eyes watched for any movement. The man knew Vaughn meant what he said sliding the knife into his boot. He returned to in his seat, covered his face with his hat, and didn't speak another word. Vaughn leaned against the seat. He smiled at Sarah but never took his eyes off the man.

I couldn't believe Vaughn had taken such risk for me. I found out quickly I needed to be more careful, and I had much to learn

Sarah had told me of her dreams of marrying a knight in shining armor and was hoping that Braxton would be that knight for her. She believed she wasn't good enough for him and after listening to that vulgar man, her self-esteem had fallen even lower.

About an hour later, Vaughn walked up to us. Sarah leaned near him and whispered, "Thank you, for making that horrible man be quiet."

"He won't bother you again, Sarah, not while I am around," Vaughn answered looking over at her.

I did have to admit that Vaughn could be my knight, even though it wasn't socially correct.

We sat quietly in our seats for a while before it was time to retire and just listened to the train make its way down the track. I wanted to remember all the sights and sounds of the train. When morning arrived, we would be in Bottle Mountain, Nevada.

Special Traveling Companion

I woke early, dressed, and sat quietly in my seat watching the sun warm the day. Hirum Freeman had explained the blaring hot days and cold nights of the Nevada desert. He had also told me about the Sierra Nevada Mountains that stretch out as a gateway to the Pacific. Hirum mentioned that Sherman, Wyoming was the highest point of the railroad at more than 8,000 feet, and that I also needed to watch for Point of Rocks, Wyoming. "The train tracks will twist as a long dark snake through Nebraska's open prairies," Hirum said.

Sarah and I had decided not to get off at Bottle Mountain, which happened to be the right decision. The loathsome man stood and walked to the door, but before he left the train, he turned his head and stared at me. Vaughn stood from his seat and the threatened man turned back around and left down the steps of the train.

The whistle blew and I felt relieved when the disgusting man had not returned.

The morning went by fast. As I arrived in Reno, Nevada, which was close to Virginia City, I was more than a little excited. I had read about Carson City, the capital of the Nevada Territory and the V&T Railroad. The Virginia & Truckee Railroad built in 1872, and intersected with the Transcontinental Railroad in Reno. This stretch of railroad was known as *The Crookedest Railroad in the World*.

The train pulled to a screeching halt and its whistle blew.

Sarah jumped up with delight.

Vaughn stood at the doorway. He followed us down the steps.

Sarah and I wandered around Reno. I stopped walking and turned quickly to see a real live Indian, but out of the corner of my eyes, I observed someone watching us. There by a doorway of a tavern, I saw a shaggy, bearded man turn inside. It couldn't be! I had to be mistaken! He had gotten off the train in another town. My eyes must be playing tricks on me, but it sure looked like the same scruffy man who had been so indecently rude.

"Miranda, is something wrong?" Sarah asked worriedly.

"No, everything is fine, but let's get back to the train," I assured. I tried not to let her see the worry in my face.

Sarah and I settled into our seats and I felt we were safe. In a few minutes, I noticed an older man slowly following the porter, Jefferson, into our parlor car. He was very distinguished in the way he carried himself. He had wild, curly, white hair and a bushy mustache. He looked about the same age as my father and dressed in a white crumpled suit.

Jefferson stepped by us.

"Miss Miranda Curry 'n Miss Sarah Reed, I would likes ta introduce Samuel Langhorne Clemens."

I couldn't believe what I had just heard and for once in my life, I was speechless.

"Ladies, it is of great pleasure to meet you both. May I join you?" Mr. Clemens asked.

Sarah couldn't say anything; her mouth hung open.

"Please, Mr. Clemens, sit down," I finally said.

"Ladies," Jefferson began, "Mr. Wilkins 'n Mr. Holt were generous ta allow ya the privilege of sittings with Mr. Clemens."

"Miss Curry, you wouldn't happen to be related to Abraham Curry of Carson City?"

"No, sir, I don't think I am, but my father would have known more about that; however, he died recently. I have never heard Poppa speak of Abraham Curry. Mr. Clemens, you sir may call me Miranda."

"I am sorry to hear about your father, Miranda. Abraham Curry was an Assemblyman and a Territorial Senator. He was a great man and helped to establish Carson City as the state capital. I had the privilege of meeting the man before he died back in 1873. Now, where are you lovely ladies traveling?"

"We are both traveling to San Francisco. I have always been fascinated with California and wanted to travel to see the city for myself. Sarah is returning home. Are you traveling there, Mr. Clemens?" I questioned, realizing that I was talking way too much in a rambling manner.

"Yes, Miranda, please call me Samuel. Mr. Clemens sounds so old, even though I am." He smiled and his eyes flashed spiritedly. I could see his mind spinning with creativity. "I have been to Virginia City for a quick visit with my older brother, Orion."

Mr. Clemens leaned back in his chair lacing his fingers together as he continued to talk. "I once lived in Virginia City back in 1861 with my brother." His mustache wiggled and his small eyes squinted. "We tried our hand at mining, but that didn't pan out," he laughed. "I was then hired by the *Territorial Enterprise Newspaper* in Virginia City. In fact, that was where I first began using Mark Twain as my "nom de plume." I then moved to San Francisco and worked for the *Morning Call* Newspaper for a spell. It was an interesting place, San

Francisco. I will always remember my stay in that great city by the bay; it's lovely."

"Samuel, I fell in love with The Adventures of *Tom Sawyer and Huckleberry Finn* when I was a child. That is my passion, reading, and I love to write in my journal. I have enjoyed reading my entire life, and you, sir, are the reason I am traveling." My head ducked, my face blushed. "So, I thank you very much."

"That is nice of you to say."

Jefferson informed us it was time for lunch. A big smile emerged on his face as he told me we would be having lunch in the state of California. I was so thrilled I could hardly contain myself. I had made it. I was now in California. Samuel's old eyes twinkled watching me.

"I see you are a true adventurer, Miranda. I am glad to have the pleasure of traveling with you, and I will enjoy talking more on our journey. Ladies," Samuel assured, standing from his chair, "I will wait with anticipation to join you later. Enjoy your meal."

Sarah and I sat at our table, and I watched the landscape flying by. Braxton walked up and leaned near with a smile on his face. "Miranda, we will be entering the Summit Tunnel soon. You will certainly enjoy the Donner Lake views as they are breathtaking."

"Thank you, Braxton. I'm so excited I can't wait to get to San Francisco."

"Well, since we are both going to San Francisco, why don't we share a carriage ride?"

"That is a great idea, Braxton. Sarah and I would be glad to join you." I could see the surprised look on his and Sarah's faces.

"It would be my pleasure, Miranda," Braxton added getting his composure back.

The day was wonderful. I pulled out some paper telling Marion my adventure of meeting Samuel Clemens. I mailed letters to Marion at all of the stops across this great country, and I told her that my dream had become a reality of making it to California. I just wished I had been able to tell my family, but as Marion said, they would know.

The next few hours were the highlight of my journey as Samuel sat and talked. "You ladies remind me of my daughters who I miss so very much. I do hate being away from them, but I will be joining them soon. I have some quick business in San Francisco, and then I will be returning home. Olivia and I have a home in Hartford, Connecticut," his small mouth twisted with a smile. "It is nice to have a place to call home."

I sat with wonder listening to Samuel tell tales of his family.

"Miranda, I too understand tragedy, and I am sorry to hear about your father. What did your mother think of your traveling across this fine country?"

"My mother and brother died of typhoid fever about eight years ago," I sighed thinking of the past. "That is another reason I love reading. As a child, I spent many nights reading book after book. Reading helped on lonely, solitary nights," I added, my eyes blinked back tears, "to escape reality."

Samuel's eyes wandered toward the window. He was quiet for a minute but then continued, "I have wanted to see as much of the world as my life would allow. I have an infatuation to see this great world, not just read the distorted version from others. I hope, Miranda," his face lit, "you never give up your enthusiasm to read and examine everything about this glorious world. If you happen to ever find yourself in Hartford, please look me up; I would love you to meet my beautiful wife and daughters. I would genuinely care to hear the tales from your journeys about this astonishing country, and hopefully, the world." Samuel became quiet and pulled a cigar from his pocket. He stood and bowed, leaving to join the men in the smoking compartment.

Our next stop was Colfax, California; we were nearing the end of our journey.

Edwin and Grady stepped near. "Ladies, it has been a pleasure traveling with you, and I hope to see you sometime in San Francisco," Edwin said.

I smiled seeing the young men's enthusiasm showing on their faces. "I wish the best for both of you," I replied, "and, Edwin, I hope someday to see your jewelry store in town."

"Thank you, Miranda," Edwin added as he bowed to us and walked away.

Samuel stepped near. "Well ladies, our adventure has come to a finale, but a new passage is beginning. The best to both of you," he concluded, tipping his hat. His hand reached into his coat pocket and handed me an envelope with my name on it. I slowly opened it and began to read.

Miranda,

Keep your faithfulness for life no matter what tragedies life sends swirling at you.

Don't lose your joy for life, for when you grow old, you may still exist, but you will have ceased to live.

Life must not be envisioned through others' eyes, It must be envisioned through your own.

I too treasure meeting travelers on my journeys. You, my child, have been an encouragement for an old man in troubled times. Your traveling companion,

S L Clemens, Mark Twain

"Thank you, Samuel; best wishes and safe travels. I hope you will be home soon with your family. I do understand how important family is for us all," I thought blessing him with all my heart.

The magnificent train began to slow, and the large black iron horse came to a stop. The whistle screeched like a banshee, and the large train hissed steam like a dragon.

Braxton scooted close. "Ladies, I will see to everything for our carriage ride. You need to meet me by the depot when you are ready to leave."

Old Grand Hotel

Samuel's right arm crossed his stomach as he bowed to Sarah and me. We blew him kisses, and he beamed a happy smile.

We stood and watched as he left. He was the most fascinating and astute man I had ever met, and I don't believe his mind ever rested. I cherished my letter from him and had tucked it safely into my journal.

Braxton waved Sarah and me to the carriage. As we walked toward the carriage, a strange feeling came over me as if someone were watching. I turned quickly getting a glimpse of a man in the depot's window as he ducked away out of sight.

"Miranda, let's go," Sarah tugged on my arm. "We don't want to keep Braxton waiting."

"Yes, you're right, Sarah," I nodded not taking my eyes from the building.

A beautiful carriage waited. Braxton offered his hand, and I climbed inside. He turned to Sarah assisting her as well, and then he climbed in sitting beside me.

At that moment, Vaughn appeared out of the blue. He held the side of the carriage and slid into the seat next to Sarah. His mischievous grin covered his face, and his blue eyes sparkled as he stared at me.

"Good afternoon ladies," he said, lifting his hat.

Vaughn was fascinating to me, but I remembered Dorothy's warning, not to be swept away by just any handsome man.

"It is a beautiful afternoon," I commented. "The weather is spectacular—so crisp." I was having the time of my life, and I didn't even worry that I was riding along with a known gambler.

"I can't wait to see the San Francisco Bay and the fascinating fog. I'm so excited!" I exclaimed.

"Calm down, Miranda," Braxton said, his hand gently patted mine. "You will have plenty of time to see all of San Francisco, and I would be delighted to show you," he added, his eyes on Vaughn.

I could see the hurt in Sarah's eyes as she turned her face from us.

The horse's hooves clapped on the stone streets as we entered into the city. Seeing the city was just as I had dreamed, breathtaking. The hills were so beautiful like waves on an ocean and the fresh sea air tickled my nose and made me shiver.

We arrived at a magnificent soaring structure and unhurriedly pulled into the center of the building. I drew in a deep breath. We were in the elaborate Old Grand Hotel. I couldn't believe my eyes. I had never seen anything like this before. I could see up to the roof. It was so enchanting and captivating. The Coachman opened the doors of the carriage, and Braxton quickly jumped out helping me down, while Vaughn took Sarah's hand.

Sarah stood next to me fidgeting as she smoothed her hair and dress. "Miranda, I won't be staying here, so this is goodbye. I have enjoyed spending time with you, and I would like to keep in touch," she said in a low voice. Her head dropped downward letting her long hair hide her face. Finally, she looked up to say, "If you wouldn't mind?"

"Where are you going to stay?" I questioned.

"Oh, I will go down the street a ways and find a decent hotel. I will be just fine. I can take care of myself, you don't need to worry," she announced pushing her hair from her face. "I have been taking care of myself for a long time."

"Sarah, there isn't any reason for you to go somewhere else. You can stay right here with me until you get your job back and find a place." I knew Sarah and I hadn't known each other long, but I couldn't get that distasteful man out of my mind. I just couldn't let her go alone; something was making me stop her. My intuition had helped me over the years, and I wasn't going to ignore my thoughts today.

"Oh, no," Sarah insisted, "I couldn't do that. Miranda, I will be fine."

Braxton's face twisted in a frown. He didn't approve of my letting Sarah stay with me in the hotel.

"I won't take no for an answer, Sarah," I declared. I knew she wasn't that different from me, and I hadn't done anything special but to be born into a great family. "Then it's settled, let's go in," I announced. I began to walk to the entrance of the hotel not giving her or Braxton a chance to change my mind.

We walked to the desk to check in, and Braxton came over by me. "Miranda, I'm getting hungry, so why don't I wait until you get settled into your room, then we can have dinner."

"That sounds like a great idea," Vaughn said looking at Braxton with a grin. "We will meet you at the dining room in a few minutes. You can get us a nice table for four."

Braxton's face scrunched tightly.

"That sounds nice, Braxton. We will see you in a little while," I announced happily intently eyeballing Vaughn.

"That will be fine, Miranda," Braxton reluctantly agreed, turning from us walking to the dining room.

We walked over to the hydraulic elevators, which were even nicer than my Poppa's elevator, and rode up to the fifth floor.

"Wow! This must cost a pretty penny," Sarah said swirling around in the hotel room. "This is huge. Oh, it's so elegant. Miranda, I have never stayed in a place like this. Are you sure this is all right. You know I will never be able to repay you."

"It isn't a lot more money for you to stay here, and I like the company," I assured. "Let me check the room and then we need to wash up. I'm sure I'm a mess."

"Oh, you look fine; you always look classy." Sarah said as she nervously smoothed her dress. "Maybe I should stay here in the room, and you can bring me a small snack." Sarah suggested. "I don't want to embarrass Braxton."

"If you don't go, then I'm not going either."

A knock at the door interrupted our conversation.

I opened the door to Vaughn who stood in front of me looking so debonair and dapper in his dinner jacket, nonetheless. "Are you ladies ready to go eat?" he asked.

"Well, we were discussing that," I said, as my eyes peered back into the room, "Sarah doesn't want to go, and I'm not leaving her."

"Sarah is something wrong?" Vaughn stepped into the room. "Oh, I see, it is Braxton. Don't worry about him. You're fine; let's get going, I'm hungry." He said reaching his hand to Sarah.

Sarah wasn't going to say no to Vaughn. We went down the elevator, and Braxton was waiting at the entrance to the dining room. He quickly took my arm, and Vaughn, Sarah's. I smiled at him, and he grinned back at me tilting his head in my direction.

During our meal, a man in his late thirties walked up to our table. He had mesmerizing greenish-brown eyes and was dressed in a camel frock coat with a double-breasted vest and a continental crosstie. He carried himself with confidence and ease.

"Hello, Braxton, I haven't seen you in a while," the man said, patting Braxton on the shoulder.

"I've been in Boston the last few weeks," Braxton answered, standing and shaking the man's hand, "helping some friends with their bank. I just got in today." Braxton turned his attention to the table. "Let me introduce my friends who I met during my train ride from Boston."

"This is Miranda Curry of Boston; Sarah Reed, a local, and Vaughn Ellsworth. This is Oliver Wilkerson."

"Vaughn and I have met," the man said earnestly, turning towards Sarah and me. "It is very nice to meet you ladies. Are you staying here with us?"

"Yes," I said, "it is a lovely hotel."

"I'm glad to hear that. I do take pride in the Old Grand Hotel, since I own her."

"You own this hotel?" asked Sarah in a high-pitched voice.

"Yes, I do," Oliver answered proudly, "and I hope you have an enjoyable stay. If you need anything, please, don't hesitate to ask. Enjoy your meal." His head bowed as he said, "Good evening."

"Good evening," we all said watching Oliver Wilkerson leave the dining room.

"I can't believe I met the owner of the hotel," Sarah kept saying.

"He seemed so nice."

"He isn't that great, I've played cards with him before and he's very tight with his money," Vaughn moaned, "and a sore loser," he announced agitated.

"Is he married?" Sarah asked blushing.

"No, he isn't married," Braxton answered smiling at Sarah. "And he lives out by me in Knob Hill, and owns a handsome mansion.

I turned the conversation to landmarks that I would like to visit, and that constituted the rest of the dinner discussion.

We finished our dinner, and I said goodnight. Vaughn and Sarah decided they were going to stay in the dining room for a bit longer.

Braxton bowed to Sarah. "Good night," he said in a soft voice.

I turned to Vaughn and Sarah. "I had a great evening, Vaughn, I hope to see you again, and I'll see you later, Sarah."

"You can bet on it, Miranda. Good night," Vaughn promised as he glared at Braxton. I studied Vaughn and Sarah. They did make a nice couple. Sarah so beautiful and Vaughn so handsome, but that wasn't what they wanted, and I could see it in their eyes.

Braxton looped my arm in his and strolled me out into the lobby.

"Miranda, when I get to work tomorrow, I will check on the businesses that are for sale, and I'll give you a list of what I come up with. If you need anything, just let me know."

"Thank you for the dinner, Braxton, and the ride from Sacramento. You have been very kind."

"You're welcome. I do hope to see you soon, Miranda. Good night."

Returning to my room, I busily began to unpack my clothes, but before I was finished the hotel door opened.

"Sarah, is that you?" I called out.

"Yes, Miranda, are you still up? I thought you might be asleep by now, and I didn't want to wake you."

"No, I wanted to unpack some things."

"I'm going to stay up for a while, if that is alright?" Sarah asked peering into my bedroom. Her long curly hair hugged her face.

"You stay up as late as you want."

"Thank you, Miranda; I still don't know how to repay you."

"Don't worry so much Sarah."

"It was something to meet the owner of this hotel, Oliver Wilkerson, wasn't it?" she added with a big smile on her face.

"Yes, it was, and he did seem nice."

"He was looking at you," she added smiling.

"You are imagining things again."

"Good night, Miranda," she whispered closing my bedroom door.

California

I woke with the morning sun bouncing off my face softly welcoming me to San Francisco. I climbed out of bed, spun in a circle, but stopped and stood frozen to look out over this magnificent city. My dream had come true.

I quickly dressed and hurried to the main room.

A knock at the door startled me. "Who is it?" I asked before I cracked the door open. "Morning messenger," replied a young man holding a letter. I took it from him and closed the door. I smiled and was pleasantly surprised that it was from Braxton.

"Dear Miranda, I am currently at the bank and have found some businesses for you that I think would be of interest. If you happen to be free this afternoon, it would be my pleasure to show you around this great city. I will be available about two o'clock. Please let me know. I apologize that I can't meet you for lunch. Sincerely, Braxton."

I was surprised that Braxton was taking time from his busy day for me, but very excited about seeing the city. Braxton would be a great guide. I twirled around the room like an excited, young girl.

Sarah walked into the room, and I spun to a stop facing her. "Good morning, sleepy head."

"Good morning, Miranda," she said trying to comb out her hair with her fingers. "Oh…coffee," she declared, quickly pouring a cup from the tray on the sideboard.

"There are some pastries and orange juice, too," I added slipping the letter into my pocket.

"This is so nice," she said sitting down in an oversize chair tucking her legs up under her as she slowly sipped her coffee. "What are you gonna do today?"

I couldn't lie. I pulled the letter from my pocket. "Well, I just received this letter from Braxton, and he wants to meet with me this afternoon and talk about some businesses he has found."

"That's nice," she said softly as her eyes turned downward.

"What are you planning on doing today?" I questioned changing the subject from Braxton and carefully pouring another glass of orange juice.

"I am going to my old job to see if I can get it back, and then I need to find a new place to live."

"Sarah, there isn't any reason for you to rush. You are fine staying here. Stop worrying."

"Miranda, I have never had anyone treat me this nice. I don't know how to act."

"Just take some time to get settled in," I said. "I'm going to finish unpacking."

I hurried back to my room and pulled out a writing tablet. I wanted to send another letter to Marion, and I knew I needed to send a telegram to Mr. Mills in Boston to get an update on the sale of the house and Curry Distributors. I would need to know about my finances before I continued with the purchase of a business.

I finished my letters and unpacking and came back into the main room. "Sarah, I need to mail a letter and send a telegram. I will see you later."

"Alright," she called from her room. "I will be back later this afternoon."

I hurried down the elevator and over to the main desk quickly handing the man my message to Braxton along with the letter to Marion and the telegram. The lobby was bustling with people, so I found a comfortable chair to watch everyone.

A young woman about my age walked up. "Good morning, I'm Grace Tanner. I work here in the hotel. Do you need anything?"

"Good morning, Grace, I'm Miranda Curry. No, I'm doing fine," I answered studying the woman dressed in a nice, white, crisp blouse and Abigail skirt. Her light colored hair was very interesting tied in a knot at the back of her head and covered in a hair net.

"How long are you staying with us, if you don't mind me asking?" she questioned with her fingers relaxed slightly laced together.

"I'm staying at the hotel until I get settled. I just moved here from Boston."

"That is some undertaking. What does your husband do?"

"Oh, I'm not married."

Her blue eyes widened. "You're moving on your own from Boston?"

"Yes, and I'm having a wonderful time."

Grace's hands anxiously twisted together. "Maybe we can get together and talk. I'd like to hear about your plans."

"I'd like that very much, whenever you have time."

"How about lunch tomorrow?" Graced asked eagerly. "I know of a great restaurant down the street."

"That would be very nice. What time do you want to meet?"

"I'll meet you right here in the lobby about noon. Will that be convenient you?"

"Yes, and I'm looking forward to our lunch."

"See you tomorrow," Grace said as she turned to the front desk. "Goodbye, Miranda," she called out.

The morning passed quickly and the smell of delicious freshly baked bread flowing from the dining room brought me to its entrance. I stopped for a few minutes at the podium to scan the menu.

"Good morning, Miss Curry."

I turned around and Oliver Wilkerson stepped next to me. Looking very distinguished and handsome, he stood just a couple of inches taller than I. He was about the same height as Poppa. Though not very tall, he gave off an air that made him the tallest man around.

"Good morning, Mr. Wilkerson," I replied heartily.

"No, my dear, that won't do. You need to call me Oliver, Miss Curry."

"Then you must call me Miranda."

"Are you meeting Braxton for lunch today?" he questioned his bushy eyebrows raised.

"No, he is busy," I replied, "I am meeting him later this afternoon."

"Ma'am, would you like to be seated," the waiter inquired interrupting us. "How many for lunch?"

"Just one," I answered.

"Well, Miranda, I don't fancy eating alone," Oliver proposed. "How about joining me for lunch?"

"That would be very nice. It's lonely eating by oneself."

"Well, I do all I can to make my guest welcome." A huge smile came on his face showing deep dimples. "Please come with me." My arm looped inside his, and he tenderly stroked my hand. We walked to the best table in the room, one sitting by a large window. "Well, what do you think about this grand old place?" He asked with affection showing his love for the hotel.

"This hotel is a marvel. I walked around this morning, but there is a lot to take in."

"After lunch, how about a grand tour," Oliver asked proudly.

"I don't want to bother you, Oliver, I'm sure you are a very busy man."

"Yes…but never too busy for a beautiful woman." His caring eyes stared at me making my heart palpitate.

"Then a tour would be fascinating. Thank you," I answered nodding my head yes feeling my face blush.

"Where," Oliver questioned as he slowly sipped his bourbon, "did you say you were from?"

"I'm from Boston. My father passed away, and I've always dreamed of coming to California, so I did." I paused. "Where did you grow up, Oliver?"

"I grew up in Sacramento," he answered. "I had a dream, too. I wanted to build the best hotel in San Francisco, and I believe I have done just that. You can be the judge."

I smiled. He made me feel relaxed and at ease.

"Miranda, would you allow me to order for you?" Oliver questioned when the waiter stepped up. "The chef prepares a special meal just for me each day. It is a surprise each time."

"That would be wonderful. I do love surprises."

I could see Oliver was always in control. That was all right to a point. I did enjoy his love for life, and he wasn't waiting around for someone else to take charge. The meal was delicious and perfect, just as everything else in the grand hotel.

"Miranda, are you ready to take our tour," he announced standing taking my arm in his.

It was amazing to see the hotel from the eyes of the man who built it. He referred to it as his lady and she was captivating. I remember how much my father loved Curry Distributors, and how he had brought it to life. That was just how Oliver was with this outstanding hotel. It was a magnificent structure and Oliver had thought of every detail to make the hotel flourish.

I had a wonderful time and enjoyed being with Oliver. He was so different from Braxton and Vaughn.

We entered into the main offices and Grace was sitting at a large desk in the center of the room.

"Hello, Grace," I said.

Grace looked up from her work. "Miranda," she said overwhelmed.

"Grace, it is nice to see you again."

"You two know each other?" Oliver asked surprised.

"We met earlier this morning." Grace assured, "We are having lunch tomorrow."

"Miranda," Oliver's head leaned to the side, "you do get around. You haven't been here a full day, and you're already meeting everyone."

I smiled at him. "Thank you Oliver for lunch. I need to go out front since Braxton will be arriving soon."

"Did you say Braxton?" asked Grace quickly standing from her chair.

"Yes, Braxton Sims," I assured, studying Grace's face. "Do you know him?"

"I have met him a few times," Grace said guardedly. "He seems very nice."

I could see a look in Grace's eyes that she'd like to get to know Braxton even better, and I knew he was one of the most eligible bachelors in the city.

I turned back to Oliver. "Thank you for the tour."

"You are very welcome, and I hope we can have lunch again soon," he answered smiling.

"I will see you tomorrow, Grace," I called out as I was leaving.

"Goodbye, Miranda," Grace answered with a faraway look on her face.

I stood in the lobby and kept thinking about Oliver and how kind he was.

My thoughts were quickly brought back. "Good afternoon, Miranda," Braxton said. "Are you ready to see the most amazing city in the world?" he asked taking my arm.

"Yes, Braxton, and thank you for taking the time to show me this great city."

My eyes gleamed image after image in amazement as we rode along the streets of the wonderful city of San Francisco. The buggy pulled to a stop at a point near the water that was called the Golden Gate, a strait that connects San Francisco Bay to the Pacific Ocean. Braxton and I sat quietly watching far out into the turquoise water.

"This is wonderful, Braxton," I said taking in a deep breath of fresh salt air.

"This spot has so many memories," his eyes had a faraway look. "My father used to bring my sister and me here when we were young just to watch the fog creeping up from the bay."

"Oh, I would love to see the fog," I proclaimed anxiously.

"When the extraordinary fog rolls into the bay, the world changes. I promise, Miranda, I will bring you back someday to watch."

"That sounds wonderful Braxton. I can't wait," I declared.

"Miranda, I have an unusual place to eat dinner if you are game. Josephine can cook the best and, of course, freshest fish that you'll ever eat. So what do you say?"

"It sounds delightful."

"Then, let's go," he declared steering the buggy.

The buggy jolted to a stop at the wharf, and Braxton leaped down tying the horse to a post. He then lifted me from the buggy.

We leisurely strolled along the creaky old boardwalk next to the worn fishing boats. The sea gulls flew overhead on their last flight before dark hoping to get bites left from the day's catch. The setting sun's rays covered everything in an orange glow.

Braxton pulled us to a stop in front of a gray, shabby building with a sign hanging above it containing faded blue letters saying *The Fishing Shack*.

The wooden door swung open and Josephine, a gray headed, plump woman greeted us.

"Good evening, Braxton," The woman said graciously. Her body wobbled leading us to a table by a large window. The old wooden chairs crackled when we sat and the smell of frying fish and fresh baked sourdough bread filled the room with warmth. I stared out the window watching the fishing boats sway in the water making a perfect picture with the sun setting behind them as the orange glow disappeared into darkness. Braxton began to tell tales of growing up in this great city and coming with his father to this restaurant when he was a young boy.

Old fishermen with sundrenched faces sat at tables near us. One man started telling tales about how the men would sing on early foggy mornings when they sculled in the bay. "That is how we know where each other is in the dense fog," the man replied with a huge grin on his tanned face.

Then two of the fishermen began to sing.

Listen lads to her tale of fishermen of yore
An' early day begins to break the sun comes up on shore
Sculling along the deep blue bay fair winds and seas, they pray
To cast upon the water as fog takes their luck away
An' in the quiet waters the songs you do hear
Out away from shore as the fishermen draw near
As pirate gulls are watching the nets they doth fill
An' so the day is darkening the cool water it be still
Lord keep us safe the light is fading fast
For 'tis another day of fishing the fisherman do request

Listening to the men's deep voices singing made me believe I was sitting on one of their boats in the thick fog gently floating along.

After dinner, I stood to leave but stopped and turned to Josephine. "This has been the best meal I've had in a long time. Thank you very much."

"I'm sure glad you liked it, Miss Miranda," Josephine said puffing up with pride. "Please come back soon."

Braxton slipped my arm in his and we silently walked along the boardwalk with the moon sparkling onto the shimmering water to the buggy and unhurriedly rode back to the hotel. I was mesmerized by the steep hills and the lights in the buildings glowing like magical eyes.

"Have you had a pleasant day, Miranda?" Braxton questioned turning to look at me.

"Yes, thank you very much. Everything was great, and I loved meeting Josephine and the fishermen."

Holding the horse's reins in his left gloved hand, he reached into his jacket and pull out a folded piece of paper. "Here are the lists of some of the businesses that are for sale. If you are interested in any of them, let me know." He slowed the buggy. "You know this is quite a venture for a woman. My boss at the bank couldn't believe I was preparing this list of businesses for a woman to choose from. You sure you are ready for this?"

"I understand what I am up against. Thank you for believing in me, but I am ready."

The buggy pulled to a stop in front of the hotel. He waited for a minute, and then leaned over gently pulling me close. Before I had a chance to think or react, he boldly gave me a kiss on the cheek. "Good night, Miranda, I hope to see you soon," he said confidently helping me from the buggy.

"Good night, Braxton. Thank you for a marvelous day," I said finally finding my voice.

I rushed to the elevators. I wanted to retreat to my room since I wasn't expecting the kiss, Marion would be having a fit if she knew. I opened my door; the suite was quiet and I was relieved. I sat at my bedroom window looking over the city and tried to figure out what to do about Braxton. I picked up my journal and began to write about my adventures. Things were moving on fast and my mind was spinning. I knew I wasn't acting like a respectable young woman. Talking to men I barely knew and riding around a strange city in a carriage without a chaperone was just unheard of for a well-bred, young heiress.

I placed the list on the table, climbed into the soft bed, and pulled the covers up to my chin to hide from the world. Tomorrow would be a fresh, new day.

The next morning, I ordered breakfast in my room to give me some more time to think. I had to stay focused about what I needed and wanted to do. Marion would be upset with me. A young woman was supposed to be planning a wedding at my age, not buying a business. She would tell me that she had raised me right and to find a husband. Braxton would be top of her list. I sat laughing visualizing Marion's large body and arms waving getting upset at me for not wanting to think of marrying Braxton, but instead wanting to start a company.

I decided to take my time on making a decision of what business to pick. I wasn't in any rush, and I sure wasn't worried about what society thought. I was fine for now. I had made a quick decision to move here, now I needed time.

Grace Tanner

The next day, the morning flew by and suddenly it was time to meet Grace for lunch. I picked my cloak from the back of the chair and reached for the doorknob to leave, but Sarah came out of her bedroom.

"Good morning, Sarah, I'm on my way to have lunch." I stopped. "Oh, how did it go at your old work?"

"It didn't go so well," Sarah's eyes swung to the floor. "They didn't have any openings. I promise I'll keep trying." She heaved a great sigh. "Miranda, could I talk to you for moment."

"Sure Sarah," I said moving back into the room. "I know you will find a good job. I told myself this morning, I'm not in any hurry to make a decision and neither are you. Please take your time and find what you want to do."

Sarah's face squinched.

"Sarah is something wrong?"

"Miranda, I appreciate what you're doing for me, and I'll keep trying, but we need to talk."

"No problem," I said, becoming concerned. "Now, what is the trouble." I laid my cloak and bag in the chair.

"Miranda," she sighed, "yesterday." She began to pace the room. "I saw that horrible man from the train. He was following me. I was able to lose him near my old work, but he's out there watching us, and you need to be careful. I could see in his eyes he's out for revenge and nothing is going to stop him," she said worriedly. She moved near me.

"Here," she said pulling a small derringer from behind her. "This is for you to carry with you when you leave this hotel."

"What!" I exclaimed leaping from my chair, "I can't carry something like that! I don't even know how to shoot a gun," I stared down at my hands holding onto a small gun. I looked up. "Sarah, you've known for a while, haven't you, that the vile man has been following us?"

"Yes, that is why I didn't want to stay here. He followed me. I want him to leave you alone."

I laughed. "That was the reason I wanted you to stay here; so you'd be safe."

"Well, now we need to protect ourselves, and it isn't hard to shoot a gun," she assured, showing me how to load the gun. "Miranda, you just pull the trigger. Please don't hesitate to use this. That man won't give you another chance, so you must get him first."

My body slipped back into the chair. "Sarah, I don't know if I can really shoot someone." My head nodded. "If you think this is right." I held the pistol in my hand and my heart raced. "I will keep the gun with me."

"Please be careful, Miranda," Sarah warned, pacing the room again. "Don't go anywhere alone."

"I'll be watchful of everyone who comes around me," I assured letting the gun slip into my bag, "but you do the same." I picked up my cloak from the back of the chair. "I'll see you later, Sarah." I walked out the door and rode the elevator to the first floor.

Grace stood poised and confident, waiting for me in the lobby.

"I hope I didn't keep you waiting long?" I called out.

"No, since Mr. Wilkerson found out we were having lunch, he let me go early and said for me to take all the time I needed," Grace assured grinning.

"He is a very amiable man," I admitted.

"Miranda, he seems to care a lot about you."

"Where are we going?" I said quickly changing the subject.

"Oh, wait a minute." Grace stopped walking and pulled out an envelope from her cloak. "I don't want to forget, this telegram came for you this morning. I hope it isn't bad news."

"Thank you, Grace. No, this is from my banker in Boston. I'm looking into buying a business and I'll read the telegram later." I slipped the envelope into my bag next to the gun.

Grace shook her head. "Wow, a business that is something. I don't know many women who own businesses, but if anyone can pull it off it'll be you," she said smiling. She slipped her cloak over her shoulders. "All right, are you ready to go? We are only going a couple blocks down the street to a small family restaurant. I met the family when their daughter, Liliana, was married in the hotel last year."

The intense sunshine and the crispness of the air hit me in the face. It was a delightful day. I pulled my cloak around my shoulders, and we walked leisurely down the street and went into a tiny restaurant.

"Good day, Miss Tanner," an older man with graying hair and long mustache said, greeting us. "I have your special table ready."

"Thank you, Mr. Agrioli. This is perfect."

"I hope you enjoy your meal." Mr. Agrioli bowed and turned back to the front door.

Grace whispered shyly, blushing. "How was your day with Braxton Sims?"

She couldn't hide her feelings for Braxton.

"Yesterday was an unbelievable day. I had the best time seeing this marvelous city."

Grace's face twisted with questions in her eyes.

"Okay, just ask. If we're to be friends then we need to be honest. What is it you want to know?"

"Wow, you do come to the point," she said. "Alright, I was curious about your feelings for Braxton." Her face blushed again.

"I thought so. I saw the look on your face yesterday when you heard I was meeting him. I haven't known him long; however, we are only friends, and we'll only be friends. Do you know him very well?"

"No, I have only met him a few times when he would visit Mr. Wilkerson, but he is so handsome and interesting."

"Well, we'll have to do something about your getting to know him even better and soon," I replied. I knew that Sarah cared for Braxton, but he would not be interested in her. Grace was ideal for him, though.

"Since we are being honest," Grace said, "I'll let you in on a secret. Mr. Wilkerson is very interested in you. He wasn't happy to hear that you were spending the afternoon and, I suppose, the evening with Braxton. So how do you feel about Oliver?"

"Honestly," I asked, "you aren't going to tell him, right?"

"No, this is between us girls," she assured.

"I think he is very remarkable, and I would like to spend more time with him too."

Grace smiled; she was happy to hear for sure that I wasn't thinking about Braxton.

"You and Braxton do have something in common."

"What could that be?"

"He likes to go to small, unusual places to eat and would enjoy this place."

"Maybe I can bring him here sometime." Grace became quiet as she stared out the window thinking of Braxton.

I was interested in Oliver, but Vaughn still was the most intriguing man I had ever met. I wasn't going to let Grace know since she wouldn't approve of him. He wasn't the class of men that she would want to be around. Vaughn was so different from anyone I had ever met. Maybe that was pulling me to him.

We walked back to the hotel and chatted the whole way. Grace was very different from Sarah, but would be a good friend. I studied the astonishing hotel as we came close; it definitely was one of the most unique places I'd ever seen.

I stopped at the entrance to the hotel and turned to Grace. "I know we don't know each other well, but I have a friend, Sarah Reed. Sarah is looking for a job; she sings and waits tables. I was wondering if there might be a job for her in the hotel."

"You tell her to come to my office in the morning. I'd be glad to talk to her. We girls have to stick together, right?" Grace said with a gleam in her eyes.

"Thank you for lunch."

"Goodbye, Miranda. You're very welcome," she called back.

The room was dark and quiet. I opened the curtains and looked out with a glad eye onto the breathtaking city. Sitting on the bed, I pulled the telegram out of my pocket, and began to read. Mr. Mills stated that he had a buyer for the house and another for Poppa's business. He had already mailed all of the papers for me to sign. The offers on both, he mentioned, were outstanding, and I should be very pleased. He wanted me to sign the papers to finalize the deals and send them back with instructions of where to send my money.

Tomorrow, I would contact Braxton. I knew he could handle my banking here and get all of the information Mr. Mills would need. I also knew Braxton was correct that this would be a great venture for me, but I was motivated and not going to let anyone interfere with finding a perfect company.

Sharkie

About an hour later, a knock at the door startled me. I swung the door open and there stood Vaughn.

"Miranda, I was hoping you were here," he said earnestly with his hat in his hands. "Get your cloak, let's go."

"Where are we going?"

"I am going to show you my town. I know you went out with Braxton yesterday, so now I'll show you this great city, my way."

"Word travels fast around here," I said smiling up at him, "Oh, I see it was Sarah, who told you." I could see it in his face; he might be a great poker player, but couldn't hide his thoughts from me.

I grabbed my cloak. I knew Marion would be having a fit. This was not who a well-cultured, young woman should be going out with in public, but I was thrilled.

Gently he held onto my arm when we stepped outside into the bright day.

"Where are we going?" I asked anxiously looking up into Vaughn's blue eyes letting his arm pull me in close to him.

"Just have patience," he grinned slowing his pace.

We turned a corner, and there in front of us was a cable car clanking and pulling to a stop.

"Are we really going to ride a cable car?" I squealed with delight, spinning around putting my hands on his vest.

"Yes, and you had better hang on," he laughed, helping me climb up into the car.

My hands gripped the pole on the cable car, and Vaughn's arm securely wrapped around me. The cable car shook as the man pulled the brake descending along the sloping hill. Wind whooshed blowing my hair; the ride was invigorating and my body was alive. I knew Vaughn was my kindred spirit. His presence made me feel protected, and he seemed to be able to look into my eyes and know my mind. He was the only person in my life who could outsmart me, and I loved every minute of that game.

Vaughn's arms kept me close as we strolled down the streets, and I could smell the earthy savoriness about him. I knew gossip would fly, and it would get around that I was out with a known gambler. I was pushing the envelope of decency. I was living the wild life ruining my reputation by letting him put his arms around me, but I didn't care and that was what made me so different from someone like Grace. I knew I talked more than I should. I told Vaughn my dreams and secrets. But, I had confidence in his wisdom, and I trusted him.

Vaughn stopped walking and turned toward me.

"What is in your bag?" he asked, his eyes squinting.

"Oh, a gun," I admitted with spunk.

"What! What? You are carrying a gun?" he questioned, a worried expression came over his face.

"Well, Sarah gave it to me this morning because that vile man from the train has been following us."

"You knew that brute has been following you and you didn't tell me?" he asked turning his head to the side. "Why didn't you tell me sooner?"

"I'm not as simpleminded and dependent as you think, Vaughn. I saw him on the first stop after he supposedly got off the train."

"You don't need to worry about anything. I will take care of him. I found out his name is Augustus Jones, and he is wanted for two murders. Miranda, he isn't someone you need to mess with. You need to get rid of that gun. Give it to me, please."

"That's nice of you to be so concerned," I gripped my purse tighter, "but I'm keeping it for now. Besides, it's not my gun; it's Sarah's"

"Okay," his head nodded yes, "but you need to be careful carrying that thing around."

"I'll be careful."

Vaughn took in a deep sigh and didn't say anything else as we continued to walk. He slowed his pace. A strange man with what I thought was known as a tripod camera was standing in front of a store. We seemed to be his target. Vaughn pulled me close and a flash went off. Vaughn didn't say anything but just kept going. We turned a corner and entered the streets of Chinatown at the intersection of Grant and Stockton Streets. It was as if we magically entered another country.

My eyes grew wide seeing beautiful women wearing dresses that had high mandarin collars and side slits−very risqué. The dresses, called "qipao," buttoned on the right side and were most elegant and a beautiful color. The alluring women looked at Vaughn. He dipped his hat to each of them as we walked passed, and they smiled back.

Vaughn had lived such an amazing life traveling the country and meeting so many exceptional people. I understood his charisma and how women were infatuated with him, just as I was. I wasn't worried about his past life, I was now thinking of his future.

"Miranda," he said, peering down, "you know we really aren't so different. You're an adventurer at heart," he said gently moving my hair from my face. His mischievous expression lit up his face. "Alright…are you ready for more escapades?"

My heart pounded feeling the tender touch of his fingers on my face.

"I'm as ready as I'll ever be," I said delightfully. I moved even closer to him. "Vaughn, where did you grow up?" I asked looking up into his deep, blue eyes, my hand caressing his arm.

"Miranda," his explanation began with sorrow, "a long time ago," his lips pursed, "when I was a small boy of five," he took in a deep breath, "a band of rustlers came to our farm. They were wild, yelling, and screaming with their guns brandishing in the air. One man aimed and fired a shot at my father. I watched his body slump to the ground. I wanted to scream and run to him, but I stood paralyzed. My mother ran from the house. One of the men scooped her up in his arms carrying her inside our home." Vaughn's head looked at the ground. "They treated my mother with shame before they killed her. I hid near the barn not making a sound. The images of each of the men stayed etched into my mind from that day." Vaughn's voice became soft. "I found those men…years later." His head rose and his eyes met mine. Not telling the complete story, he continued, "Well, I buried my parents, I left our farm and home, and I never returned. I lived from that day on with anyone that would let me. My parents were all the family I had.

One hot day, I met a man named Brett, out on the street when I was being beaten by a drunken man not wanting to pay me for taking care of his horse. The man fell to the ground from Brett's blow. Brett stood with compassion in his eyes looking at me as he handed me the money the man owed me. I was awestruck and began to hang around the saloon that he owned and helped him with whatever he needed. He paid me well for my work, and we became friends. I took out the garbage, shined his boots, and watched his back in card games. He taught me everything I know about cards, guns, and how to make it in life.

At the age of fifteen, while I was out running an errand for him, a man drew his gun in a card game. Brett, the only person who I cared for, lay dead on the floor of the saloon. I learned a hard lesson that day why he had me watching his back, and I will never forgive myself for not being there for him."

Vaughn became quiet. He wasn't going to elaborate on his childhood, and I knew he had secrets from his past just as Sarah had.

He slowed down and stopped in front of a tavern. "Well, Miranda," he asked pausing, "what do you think, will you go inside with me?"

"Yes, if that is what you want."

He held the door. I walked into the dark, smoke-filled room, my eyes finally adjusting to the light.

"By George! Well now, if it ain't Nicholas Vaughn Ellsworth! How ya doing, ya son of a gun!" A very short, chubby man shouted as he came from behind the bar and gave Vaughn a hug.

"Doing great, Sharkie, how's the wife and kids," Vaughn said patting the short balding man on the back.

"Oh, I have another boy, since I seen ya last," Sharkie added with pride.

"How many does that make?"

"Eight, and I think that's it. What can I do fer ya?"

"Does Helen still make the best fish stew in California?" Vaughn questioned with his huge grin across his face.

"Yep, she sure does. Now, who's this?" Sharkie asked wiping a table off.

"This is Miranda Curry from Boston, Massachusetts."

"Nice ta meet ya, Miranda," Sharkie said warmly, grinning with a couple of teeth missing in front. "Now why's a nice, ace-high girl like ya hanging out with this character?"

"I have asked myself that a few times," I added with a laugh, "but we've had fun today."

"Well, that's what life is about, girl. If ya ain't having fun and enjoying life, then there ain't much else. I have a good time with my little ankle biters and wouldn't give 'em up for all of the money in the world. Most people think I'm crazy having eight of 'em. Maybe I am, but I love my life and that's all that counts. Many people do what everyone expects 'em ta do and would never change their thinking, but this guy right here," hitting Vaughn on the shoulder, "doesn't do what is expected. He's very dependable, but unpredictable. No one can hold a candle ta him. Ya won't be bored around him."

"Okay, enough talk, Sharkie. How about some of Helen's fish stew," Vaughn interrupted.

"Sounds good, stew's coming up." Sharkie chuckled and his round body shook as he hurried to the back of the room.

I looked at Vaughn, "How did you find this place?" I could see sadness in his eyes.

His hands clasped together, he lay them on the table. "I grew up here. I lived above this place for awhile. Not where Braxton or some of the other men you know came from, is it?" he offered, with pain in his blue eyes. "I'm sure," he paused, "it isn't like your home back in Boston, either."

"No, it isn't like how I grew up, but it is how my father grew up, and he was the best and most caring man I have ever known in my life."

Vaughn sat looking at me with those blue eyes. He didn't say anything else for a few seconds. I could see the hurt that he had lived through, and it made my heart ache knowing that life had been so hard on him and society hadn't helped.

He took a bite of stew and was quickly his old self; he had learned not to take life seriously. "The stew is delicious as usual. Helen's a great cook."

I nodded my head yes. I sat searching Vaughn's face wondering what he was thinking. Why had he taken the initiative to show me his city? I knew he thought of girls like me as snobby, spoiled, little, rich girls. Could it be, he felt the special bond we had from that first time our eyes met on the train? I hoped it wasn't just curiosity to see if I would go out with him. I finished the last of my biscuit and stew, we stood to leave, and Sharkie came over.

"It was nice to meet ya, Miranda, and I hope ta see ya again."

"I hope so too, and please, tell Helen thank you for the meal."

"Sure will," he said as he patted Vaughn on the back, smiling at him.

We strolled down the street toward the hotel, Vaughn had his arm around me, and he drew me close. My head snuggled against him and my insides tingled with warmth as he held me tight. I felt safe; the loneliness vanished. I didn't even know Vaughn very well, but it was as if we had known each other our entire lives.

Moving at a snail's pace we each wanted the day to go on forever. I twirled around facing him and lay my hands on his vest. "Okay, I have to ask, why is he called Sharkie?"

Vaughn started laughing as his hands stroked my hands.

"I wondered when you'd ask. It became his nickname when we were kids. His father was a fisherman during the day and a bartender at night. He literally worked himself to death to support his family. After Brett died, Sharkie's dad let me live with the family, which consisted of seven kids. Even though it was hard for him to support his own family, he took me in. He was a great man.

You see, one day Sharkie's dad went out on his father's boat when he was very young. That day the only fish he caught was a shark, and it scared the fire out of him." Vaughn chuckled. "He never would go back out on a boat. His father was a kind man and he didn't force Sharkie to go fishing, but Sharkie became his nickname from then on."

"He seems so kind and works very hard," I said gently wiggling my fingers in Vaughn's hands.

"Sharkie is the closest thing I have to a family," he said getting quiet.

The oil lights hanging on the building were flickering with their orange glow. People passed us, but I didn't pay any attention to them. It was as if we were in our own world. It had been an enrapturing day, and this time, I hated for it to end. I knew I had fallen in love with Vaughn; he was my life, not Braxton, nor Oliver. I had my answer.

Vaughn walked me to my door, and I was ready for him to kiss me, but he didn't. He said good night holding onto my hand and turned. I started to go inside, but something pulled me back. I watched him leave. He slipped on his hat, as he slowly sauntered with his shoulders taut and head held high, disappearing around a corner. I knew he was more of a gentleman than my old traveling companion, Dorothy, believed.

Sarah's New Life

I swing the door open to my suite. Sarah sat quietly in the over-stuffed chair next to the window with her legs pulled to her chest. She had been staring out into the night but turned around. "How was your day?" she asked giving me a questioning look.

"It was the best day I've had ever," I assured spinning around like a schoolgirl.

"Okay," she sat up in the chair. "All right, out with it. What's going on, and who were you with today?"

"I was with Vaughn this afternoon," I answered breathlessly.

"I see," she said grinning and then letting her legs fall to the floor. I plopped down in the other overstuffed chair.

"Oh, Sarah, I also had lunch with Grace Tanner. She works here in the hotel. I told her you were looking for a job, and she said for you to come and see her in the morning."

"Did you tell her what kind of job I've done before?" she asked nervously.

"Yes, you need to talk to her."

"Thank you is all I can say." Her shoulders tensely tightened. "I still don't have any idea how to repay you."

"You don't have to keep thanking me. Friends shouldn't have to say thank you all the time. I know you are grateful."

I stood from my chair and turned back to face her. "You and I are two of kind, whether you believe it or not. I'm tired and going to bed."

"Good night, Miranda," she giggled, "I know that you'll have wonderful dreams."

"Good night," I said.

"Miranda, I'm glad you went out with Vaughn," she called out.

I smiled back. Of course, Sarah wouldn't judge Vaughn or me and would never worry about what society would think.

My bed wasn't as fluffy as my old bed back in Boston, but it was a great place to hide. I couldn't sleep; I just couldn't wind down. I moved to the window to watch the kerosene lamps shine dimly through the fog and a calmness came over me, recalling every second with Vaughn.

I finally fell asleep from exhaustion. I woke with the same peacefulness of the previous night. I walked into the parlor and stood shocked. Sarah sat dressed ready to go downstairs. "Wow! You're up early!"

"I wanted to be sure I was on time to meet Miss Tanner," she said excitedly standing. "Do I look all right?"

"Yes, your dress is perfect," I said. "Let me dress and then we can go downstairs and have a nice breakfast." I turned back to my bedroom, but stopped to offer, "I'll even go with you to Grace's office. How does that sound?"

"Oh, that'd be nice. I'm so nervous. I've never tried to get a job in a place like this." Her hand flew in the air. "Are you sure?" she queried. "She wants to talk to me."

"Yes, you're right," I called out from my bedroom as I dressed. "You'll be fine." I peeked my head out the door, "Look, you don't have anything to worry about."

The dining room was quiet. Finding a table by the door, we sat down and ordered our breakfast. I tried to have a normal conversation, but Sarah was too anxious to talk or eat. As each minute passed, she sat playing with her food and rehearsing what she wanted to say during her interview.

I smiled taking the last sip of my orange juice. I stood from the table. Sarah, realizing the time had come, stood and tried nervously to straighten her dress.

We walked silently into the lobby and to Grace's office. The door was open and quiet. Sarah fidgeted wringing her hands together.

Grace looked up with a smile.

"Good morning, Miranda. This must be Sarah," she said kindly. "Sarah, I'm Grace Tanner. Please, have a seat."

Sarah forced a distressed smile as she entered the room. She sat in a chair across from Grace.

"I see you're in good hands, so I'll talk to both of you later," I excused myself.

Grace smiled at me as I pulled the door closed.

Time slowly moved on as I sat in my bedroom waiting to know the outcome. I was more anxious than Sarah. After what seemed like hours, she came running into my room.

"Miranda, I got the job," her voice trembled with excitement and her face beamed.

"Alright," I said nervously scooting to the edge of my chair. "Don't leave me in suspense. Tell me what happened."

"Grace and I talked for a time. You were right; she's so nice."

"Yes, she is. Come on, what did she say?"

"She said they had an opening in the men's bar upstairs, and they need someone to oversee the entire group of servers." Sarah shook with delight. "Oh, I can't believe I'm getting the job. The pay is more than I've ever made. I also get a room here in the hotel. It ain't anything like this," her eyes studied the room, "but it comes with the job. I know everything about running a bar and serving drinks. It's perfect; I can't wait to start. I'm meeting the manager and bartender this afternoon after lunch. The hours will be long for a while, but the job is great. Miranda," Sarah sighed, "I'm not saying it because you said I don't have to repay you, but you know how I feel. You're the best friend."

"You got the job because you are qualified, and you'll keep the job for doing a great job." We stood from our chairs and went into the parlor.

"I'll show everyone I can do this job. They've never had a woman as manager," Sarah said assuredly.

"I know you will," I agreed. "When do you move to your new place?"

"Tomorrow, if that is alright? I have a lot to do before then," she said excitedly.

"Sure, tomorrow it is, but I'll miss you."

"Hey, I'll just be downstairs," she added with a new confidence in her voice.

The morning went by fast. Sarah came to my bedroom door, "Wish me luck," she said.

"Sarah, you don't need luck. Just be strong. You can handle this job."

Walking out the door, she smiled at me. I lifted my book to read, but I couldn't concentrate. I was in San Francisco, in love, and had wonderful new friends.

My Knight in Shining Armor

bout two o'clock, a young messenger stood at my door. He was holding a long, white flower box.

When I lifted the top, I couldn't believe my eyes. Inside the box, more beautiful than I could imagine, were thirteen long-stem, light pink roses. Lying with them was the locket from the train; the locket I had fallen in love with.

I cradled the roses in my arms and smelled their sweet fragrance. I was ecstatic remembering what Dorothy had said. Thirteen roses meant a secret admirer. I couldn't believe I was looking at my special locket. I knew it had to be Vaughn or Braxton who sent the roses. I was hoping it was Vaughn.

I carefully opened the locket. Inside was a photo of Vaughn and me. My heart pounded. This was a dream come true. Now, I understood why the man took our picture. Vaughn had all of this planned. I slipped the locket around my neck closing the clasp. I would cherish it forever. My fingers held onto the necklace as tears swelled in my eyes. Underneath the roses was a note.

"Meet me on the balcony at 6:30 for dinner. If you aren't there, I will understand. Your secret admirer."

Patience was difficult for me as I waited with suspense for the clock to chime off the hours. I carefully picked out the perfect dress —my new, light orange one that fit snug in the front and gathered into pleats in the back. I also had a cashmere shawl that had flowers to match the dress and the most fabulous hat with small feathers.

The time finally arrived for me to leave. I opened the door and walked down the hallway and around the corner. Standing on the balcony was Vaughn just as handsome as ever holding one pink rose, meaning love at first sight. He had listened to Dorothy that morning at breakfast, explaining the meaning of roses. He remembered I said pink roses were my favorite. A feeling of completion welled up in my soul.

His strong arm looped my arm, and we stepped into the elevator. I didn't notice if anyone was around me. My thoughts and eyes were only on Vaughn. The elevator doors opened wide, and he led me to the entrance of the lobby. A doorman bowed when he opened the lobby door, and we stepped into the courtyard. The night air wafted with the scent of fresh cut flowers and the most elegant white coach stood before me. Vaughn held onto my arm and helped me inside the fairytale coach. The horse trotted down the street stopping in front of the most romantic restaurant in the city, The Coppa on Montgomery Street.

The Tuscan dinner was more spectacular than I could imagine and my mind kept dreaming of growing old with Vaughn always by my side. This was my new life and no one was going to tie me to old, worthless traditions. I didn't care that Vaughn wasn't the reputable man society wanted me to marry. Fate had brought us together, and nothing was going to tear us apart. I knew that night I never wanted to live without Vaughn. He was my knight in shining armor.

I sat thinking of Marion with her hands on her hips calling out, "Lordy mercy, child! What has ya dun." Then a smile would appear on her face because all she wanted was for me to be happy.

I was so intrigued watching and listening to everything Vaughn said. He ordered lobster arrabiata for us to share. For dessert, we ate tiramisu. We only had eyes for each other and there seemed to be no one else in the world. At the end of our feast, he stood taking my hand and led me out of the restaurant and into our coach.

He climbed into the coach and slid in close next to me. The coach slowly moved along through the fog. The fog enveloped us on the most fantastic evening of my life. Vaughn's arm wrapped around me and kept me warm in the chilly night. We sat quietly in the silence of the evening with our breathing to coincide and became as one person.

He caressed me and pulled me close as our lips met for our first kiss.

We sat holding onto each other not having to talk. Our emotions were doing the talking for us both. He held onto me as we snuggled and new feelings stirred inside me. I knew neither one of us could deny the thoughts we had. I looked into his eyes reaching up tenderly touching his face, kissing him once more knowing I wasn't behaving properly, but I wasn't worried about anything at that moment. I wanted to stay safe in his arms and never leave.

The sound of the horse's hooves were soothing and calming. This, I believed, was my new life. The carriage pulled to a stop. The amazing night had ended with Vaughn helping me out of the coach. He put his hands on my waist and twirled me around just as my Poppa used to do when I was a child. I looked into his eyes, and I believed we would have many nights just as this one.

Vaughn walked me to my door. I looked into those enchanting blue eyes full of mischief and love. His face was radiating with happiness as he leaned down and kissed me. Softly he whispered, "Miranda, I will love you forever." He opened the door, and I said good night. Reluctantly, I went in my room. My mind swirled with dreams about the life Vaughn and I were to have.

A Love beyond All Loves

The next morning, I woke with inexplicable happiness. Sarah was up early getting her things ready. I had so much to tell her before she moved to her new room. She had seen the pink roses earlier, and I explained the meaning of thirteen roses. I showed her the locket. She knew Vaughn had been in love with me from the beginning, just as Dorothy did.

Finishing dressing, I helped Sarah prepare to leave. It was going to be lonely without her here, but I would have Vaughn.

A knock sent me rushing to the front door. When I opened it, there stood the same man with another long flower box. I couldn't wait. I pulled the lid off. This time, inside the box were 15 pink roses. I gasped and became dizzy. I felt as if someone was chocking me when I remembered 15 roses meant I'm sorry. My trembling hands lifted the card out of the box.

Miranda, my love, I realized last night just how much I do love you. I love you enough to know that I am not right for you or worthy of you. You are extraordinary and deserve someone better than I am. I'm a known gambler and that wouldn't be the life for you. You deserve the life someone like Braxton would give you—the mansion sitting up in Knob Hill, not traveling from hotel to hotel. I am not the settling down type.

I love you enough to let you have the life you deserve. I had hoped it could be different, but I knew last night our dreams were unusual and society wouldn't approve, causing you pain. The time we have spent together, I will always remember.

I will love you forever. Please find it in your heart to forgive me. With all my love to the end of time, Vaughn.

I slipped down into a chair. Tears flowed and my body shuddered. My dreams and thoughts of happiness had just disappeared.

"Miranda, what's wrong?" cried out Sarah running into the room. She took the letter from me and read it with her eyes growing wide. "No, he can't do this to you! I'll put a stop to this!" she yelled swinging the note in the air.

"No, Sarah, I'm sure he is gone." I sniffed with tears flowing down my face. My body paralyzed, loneliness was taking over. For the first time in my life, I believed loneliness would win.

"But, Miranda, he doesn't understand you don't love Braxton," she shrieked. "Vaughn's right for you! You two are meant to be together. I'm going to go find him. He is just confused," she called back running out the door.

I couldn't stop her or maybe I didn't want to. I sat thinking about last night—about my dreams and how they had just vanished. I knew I'd never love anyone as I loved Vaughn.

The door opened after what seemed like hours, but it had been only a few minutes. Sarah walked into the room with her head down shaking no.

"Vaughn has checked out and didn't leave an address. He's gone, Miranda. I'm so sorry."

"Don't worry about me, Sarah. I have lived through a lot of sadness, and I'll live through this. I'm a survivor, Vaughn knows it," I said in a soft voice with my fingers caressing my cherished locket.

Sarah didn't move. "I don't want to leave you, Miranda."

"I'll be alright; you go and get settled into your new place. I'll come down and visit soon. Good luck with your job."

She still didn't move.

"Stop worrying about me; this is an exciting day for you."

I gave her a hug, and she walked out the door carrying her bags.

The door closed, and I was alone again. I held Vaughn's note in my hand, and I began to read it repeatedly, letting tears race down my face. I imagined a crestfallen Vaughn as he sat and wrote the short but powerful note.

A deep breath filled my lungs as I whispered, "Vaughn…Why did you leave? Why didn't you talk to me first?"

I gripped my fist with anger building. I should have said something to him last night. I should have told him I would fight for him and not let anyone tear us apart. Why didn't I tell him how I felt? Now I might never have the chance.

I laid the tearstained paper on my bed. I couldn't breathe feeling as if I was being smothered. That was the only thing I hated in life, feeling so alone. I couldn't live like this; I needed something to keep me busy. I would find a business. Then I'd find a way to bring Vaughn back. I would convince him that everything would be all right. I wouldn't let my dreams vanish. I would do as I used to say, making Marion cringe, "Come hell or high water, I will be all right."

I stood in front of the mirror glaring at the young girl staring back with swollen red eyes. "Miranda, you'll make it."

I wiped my face and combed my long wild hair. I couldn't stay in my room any longer.

I was walking around the lobby when Grace came over. "Are you alright, Miranda? Sarah explained what happened. I'm so sorry."

"Yes, Grace, I'll be fine." My head shook no, "Don't worry. I'm not going after Braxton; he's yours," I assured trying to smile.

"I wasn't worried about that. I see the pain in your face. We need to do something fun. Why don't we invite Braxton and Mr. Wilkerson to dinner at my place tonight? What do you think?" asked Grace.

"I don't know if I'm up to helping with a dinner party, but if it'll help you get to know Braxton, all right."

"And you a way to get to know Mr. Wilkerson."

"That, I'm not interested in. Let me know what they say."

A heavy morning mist hovered over the city. I left the hotel and began walking aimlessly. I knew I shouldn't be out around the city alone, but I needed to get away for a while. I kept my purse close feeling the gun inside. I had planned in my head how to use it.

The streets were busy and people were going everywhere, but I was still on alert. I turned down a street and I stopped walking. A beautiful old church sat in the distance. I began to walk toward the church with something drawing me there. I stopped in front of the tall steps reading the sign, "Old Saint Mary's." This was Sister Margret Mary's church.

My shoes tapped on the stone steps making my way up to the beautiful church. In the dimly lit sanctuary I smelled the scent of burning candles, and it relaxed me. I stopped moving. A young nun was sitting in the front pew. I didn't want to disturb her so I turned to leave, but she saw me.

She stood. "Good morning, my child. May I help you? You look very sad."

"I'm fine, Sister. I met Sister Margret Mary on the train when I was traveling from Boston. She told me about this church, and I wanted to see it."

"Yes, this is a warm inviting church, but I have a surprise for you," she said earnestly. "Please sit. I'll be right back."

The young nun hurried through a side door. I sat quietly thinking about Vaughn. Footsteps behind me were getting closer. I turned seeing the nun standing with a big smile on her face. Next to her was an older nun with the same warm smile that I remembered from the train.

I flew from the pew.

"Sister Margret Mary," I called out.

"Miranda, my dear child, what is the problem?" she asked wrapping her arms around me. "Something has happened."

"Sister, it is so good to see you. When did you get in?"

"I arrived last night, late," she announced leading me to a pew. "Please sit and let's talk. Tell me what the trouble is."

The words began without even thinking, telling my tale about the message from Vaughn. Believing he wasn't the right man for me, he had left to give me a life. I told her how much I loved him.

"Yes, I know he left town."

"How do you know?"

"I saw him last night at the train station in Sacramento. He looked as sad as you; he wasn't his usual confident self." Her head shook. "I now understand."

My heart sank. "So," I sighed, "he did leave town?"

"Yes, you know, I didn't approve of your seeing him, but you also set me straight on Sarah. I had to reflect and ask for forgiveness for judging people. Even I am not perfect. I'm so sorry. I did believe that he was wrong for you, but I know he loves you. He loved you enough to give you the life you should have. I could see by the look in his eyes that he isn't coming back. I'll do everything I can to help you get through this."

"Thank you, Sister. I needed to talk this out, but I know how tired you are."

"I'm never too tired for you, Miranda."

"One more thing before I leave, I have to tell you about Sarah and her new job at the hotel."

We sat in the quiet of the church and her smile grew as my words continued about Sarah.

"Sarah does deserve happiness. Please give her my best and let her know she is always welcome, too."

"I know she'll appreciate hearing that you would like to see her; thank you for listening. I do hope to see you soon, and I'm glad you're home."

"Please, visit me often."

"I will Sister. Goodbye."

"Good bye, Miranda." She stood and gave me a hug and we walked to the massive doors. "The Lord will be with you."

I sighed stepping down the massive steps and passing a few more souls entering the church who needed reassurance that life would continue. I moved on quickly down the street to the hotel. I kept a watchful eye, even though I believed Augustus Jones had moved on. I hadn't noticed his standing around, and I didn't feel his stares, but something still worried me.

The doorman ducked his head as he opened the door, and I stepped into the busy lobby. Grace ran over her arms flying in the air.

"Miranda," she grabbed my arms. "They both said yes. Now we have to plan a meal. Oh! These letters also came for you today."

I peered down at the return addresses. One letter was from Mr. Mills. I looked and the other was from Marion. I put them inside my cloak. Grace's body was trembling with excitement. I had to smile at seeing love would never die.

"That may be a problem," I added. "I don't know how to cook."

"Oh, you can't cook," she said, laughing.

"No, I can't cook, I'm sorry."

"That's alright, I'll see to everything. We need to get ready to leave by four o'clock. Mr. Wilkerson said I could leave early to prepare. Don't look worried. I'll teach you to cook, and there's plenty for you to do."

"I don't mind helping, and I'll meet you in the lobby at four."

"Miranda, you seem to be feeling better, I'm glad. You'll see you're going to have a good time tonight."

"I'll be fine," I assured.

I pulled out my key, the door swung open. I sighed seeing the huge room so empty, so lonely in front of me. I would have to switch to a smaller room. I would talk to Grace about that tonight. I could see the flower box in the trash can over to the side, a reminder of my life.

I knew I needed to eat, but I wasn't hungry. My insides were a mess, just like when Poppa died. I couldn't think about food, and I hoped I would be able to make it through dinner tonight.

My fingers pulled the letters from my pocket. The sun shone in the window letting the rays flicker across the room. I laid Mr. Mills' envelope on my lap and tore open Marion's envelope first. The words flowed, not from the page, but from her voice. A tear dropped onto the page, not a tear of sadness but of joy. She was doing fine and would be moving in with her older sister who needed help. Marion had to stay busy and couldn't sit around all day. It was uncanny how she knew just what to say to make me smile. I folded the pages sliding them back into their envelope.

The letter from Mr. Mills was only one page. I sat up in my chair. I was stunned at the offers he had gotten for the house and business. I knew why he was excited. I would have plenty of money to buy my business. I did feel guilty; this was Poppa's money, but I hoped he would have approved of what I was doing. I decided to give Braxton the papers tonight at dinner. I needed to mail the paperwork back to Mr. Mills very soon; I had to get my banking settled.

I closed the bureau drawer which was already laden full of letters from Marion. I place Mr. Mills' papers on top, I didn't want to forget them. I sat in the chair by the window, laid my journal in my lap, and began to write.

Tears dripped discoloring the pages. I wrote of my happiness with Vaughn, the sadness, the changes in my life from minute to minute. How can dreams vanish before they become a reality? I sat remembering Vaughn's last kiss of the night. His soft deep voice, whispering in the quiet hallway, "I will love you forever." The words kept playing in my mind without an end. I had to remember his voice. The voice I swore I would never forget.

I placed one pink rose in the front of my journal. A reminder of a love beyond all loves, a love I hoped someday would become a reality.

The clock on the bureau struck three. I stood in front of the mirror and wiped the tearstains from my face. "Miranda, this is a big night for Grace, a night of happiness. Life will move on with or without you."

The hurt I hoped would stop someday, but the pain of missing Vaughn would always be in my heart. I wished I had Jonathon with me now. I needed all the encouragement I could get to move on with my life. I felt such emptiness inside my heart.

"Okay, Miranda, there will be no more tears," I said with a strong voice.

After a few minutes, I grasped my locket. I had to smile, and I believed someday I would be reunited with Vaughn. I picked up my cloak and Mr. Mills' papers and slid them in my pocket. I was ready to leave. The door closed echoing in the silent hallway.

The elevator dinged as it opened in the lobby and standing waiting for me was Grace fidgeting as she paced back and forth. Her face flushed with excitement.

"Are you ready, Miranda?"

"Yes, let's go."

Grace didn't live far; it was only a few blocks, but again I was very careful traveling along the street. She opened the door to her small home and hurried into the kitchen. In a matter of minutes, pots and pans were banging, and the kitchen began to smell incredible.

"Miranda, the dishes, tablecloth, and napkins are in that sideboard. If you don't mind, please set the table?"

"That I can handle," I assured. "Now Grace, take a deep breath;

everything is going to be wonderful."

I shook the freshly ironed cloth spreading it out and set the candlesticks in the middle of the table. This was going to be a perfect dinner for Grace, and I hoped Braxton understood.

"Alright, now we need to freshen up, and then we're ready," Grace said briskly coming from the kitchen. She stood very proud looking at the table. "You did a great job, its perfect, so elegant," she added with anticipation.

"How do I look?" she questioned. She spun around smoothing her clean dark blue dress down with her hands.

"You're beautiful; now relax; have fun," I insisted going into the parlor.

Grace hurried to the table and lit the candles. Their warm glow danced around the room. "The candles are perfect," she said in a high-pitched voice, clasping her hands together. "Everything is perfect."

A knock at the door made Grace jump. Here she had invited her boss and the man she cared about to her home.

I smiled with her enthusiasm becoming infectious and hurried to the door, opening it wide, and letting the two very distinguished men enter the room.

"Good evening, Gentlemen. Please make yourselves at home."

"Good evening, Ladies," Oliver said walking ahead of Braxton and handing me a beautiful bouquet of fresh flowers.

"These are lovely," I said. "They smell so fresh," I assured taking in a deep whiff of the sweet aroma.

"I grew them myself in my garden at my home," said Oliver as he puffed up proudly.

"They're gorgeous. Oliver, I can't believe you have the time to see to flowers." I handed the bouquet to Grace when she finally snapped out of her daze.

"Please, let me take your hats and coats," I insisted holding out my arm.

"Let me help you, Miranda." Oliver said kindly. He stepped near me, his firm hand taking the coats from my arm as I opened the wardrobe door and pulled out two hangers.

Grace had finally found her voice and asked Braxton to sit. She left for a few minutes to put the flowers in a beautiful vase and set them in the middle of the dining room table.

I sat on the sofa, but was surprised when Oliver sat next to me. His arms crossed over his chest with an air of confidence. Braxton sat in a flowery chair to my side. I wondered if he knew he was being set up, and I had to smile thinking about the trap we had set for him. This is what Marion had trained me to do. I was supposed to be catching a husband, but I must not have been trained very well, since I let Vaughn vanish out of my life. My head shook; I had to stop thinking about Vaughn. I looked over at Oliver, and he had a smile covering his face bringing out his dimples. I wondered if Oliver knew what Grace was up to. I smiled back at him.

I walked to the sideboard full of beautiful crystal decanters sitting on top. "Gentlemen, would you like a drink? I believe Grace has some brandy and scotch."

"Yes, I would," Oliver answered, standing up. "Miranda, I'll fix the drinks. What would you like Braxton?"

"A little brandy sounds good, thank you."

Oliver lifted the decanters and poured their drinks.

"Thank you, Oliver," I said softly touching his arm.

"My pleasure," he answered picking up the drinks and following me to the sofa.

"This is a nice place you have here, Grace, I must pay real well," Oliver called out with a comforting laugh looking around the room.

I turned to Braxton. "I have the papers from my banker, Mr. Mills, and the instructions for him to finalize the selling of my Poppa's house and business." I handed the papers to him. "If you don't mind, can you help me out?"

"Yes, it won't be a problem. I will be happy to see to filing the papers first thing in the morning."

"Now that I have my banking intact, I believe it is time for me to choose a business from the papers you gave me."

At that point, Oliver quickly spoke up.

"Miranda, I don't mind helping you. I would be glad to look over the business you are thinking about buying. Why don't we have lunch tomorrow? You bring the papers about each of the businesses, and I will look them over."

"That would be very nice. I could use some advice."

I saw the look on Braxton's face that Oliver was going to help me and not him. Grace had gone into the kitchen to finish our meal, and I could tell she was overly anxious. It was hard for her knowing Braxton wasn't paying attention to her and her special dinner party wasn't working.

"Grace has worked a long time cooking. I had better give her a hand, even though I can't cook."

"She cooked all of the meal by herself?" Braxton questioned.

"Yes, this was her idea, and she has worked nonstop," I assured. "I had better help. Will you excuse me?"

"No, Miranda, you just sit still. I'll help Grace. I love to cook," Braxton insisted.

He set his glass on the dining room table and pushed the kitchen door open. I would love to have seen Grace's face when Braxton walked in the kitchen.

After a few minutes, Braxton came into the room and announced with his big crooked smile, "Dinner is ready."

Oliver stood looping my arm in his and let me to my seat at the food laden table. I smiled knowing he was always in charge.

Braxton opened the wine and poured each of us a glass. The evening was going well for Grace. Her anxiousness had eased, and she began to tell stories and laugh. The food was delicious; the evening fantastic and, I had to admit, I was having a good time.

When we were done with dessert, Oliver stood. "I think I need to be on my way. Tomorrow, I have a big day ahead. The meal was spectacular Grace. I didn't know you were so talented. I will see you in the morning." He turned toward me. "Miranda, would you like to accompany me back to the hotel. I'd be honored?"

"That would be very nice, Oliver."

He reached out his hand to help me from the sofa.

Grace handed us our coats, and I smiled at her. She grinned back as I slipped on my cloak.

Oliver opened the door and led me out into the cool crisp night. The sparkling city was beautiful as we strolled along the street to the magnificent hotel standing tall in the distance.

"The evening went rather well, didn't it?" Oliver said calmly, "I'm not going to beat around the bush. I know this was what Grace has wanted for some time."

"You knew all along what the dinner was about?"

"Yes, I think Braxton was the only one who didn't," he said laughing. "I also know about you and Vaughn."

I gave him a look.

"I'm not trying to pry, but in a hotel, gossip does get around. I am sorry it didn't work out for you; however, I knew tonight was for Grace."

"You didn't mind coming to dinner, even though it was a trap for Braxton?"

"Hell no, if it makes Grace happy, then it is fine with me. Braxton is a great man, and Grace has been crazy about him for years. He has been too busy to notice, and I do hope he's taking notice now. She is a wonderful person."

How nice and honest Oliver was! Most men would have hidden the truth as to what he had found out about Braxton and Vaughn.

"Thank you, Oliver."

"What for?"

"For being you."

We were nearing the Old Grand Hotel, and I saw the pride he had as we walked up to the massive door going into the lobby. He stopped and turned to me, "I will see you tomorrow at lunch."

"I will meet you at the dining room, but first I have to move to a new room."

"A new room! Is something wrong with the old one?" he asked in an alarmed voice causing him to frown making his bushy eyebrows almost come together.

"Well, you don't know everything," I added grinning. "Sarah Reed was staying with me but is working for your hotel now so she has moved out of my suite. I'm going to downsize now that I don't need such a large room."

"Well, I have the perfect room for you on the top floor. You can really see the city. The views are unbelievable."

"Did you say the top floor of the hotel?" I wheeled around and faced Oliver. "Those rooms are far too expensive."

"They're not too expensive," he snapped back smiling, "not when you own them. I insist. Tomorrow I will send someone to help you move," he paused, "about nine o'clock. Is that too early?"

"No, that's not too early, but I can't afford that room."

"Yes you can, don't worry about that. I'll see you for lunch tomorrow. Good night, Miranda," he said as he made a slight bow and walked away.

I had enjoyed the night, but couldn't help thinking about Vaughn. I missed him. I didn't feel as hopeless as I had earlier, but I did feel alone and my heart was breaking.

Life Moves On

The next morning, I was up early before the sun rose. I had worked hours repacking my trunks, and now I was ready to move to my new suite. I was so excited. I knew I shouldn't accept a suite from Oliver, but then why not, I needed something fun in my life.

There was knocking at the door, and I swung the door open. Standing in front of me was a young man who looked to be about seventeen. "Miss Curry, I'm here to help you move. My name is Mark."

I backed up letting the young man step inside the room.

He piled the two trunks on a cart, and I followed listening to it squeak as it rolled down the hallway and continued to a private elevator that only went to the top floor. The wheels continued to squeak rolling along a marvelous hallway on the top floor, and then all became quiet. Mark graciously opened the door.

I walked in. Breath escaped me. The most splendid room I had ever seen was sprawled out before my eyes. The ceiling was tall and the room elegant. I hurried from room to room trying to take in the splendor of the massive suite.

I stopped at one of the wide windows. The view was breathtaking, just as Oliver had said, and I could see forever. I did love the suite, but this was more than I should accept and felt guilty about accepting Oliver's generous offer.

"Wow," came a voice from the doorway, "I can't believe this place.

It is way bigger than my entire apartment. You know, I've never been to this floor," said Grace. She smiled at me. "Even I'm not allowed on this extraordinary floor of the hotel. This is only for special guests."

"Good morning, Grace. It is amazing isn't it? How did your night go?"

"It was a dream," she said letting her body flow down into a chair like a feather floating on air. "Braxton stayed until late, and we talked about everything." She brushed her hair from her face. "We have so much in common. I still can't believe it. Thank you, for your help."

"I'm so happy for you."

"Mr. Wilkerson said he talked to you last night about changing rooms. He asked me to check on you and not let you back out. He does want you to have it."

"Now," I said sitting in a chair next to her, "tell me all about last night."

Her face beamed the more she told her story. "We're going out to a nice restaurant tomorrow night. I can't wait."

"See everything worked out," I replied.

"Except for you, I'm sorry."

"Let's not think about that. I'll be fine," I assured.

"Well, I had better get back to work, and I'm telling Mr. Wilkerson that you are staying here, right?"

"Yes, I'm staying, Grace," I called out, closing the door behind her.

I stood at the door to the elegant bedroom. A desk and an overstuffed chair were by the window, just as my home in Boston. Oliver did think of everything in this magnificent hotel. I began to unpack, but my eyes were pulled to the window. My fingers grasped the locket as my mind began to wonder looking out at the city. Was Vaughn out somewhere in the city and would he ever come back to me? My life had been a whirlwind the last few weeks. Falling in love with him, I couldn't let go of the thought of believing and hoping he would return to me. Even in this large hotel full of people, I felt lonely.

The small clock sitting on the bureau began to chime twelve o'clock. The locket was secure around my neck. It was time to meet Oliver for lunch. The morning had gone by quickly, and I knew the reality was that I needed to stay busy.

I picked up the papers Braxton had given me and slowly made my way to the private elevator.

Oliver was standing waiting for me by the dining room door. "Hello Miranda, I hope you like your new suite?"

"The suite is an amazing place, if I had any propriety, I shouldn't be staying there. But Oliver, it's so wonderful and luxurious."

Oliver laughed, "you are well within the bounds of propriety, Miranda. Why not? I own the place, and I can do what I want. It wouldn't be any fun if I couldn't make my own decisions. You have to enjoy what you do, and I enjoy seeing you happy."

I believed he really meant what he said as he stood looking at me with his kind eyes.

I handed him the papers that Braxton had given me. He studied and read each business, and then looked up. "I believe, The Golden Gate Bank of San Francisco would be perfect. The bank is a small, up-and-coming bank, and it needs someone aggressive to take it over."

My head nodded yes, and I smiled. I had also chosen The Golden

Gate Bank of San Francisco.

"Miranda, San Francisco is growing fast. A bank will make you a lot of money. It will be perfect."

"Owning a bank would be great, but I don't know anything about banking. This could be more than I could handle," I said earnestly, feeling a little overwhelmed.

"I understand, but you do know someone who does," he said smiling, "Braxton."

"I see," I said breathlessly getting excited. "Do you think he would take a job from me?"

"If the offer is as it should be, why not. I will help you negotiate his deal and the bank deal if you'd like. I have worked with these men before, and I do know a few tricks.

"That would be great. I could use some advice."

"Miranda," he declared in a business voice, smoothing his long wavy hair from his face, "I will draw up the plans and send a copy this afternoon for you to go over. If you agree with the offer, then we'll send it to the bank. This is an amazing opportunity; it will also be a great break for Braxton to be able to run a bank."

"Thank you, Oliver, for all of your help."

"You're welcome," he assured looking at me with his caring eyes.

I did have to admit when I was with Oliver I had a great time. The meal, of course, was delicious, and I could see the determination in his face to help me with the negotiations. I also knew he was a very powerful man in this city. We stood to leave and many of the men in the dining room began to speak to him. I leaned over and whispered, "I'll see you later. Thank you again for everything.

He smiled. "Goodbye, Miranda."

I decided to go to the men's bar upstairs and see Sarah. I wanted to inform her of my move. The men in the room stared at me strangely, but I ignored them as I rushed past everyone to the back of the restaurant.

Sarah looked up from her desk and a surprised but elated look came on her face. "Miranda, what are you doing here? Is something wrong?" she questioned scooting her chair back standing up. "Come in."

"No, Sarah, nothing's wrong. I hope you're not too busy to talk for a few minutes. I'd like to catch you up on some things."

"I'm never too busy for you. Sit," she assured waving her arm in the air.

"First, how are things going?"

"I love it here. This is perfect. I can work in the bar when I want or work in the office. I have so much freedom. I also love my new home. I haven't lived anywhere so nice, except your place."

"There is another reason I'm here. I wanted to let you know I've moved."

"What floor and room are you in now?"

"I'm on the top floor in Room 702. Here's a key for you, so you can use the elevator anytime you want to visit."

"I thought you were going to get a smaller room. Those are gigantic and astonishing on the top floor. I've heard guests talking about them."

"It is, just wait until you see it, but Oliver insisted that I move to my new suite. I couldn't say no."

"Right, you couldn't say no. Is something going on with Mr. Wilkerson that I need to know?"

"No, he's only a friend and that is all. I also wanted to tell you that Sister Margret Mary is back in town, and she is at Old Saint Mary's. She wanted me to let you know that she would love to see you anytime if you would like to talk."

Sarah sat back in her chair. "She really told you I'm welcome to visit? Another miracle! I can't believe it, one phenomenon after another."

"Of course you are welcome to visit," I assured.

"I also have some news," she began. "I've met a man named Albert Johnson. He's so amazing, and we've been spending time together," Sarah declared spinning her chair in a half circle. She leaned over to me; her head shook from side to side. "He isn't like Braxton but he's kindhearted and makes me feel," she smiled, "so special. He works here in the bar with me. But, I'm still having a hard time trusting anyone."

"Sarah, Albert sounds perfect, and you need to move on from your fantasies of Braxton. I understand how disappointments are," I paused. "Go with your feeling and give Albert a chance."

"Alright, I will only if you will give yourself a chance to find love."

I had to smile knowing she was talking about Oliver. "Well, that's all that is happening now, so I'd better be going and let you get back to work. I'll talk to you later. Please come by anytime you can."

I stood to leave, but turned back to Sarah. "Sarah, Sister Margret Mary really would love for you to stop by the church. She has helped me a lot by just listening."

Sarah stood and walked to the door. "Miranda, if you need to talk, please don't ever worry about bothering me. I know how hard

Vaughn's vanishing is on you. But, like you just said, move on and give someone else a chance."

"I know Sarah. My heart just has to catch up with my head. Don't worry I'm fine, as long as I stay busy. I'll see you soon. Bye."

"Goodbye, Miranda."

I went out the door and caught the private elevator.

That afternoon, I received the offer Oliver had worked on, and it was amazing. He did understand business and the offer was perfect. I just hoped the men at the bank would accept it. I signed the document, sent it back, and told him to proceed.

About an hour later, I received a note stating that Oliver had the negotiations going with the bank. He had set up a meeting for Thursday morning at ten o'clock. If I agreed, he would continue with the plan. I sent back a note that said to continue, and I thanked him again. Concluding the note, I said I would see him Thursday morning. I paused to count my blessings and to relish in the events of the day.

Augustus Jones

Believing that Augustus Jones was gone I spent time the next few days walking around the city, but I stayed around a lot of people. I couldn't sit in my room, I was too anxious. Could I really become the owner of a bank? I knew I was also pushing the bounds of what a woman should be doing, and I had to be assertive and confident at the meeting with the bank officials.

One beautiful crisp day, I walked down by the cable car. My mind swirled with memories, and a pain shot through my heart. I continued to walk and without thinking, I was standing in front of Sharkie's Tavern. I knew I shouldn't be alone in this part of town.

The large door opened as patrons left, and I walked into the dark bar full of cigar smoke and the stench of liquor. Sharkie stood behind the bar busily wiping glasses. His eyes peered up.

"Miranda, this is a special surprise," his chubby body scooted around the bar. "Honey, how ya doing?"

"I'm fine, Sharkie. I'd like to have a bowl of Helen's stew if that's alright?"

"Sure, please sit." He began to clean a table for me. "I hope I'm not being too blunt," he said fidgeting with the wet rag in his hand, "but I think ya know me and I say what I mean. I'm sorry that crazy son of a gun left. He told me what he was doing, and I couldn't stop him. He believed he wasn't good enough fer ya. He's as stubborn as the devil. When he sets his mind ta something ya can't change it, no matter how ya try. That's the only thing I've ever seen him walk away from. He really believes he's giving ya a life. I know for sure, he loves ya. I'm sorry; I wish I could've helped. If ya need anything, anytime, please let me know."

"Sharkie, have you heard from him?" I asked reaching out gently gripping his arm.

"No, ma'am, I haven't," he said. He turned from me.

A woman walked up next to Sharkie. "Here's your stew, Ma'am. Enjoy."

I could see in Sharkie's face that he wasn't going to tell me anything, not because he didn't want to, but because he couldn't. I knew he had made a promise to Vaughn, and he was going to keep it.

I sat at the small leaning table and remembered that unbelievable day sitting right in the same place with Vaughn's hand touching mine. How safe I felt when he wrapped his arm around me! I knew I had to move on and try to forget about that wonderful day, but I couldn't–not yet.

I stood to pay, but Sharkie quickly came hurrying over. "Miranda, family don't pay fer food. Y're welcome here anytime."

"Thank you, Sharkie. I'll be staying at the Old Grand Hotel for a while, if you do hear anything from Vaughn."

"I understand and ya take care, goodbye."

"Good bye, Sharkie."

I stepped from the bar; the sun was lowering in the sky. The crowd of people from earlier had dwindled. I turned walking in a faster pace to the hotel.

Someone grabbed me around the waist! I panicked smelling the man. I turned my head to see those eyes full of hate and malice. It was

Augustus Jones! The man's nasty, foul-smelling hand cupped over my mouth before I could scream.

"I've got ya now ya uppity wench. Ya think ya're better than everyone else `cause ya have money," he growled. "I'm gonna show ya a good time," he laughed. "I've got class too," he said showing his toothless grin with tobacco all over his remaining teeth. His other hand groped around my breast.

My heart pounded. Sarah's words flowed through my mind. I had to act fast or I wouldn't have another chance. Carefully, without his noticing what I was doing, I reached inside my purse for the derringer. The heels of my shoes dug into the dirt trying to slow him as he dragged me into an alley behind Sharkie's building. My purse dropped to the ground, but I held on tightly to the derringer. My heart was as ice cold as the metal gun. When his grip loosened on me, I used all my strength to escape, turned toward him and shove the barrel against Augustus' nasty vest.

His eyes turned downward as a surprised and terrified looked came on his face. He stopped moving and stared, shocked.

I didn't hesitate. I pulled the trigger on the gun. His body fell to the ground.

I let out a piercing scream and watched in horror as the blood flowed from his body. Someone grabbed me. I turned around with the gun still grasped in my hand.

"Whoa, Miranda. It's me, Sharkie! Ya're all right! Did he hurt ya?" he questioned, trying to pry the gun from my fingers. "I don't want ta know what happened, but ya're coming with me! I'll see ta everything," he exclaimed, leading me into the back of the tavern.

"Helen, this is Miranda. She's jus' shot a man out back of the tavern. Ya see ta her, and you be sure she's alright."

"Miranda, sweetie, you're fine now," the large woman announced in a deep voice. Her dark eyes full of compassion gazed down on me as she helped me sit down.

I felt numb, not seeing or feeling anything. Mumbling voices around me seemed to be in a distance.

"Miranda. Miranda! Sharkie will take care of everything." A hand touched my shoulder. "Here's something to drink," Helen said, as she lifted a glass to my lips. The liquor burned my throat all the way to my stomach. My hand tried to push the glass away, but the liquid continued.

"Miranda," I heard Sharkie's voice, "Is there someone I can call ta help ya?"

"Vaughn."

"I know girl, but he ain't in town right now. He's back East or I'd call him. Anyone else that ya can trust?"

"Sarah Reed."

"Where does Sarah live?"

"In the hotel; she works upstairs at the men's bar." The words came from my mouth as if someone else was talking. My hands held my head and my mind swirled, confused, as tears flowed. My body shook, and I could still smell the stench of the horrible man, feel his arm wrapped around my waist, and sense his fingers pawing at me.

A young man about sixteen, who looked like Sharkie, walked up.

"Jacob, ya go ta the Old Grand Hotel upstairs ta the men's bar. Ya get Sarah Reed, and ya tell her Miranda Curry needs her," Sharkie briskly said. He turned around. "Ya lean back Miranda," Sharkie said kindly, covering me with a small blanket. "Jacob'll bring Sarah back. Ya jus' rest."

I looked up into his sympathetic eyes. My body weaved back and forth. My stomach was nauseous remembering the eyes of Augustus looking up at me as he lay on the cold ground with blood pooling underneath his nasty body.

"Sharkie, did I really shoot him?" My body shook. "Is he dead?"

"Yep, Miranda, that bastard is dead, but ya don't need ta think about that. I've taken care of everything, girl, and ya'll be jus' fine."

It only seemed like seconds, and Sarah was standing by me. Time wasn't making any sense.

"Oh, Miranda… Are you all right? Sharkie told me what happened. I told him about Jones and how he had been following us. You did good," she said, squatting down looking into my face. "Sharkie is seeing to everything. You don't have to think of anything. Can you stand? Jacob and I'll help you back to the hotel, whenever you're ready."

"I don't feel well Sarah." I gulped, "but I want to go to the hotel."
Sarah wiped my face with a cool cloth.

Sharkie wrapped his arm around me. I stood. My body wobbled as I looked up into his eyes. My arms draped around his neck and I sobbed mumbling, "Thank you."

"I'm so sorry. If I'd known about that guy, I'd have taken care of him myself. He never would've laid a hand on ya," the small man declared. His eyes were pulled to my torn dress sleeve where Augustus Jones had grabbed hold of me.

"He won't be bothering anyone anymore, Sharkie. Don't worry, I'll see to Miranda," Sarah added, enveloping her cloak around me. "Thank you for all of your help."

"We take care of family, Sarah," Sharkie assured. "Ya see ta her, and if ya need me fer anything, send someone." He went to the back door of the tavern pushing it open.

Jacob put his arm around me and the three of us walked outside. The cool air hit my face. My eyes were pulled to the spot where I had left Augustus lying on the ground and I stopped walking. The body was gone, but the blood was still on the dirt making the memories so fresh in my mind. Helen came outside with a bucket of water, and Sharkie followed with an ash bucket. My hand pressed against my waist. My stomach muscles knotted, and I began to weave back and forth as I watched them camouflage the scene. Jacob held me close to him as he led me down the long alley and back out onto the street into the real world.

Sarah walked next to me; no one was going to come near me. She was like one of her knights in shining armor protecting her Queen. She was a fighter, and I knew she sure wouldn't have hesitated to use a gun on Jones. I could see in her eyes she wished it had been her rather than me to have pulled the trigger. After a few minutes we turned a corner, there stood the entrance to the Old Grand Hotel.

"Jacob, I'll see to her now," Sarah declared. "Thank you for all of your help."

"You're welcome, Miss Sarah, shand it's like my Pa said, if Miss Miranda needs us, you jus' let us know. I wouldn't let anything happen to her. Uncle Vaughn would tan my hide."

A twinge of warmth came over my body thinking of Vaughn being Uncle by Jacob.

We hurried to a side entrance. I was relieved that neither Grace nor Oliver was in sight. We quickly made it to the elevator, and Sarah opened the door to the suite. She led me to the bedroom and slipped off the cloak that had hidden my bloodstained dress. My body collapsed into the big overstuffed chair by the window that looked out over the once peaceful city.

"You need a nice warm bath Miranda, some clean clothes, rest, and then we will order up some dinner."

Rest—I didn't think I could sleep, but before I had time to think, Sarah came back into the room.

"Come on let's get you out of those clothes," she insisted. Her hands lifted off my beautiful violet dress reeking of sweat, smoke, whiskey and blood.

I looked down and saw the torn dress with blood covering the front. I became sick. My stomach churned as it had before. I leaned over into a can and began to vomit the liquor and my last meal. My memories of the loud explosion when I pulled the trigger came vividly back. Augustus Jones falling backward and his body thumping to the ground replayed in my mind. I began to shudder.

Sarah grabbed the dress and got it out of my sight.

The claw-footed tub swallowed me as I slid deep into the warm water. I didn't want to leave my safe, clean haven. I soaked with the stench disappearing from my body and my stomach quieted.

I unwillingly climbed out of the tub and put a fresh dressing gown on. I staggered as I made my way into the parlor.

"You look better Miranda. I am going to order some dinner. Is there anything you would like?"

"No, Sarah I don't think I can eat anything."

"Yes, you're eating. I'll order some stew and biscuits. That'll make you feel better. Now, go into your room and lie down for a while. I'll let you know when the food arrives."

My body weaved from side to side. I gripped the back of the chair by the door and lunged for the doorknob but grabbed the wooden trim instead and fell into the bed. I lay back on the pillows and shut my eyes to close out reality Oh, if only my Vaughn were here.

"Miranda," Sarah called peeking in the bedroom, "Your dinner is here. You need to try and eat a little."

I slipped out from under the quilts and sat on the edge of the bed still in a stupor. Tears started to fall and the realization hit me; I had just killed a man. This is what everyone had warned me about going West, how dangerous a life it could be, especially for a young woman who had been as sheltered as I. I was raised for social occasions—to defend myself with words, not a gun.

Sarah came into the room. She sat by me and held me in her arms as I sobbed.

"Miranda, you'll be alright. You did what you had to do."

"I know Sarah, but I killed a man," I said repeatedly.

Her face squinched. "Yes, an evil man, Miranda. You had no choice. You had to defend yourself. It's unspeakable what he planned to do."

"Sarah, you..." my words fell into silence.

Her head nodded yes. "When I was young, thirteen," she nodded her head. "Now, you will be fine, you aren't a quitter. I sent for Sister Margret Mary, and she's on her way to talk to you. She'll help you sort this out in your mind. All right, now you need to eat before she arrives."

I looked at her. She wasn't telling anymore of her story, and I wasn't asking. She seemed to know what I was thinking. "Miranda, my story won't help you. Stop worrying, this is my way of paying you back, just as you said friends do."

"Yes," I assured, "you are an unbelievable friend."

My body sat in the chair at the table, but my mind was miles away. I could only eat a few bites. A knock at the door startled me, and Sister Margret Mary dashed into the room.

I jumped out of my seat and was able to run to her, "Sister, I killed a man," I sobbed.

"Yes, I have heard. Miranda, I know you would never hurt anyone without a reason. God knows that, my child," she said tenderly moving my hair from my face. "Please, stop blaming yourself. Sit; eat some more of that wonderful smelling stew. Then, you need to get some rest. Tomorrow will be a new day for you."

"Oh, no," I cried out. My mind swirled frantically. "Tomorrow, I have my meeting with the bankers and Oliver." I flopped into a chair. "How can I face Oliver?"

"Life will go on just as it always has," Sister Margret Mary declared. "You will go to your meeting, and you will put this horrible episode away deep in your mind to never think of it again." Her soft brown eyes stared down at me. "You should never speak of this again to anyone."

Sarah agreed with Sister Margret Mary, "She's right, Miranda." Sarah moved next to me. Her hand patted my shoulder. "You have your new life, so don't let that scoundrel destroy you. Now, it's time for you to rest, and I'll be here all night if you need me."

I stood hugging them both. That night, my safe bed cuddled me. I knew they were correct, but could I put this behind me? My mind wanted to, but the memories stayed etched in my brain. The day had been exhausting. I lay in my bed and would think about all of this another day. I had to go to sleep. Tomorrow would be a paramount day for me. But, how could I dismiss the fact that had killed a man.

The Rolling Fog

The next morning, I lay in my bed with the covers tucked around my neck. Tears welled in my eyes. My life had become a nightmare. The gentle voice of Jon whispered in my head. "We will have no more tears." I wiped the tears from my eyes and threw off the covers.

The parlor was quiet. Sarah sat by the window drinking a cup of coffee, her green eyes peered up. "Oh, good morning, Miranda. How did you sleep?"

"With your and Sister Margret Mary's help, I did sleep. I'm glad I did get some rest because I'm going to be the leading lady in the hardest act I've ever been faced with in my life. Today, I will be fulfilling my dream, or I, at least, am confident that I will."

"You're a fighter, and nothing has ever stood in your way. I hope you never give up. I am sorry that you had to live through this, though."

"I'll make it, just as you have. Now, I need to finish dressing." I picked up my glass of orange juice. "I know you need to get to work. If you have any problems about missing work, I'll talk to Oliver."

"Don't worry about me, I'm fine. No one says anything to me since Grace helped me get the job, but I do need to get going." She moved next to me, laying her hand on my shoulder. "Only, if you're okay."

"Yes," I assured, "I think I am and I'll talk to you later." I gave her a hug and she left. I sighed deeply. I was alone to collect myself and my thoughts.

I finished dressing and fixing my hair. I was ready for my meeting with the bankers. I had to remember to be strong like Jon would have wanted. My strength would have made my entire family proud.

Mustering all the willpower I had, I marched out of my suite and rode the elevator to the first floor. I sat in one of the flowery chairs in the lovely lobby to watch people coming and going, trying not to think about Augustus Jones.

I watched the time on the grandfather clock sitting in the corner of the room. It was time for me to leave. I stepped outside into the courtyard and a blustery breeze hit my face. Oliver stood waiting.

"Good morning, Miranda. It is a spectacular day to purchase a bank. Don't you think?" he inquired as his fingers brushed the wild hair from his face.

"Yes, Oliver, it is," I nodded.

"Are you ready to leave for the meeting? This should be interesting." His hand cupped my arm. I flinched at his touch. I tightened my mouth trying to catch my breath as flashes of the evening before blared in my mind. This wouldn't do—I had to put these thoughts away. I heaved a deep breath. My eyes looked into Oliver's kind face and my body calmed.

"Yes, I'm very excited."

"Great, let's go," he said enthusiastically.

Oliver helped me into his carriage and waved to the Coachman that we were ready to leave. We rode a few streets from the hotel, and the carriage stopped. I stepped out, peering up at the old, red brick building that seemed to be welcoming me in. This was going to be my new life. Oliver opened the large, wooden bank doors. I took another deep breath and entered the Golden Gate Bank.

Observing my demeanor, the bank officials shook my hand. Oliver introduced me to each of the men. The large cherry table sat in a cold, stark room with eight chairs surrounding it. I sat next to Oliver; his face was firm, eyes on the men. He was like Poppa. They weren't going to intimidate him. One man, Mr. Tate, resembling Mr. Mills with his round body and bald head, did most of the talking. The other men sat and listened. I sat with my mouth tight trying not to smile at recalling Mr. Mills looking like a fat pink-cheeked baby.

I stayed strong answering Mr. Tate's questions and wasn't backing down. It was as Jonathon said; don't let them see fear, or they will have you. I held my ground on the negotiations.

It seemed like hours, but it was only thirty minutes when the men stood shaking our hands. I now owned a bank, The Golden Gate Bank of San Francisco. My body tingled with excitement.

Oliver took my arm and held his hat in his other hand as his head nodded saying hello to the bank employees as we walked away from the meeting.

We stepped outside. "Now, Miranda, we have a meeting with Braxton back at my office." He turned to me lightly squeezing my arm, "This meeting did go well, didn't it?" he whispered leading me out of the bank.

"Yes, everything was perfect," I tenderly answered staring into his eyes. "I can't believe how you handled those men. You were amazing, Oliver."

"You did very well yourself. You won't have any problems running this bank." He chuckled. "Those men thought they had it made when you walked in, but you sure showed them a modern woman is no shrinking violet," he assured sweeping his hair back with his fingers.

"Thank you, Oliver," I said smiling back at him.

I knew Oliver had the status in this town just as Poppa did in Boston, and I did hope someday to be that strong.

"You and Braxton will make a fine banking team. I have no doubts about that," he added, helping me into the carriage.

The carriage began to roll along the street. I leaned my head out the window staring at the bank in amazement. "I own a bank," I kept whispering.

When we arrived at the hotel we walked into the hotel office, Braxton was anxiously talking to Grace. He touched her hand gently looking into her eyes. I smiled at Grace.

"Miranda," Braxton turned offering me his hand."

"Braxton, how are you doing?" I asked politely.

"Wonderful," he assured smiling. His eyes swung to Grace.

"Come into my office, Braxton. Let's get this meeting going. Grace, he will be back in a little while," Oliver said patting Braxton on the back.

The meeting began with negotiations of Braxton running the bank. He would be President of the bank and in charge. I would work alongside him learning the world of banking. I knew in time I would learn what I needed.

Braxton's face looked at the floor then back at me. "Miranda, this is my dream. Thank you."

I sat thinking, astonished how one train ride could change so many people's lives. I laid the pen on the desk and handed the papers to Oliver.

He stood. "Now, let's all go and have a nice lunch to celebrate."

Oliver walked out and looked at Grace. "Would you like to join us for lunch?"

"Is it alright for me to leave?" she questioned.

Oliver grinned showing his dimples. "I think your boss will approve."

Braxton gently took Grace's arm. "Let's go," he said, smiling from ear to ear.

Oliver pulled me close as we walked to the dining room, and he led us to his special table.

I sat quietly looking over the dining room remembering when Braxton, Vaughn, Sarah, and I had met Oliver for the first time, but it seemed a lifetime ago.

"Here is a toast to Miranda and her new bank, The Golden Gate Bank," Oliver announced, holding up his glass in the air.

I sat proud with my mind thinking, *"I own a bank."* I hoped Poppa would have approved of my decision.

Our luncheon was eloquent as well as elegant. Oliver had ordered specialty seafood dishes and French desserts.

"Miranda," Braxton added, "for the next few weeks we are going to be busy. I would like you to be involved in all aspects of the bank."

"Sounds great. I'll be at the bank early in the morning. I can't wait to get started."

"Why don't I pick you up around eight o'clock? It isn't that far for me to circle around."

"That would be nice. I'll see you then," I answered excitedly.

Braxton and Grace stood to leave. "Good afternoon Miranda,"

Grace said beaming with Braxton's arm wrapped around her waist.

Oliver's eyes followed as they walked away. "Well, Miranda, matters are moving forward and I am elated at your prospects."

"I'm very happy about the bank and I think it is great for Braxton and Grace. Thank you again for everything."

"I do hope it works for you," he said caringly, "With Braxton's help I don't foresee any problems."

"Thank you for lunch and the assistance. I hope to see you again, soon."

He smiled. "That can easily be arranged."

I went to my special elevator, and Oliver headed for his office.

The next few weeks seem to go by fast, and then months zoomed by. Braxton was doing an amazing job at the bank.

One early evening, after work, Braxton and I rode in his buggy, just as we did most days, but this evening we didn't ride to the hotel.

"Where are we going?" I hastily questioned.

He smiled his crooked grin. "I have a surprise for you," he said as he pulled the buggy to a stop.

"Oh! Braxton," I shouted breathlessly, "you brought me to see the rolling fog!"

"I sure did. I promised you when you first arrived I would show you the fog as it rolls into the bay, and I always keep my word. Well, what do you think?"

My eyes stayed glued on the misty clouds as they consumed the bay making its way to the wharf. "It's more wonderful than I could have ever dreamed. I'll never forget this."

There had been many foggy days since I had arrived, but watching the mysterious fog move into the city was breathtaking. I thought about the fishermen who were out sculling and singing in the bay. It was an event never to be forgotten.

Time moved on, and my days were busy, but my nights were lonely since I missed Vaughn. I took time to visit Sister Margret Mary, and one day we even went to Sharkie's Tavern. It was fun watching his reaction when the two of us walked in. After Sharkie calmed down, he and Sister Margret Mary became good friends. They were also two of the people that knew my secret about Augustus Jones.

April 19th

Time kept flying by faster and faster. Before daylight one Saturday morning, I suddenly woke hearing a knock at my door. Hurriedly, I grabbed a robe and peeped out the pinhole in the door seeing it was Grace. I worriedly opened the door, and she rushed into the room.

I grabbed her arm. "Grace is something wrong?"

"Look, Miranda," she said enthusiastically lifting her left hand swinging it in the air. "Braxton asked me to marry him last night," she paused, "and I said yes. I couldn't wait any longer to tell you. I haven't slept, I was too excited."

"I'm thrilled for you. I wondered what was taking him so long," I said happily. "Have you set the date, yet?"

"Yes, April 19th," she squealed. "What do you think?"

April 19th the date repeated in my mind as my breath seemed to be sucked from my lungs. I felt as if someone had punched me in the stomach. That was the anniversary date of when I stood in the cemetery telling Poppa goodbye?

"That sounds ideal," I answered, trying to get my composure back.

"Now, I hope you will accept; I would like you to be my maid of honor. What do you say?"

"Yes, of course, I would be delighted, but now you need get some rest. We'll talk later and plan the wedding. Everything will be perfect, and I promise I won't let you down. Come on; let's get you settled into the guest bedroom."

I lifted a sleeping gown from my bureau and handed it to Grace. She climbed into the large bed and fell immediately to sleep from exhaustion.

I quietly closed her bedroom door and walked into my room and over to the window. I stared out into the early morning. My fingers caressed my locket as thoughts of Vaughn swished in my mind. My life had been a whirlwind; I had traveled across the country, met many people, and bought a business. But, was as I happier than I would have been in Boston? I thought about Braxton, Grace, Sarah, and Sister Margret Mary. Yes, I did have good friends and even Oliver was a good friend. I still missed Vaughn every day, and I hoped I could make it without him. "Come on," I said to myself. "You can't dwell on the past. Only think of the future."

Later in the morning, Grace and I dressed and began all of the plans for the wedding. This was going to be the social event of the year –Grace's dream.

Over the next few weeks, planning the wedding kept me busy. The wedding was to be held at Saint Ignatius Church on Hayes Street and Van Ness Avenue, and it could hold up to four thousand guests. It was the most impressive church in San Francisco.

Oliver agreed to be the best man and the plans were coming together.

The wedding day quickly was approaching. Grace's parents had arrived from Salt Lake City and her father would walk her down the aisle. My heart ached with thoughts of Poppa.

The afternoon of April 19th arrived. I walked into the sanctuary to a room set aside for the bride. The door was open and standing in front of me was Grace dressed in a white, silken, lace-wedding gown. Her light hair was pulled up on top of her head with ringlets hanging around her smooth face.

"Grace, you are the most beautiful bride I have ever seen!"

She spun around, her hands nervously wringing. "Miranda, do I really look alright?"

"Yes, you are beautiful. Just calm down, and remember this is your dream."

Her father walked into the room and radiated with a smile across his face. He lifted Grace's hands and lay them in his. His presence calmed her immediately.

I left them and peeked into the sanctuary. It was full of beautiful white roses lining the pews. I smiled remembering Dorothy telling the meaning of the white rose, innocence and purity, perfect for Grace and Braxton. Candles lit the sanctuary gave it a warm glow making the stained glass windows sparkle. The church was magical. Grace's dream was coming alive.

As the processional music began, I slowly walked down the aisle. Braxton and Oliver stood elegantly in front of me. My dream of Vaughn standing waiting for me was flowing through my mind, but I knew that would never happen. It would always be…just a dream. I maneuvered into my spot and slowly turned around.

The wedding march reverberated throughout the church. Everyone stood. Grace and her father marched down the aisle to the music. Braxton's face beamed, watching his bride.

After the service, the reception was held in the largest ballroom of the Old Grand Hotel, Oliver's gift to the couple. I stepped into the grand room with white roses all around. The string ensemble began to play, and Oliver held me as we swirled around and around on the dance floor. He was an amazing host, and I had not laughed and enjoyed life so much in a long time.

Sarah beamed with her reddish brown hair surrounding her face. She was dressed beautifully in her extraordinary emerald dress. This was one of her fantasies, but her dream of marrying Braxton didn't happen; however, Sarah was resilient. She turned to me and smiled with her eyes glistening. Sarah was genuinely happy for Braxton and Grace. Just as her life had moved on without false hopes of a life with Braxton, I knew I must move forward as well.

A New Beginning

My life changed the day of the wedding. I made up my mind to live in the present, not the past. I knew my dream of a life with Vaughn would never become a reality.

Months flew by, and I began to spend more time with Oliver. We had so much in common, but at times, it was hard to tell which one of us was more head strong or stubborn, him or me.

The Christmas holidays were coming, and life was very different for us. Grace and Braxton were expecting their first child in a couple of months. She was glowing with so much anticipation.

I stayed busy helping Grace with her plans for the little one and working at the bank. My nights weren't lonely anymore because I spent most evenings with Oliver. It was a contented life.

Christmas Eve, my elegant midnight-blue gown brushed against my legs as Oliver and I strolled into the magnificent ballroom with my arm looped inside of his. My eyes stared in awe at the greenery draped with large red bows which hung all around the room. The enormous tree decorated with ornaments of every color sparkled from the chandelier's light. I had fallen into a fairytale right out of a princess book.

Oliver took my hand tenderly in his; he kneeled down on one knee.

"Miranda, will you marry me?" he said softly, smiling, making his dimples appear deep into his cheeks. "I love you and I will give you the world."

I couldn't find my voice for a second. "Yes, Oliver." My mind began to spin. Where did the *yes* come from?

He stood, pulling me in close, kissing me with so much passion. He reached into his breast pocket pulling out the largest, most exorbitant ring I had ever seen. Gently he lifted my hand sliding the ring onto my finger. He led me to a table beautifully decorated with a long flowing white linen tablecloth and flickering candles in the center.

The evening seemed like a blur in my mind as we danced until late.

Later that night as I stood in my room, my eyes peered back at my image in the mirror. I couldn't believe what I had done. I really had said yes. I couldn't sleep all night, but unlike Grace, I was anxious and confused with more questions than answers. I enjoyed being with Oliver, but I loved Vaughn and always would.

I slept for a short while, but I awoke with a start early the next morning, Christmas Day. I dressed and hurriedly grabbed my cloak and gloves. I needed to talk with Sister Margret Mary. I made my way down the street, dashed up the tall steps, and rushed into the church.

"Miranda," Sister Margret Mary called out to me rushing down the aisle, "what's happened? I can see something is wrong by the look on your face. Are you alright?"

I quickly showed her the ring. "Sister, I don't know what happened. Oliver asked me to marry him last night, and I said yes. I don't know what made me say it."

"My child, do you love him?" She asked with a warm soft voice, her fingers touching my arm.

"Yes, I do love him, but not like Vaughn."

"You have to forget Vaughn. You have to let him go. Your mind is telling you what you need to do. Oliver loves you. I have seen how he looks at you; a man's eyes don't lie. It is time to make a life now without Vaughn. He isn't coming back." Her hand gently patted my arm. "I'm sorry to have to be so blunt. Oliver cares and loves you; this is your new life."

"How can I forget Vaughn and move on?" I asked staring at her caring eyes.

"You have to child; this is what the Lord wants for you. Go and spend time with Oliver." Her hand fell from my arm. "It's Christmas Day, a time of hope and joy. You have your entire life ahead of you. Go; be with Oliver."

I sighed understanding she was correct. "Thank you, Sister. I'll find Oliver. Merry Christmas."

"Merry Christmas, Miranda."

It was almost eight o'clock, and I knew Oliver would be in his office. I took a deep cleansing breath, straightened my hair, and grabbed hold of the doorknob turning it and pulling the door open. Oliver sat at his desk with a sad, worried look in his eyes. He stood and came around the desk to me.

His hands gripped my shoulders. "Miranda, I was worried about you. You weren't in your suite this morning. Where have you been?"

"I went to see Sister Margret Mary this morning."

"Oh! I see," he answered, his thick eyebrows rose, his face became rigid, "so, what did she advise you to do? Marry me or wait for Vaughn to return?"

I could see the hurt in his eyes. He knew I would never love him as I did Vaughn, but I did love him.

"She was thrilled about our getting married. I wanted her to be the first to know." I wasn't going to hurt him anymore. I was going to do as Sister Margret Mary had said. My mind, not my heart, said to love and marry him and that was what I was going to do. I would never hurt him again.

He smiled and the hurt look disappeared from his face. "Let's go and have a wonderful Christmas. I have a special gift for you."

He wrapped his arms around me bringing me close. We left the hotel to go to his home on Knob Hill to spend Christmas Day, the start of our new life.

Oliver's home was smaller than my home in Boston, but impressive to say the least, sitting tall on the sloping hillside. The smell of fresh Christmas cedar was strong as we stepped into the stunning vestibule. He led me into the parlor. In front of the plate glass window, a Christmas tree stood decorated as striking as the one in the Old Grand Hotel. I sat in a comfortable chair next to the blazing fireplace.

Oliver shifted his feet, nervously lifted a tiny present from under the tree, and gently placed it in my hand. "Merry Christmas, Miranda," he said, a warm smile grew on his face letting his dimples show.

I gently tugged the beautiful bow carefully peeling the paper off the small box. I lifted the lid and lying there was the most brilliant, sparkling platinum and diamond necklace I had ever seen.

"Oh, Oliver, this is gorgeous." I said as I carefully lifted the necklace from its velvet resting place laying it in my hand.

"Put it on and let me see what it looks like," he said, anxiously pacing the room.

I stepped in front of the mirror seeing Vaughn's locket hanging around my neck. Oliver had never asked about it. I believe he thought it was my mother's, and I never said differently. I had promised never to hurt him. The diamond necklace sparkled from the light of the chandelier. My fingers gently touched the smooth stones laid out in the shape of a heart.

"The necklace is perfect. Thank you, my darling."

I turned from the mirror and his gentle hand caressed my face. Standing there in front of me was the kindest, sweetest man, and I knew that I didn't have any regrets. I loved him.

The day was amazing. Melodies' flowed from the Porter music box and the fire flickered in the fireplace, its soft glow hitting the wall with splashes of color. I knew living with Oliver would be as secure as this day. I would never be lonely.

Later that afternoon, we drove to Braxton and Grace's home for Christmas dinner. Grace was ecstatic seeing my ring. This was her dream for me, and she vocalized ideas for the wedding.

"Now, you will have to wait until after the baby is born. I hope that is alright?" Grace assured.

"That won't be a problem Grace, but this is going to be a very small wedding. I want to have it at Old Saint Mary's Church." I could see the disappointment in her face, but I knew she would be busy with the baby.

Braxton lifted his glass. "Here's to Miranda and Oliver's new life and our new arrival."

That was the best Christmas I'd had in many years.

The next couple of months went by rapidly as we prepared for the wedding and baby. On February 22, 1897, Grace and Braxton welcomed a new baby boy whom they named Carlton Lambert Sims after both of their fathers.

Grace stayed too busy with Carlton, so I asked Sarah to be my maid of honor. She didn't know what to think, but graciously said, "Yes.

The wedding day, May 22, 1897, was approaching very quickly and the plans were finished. Even with Grace's input, we kept the wedding simple.

That beautiful spring day, the morning of the wedding, Sarah and Sister Margret Mary helped me dress. I had picked a flowing silk, pure white dress with lace from top to bottom. I had the most gorgeous light pink roses in my veil and a beautiful bouquet of long stemmed roses to carry down the aisle. My new diamond necklace lay around my neck along with my locket.

I turned my eyes and peered into the mirror. I couldn't believe I was really preparing to marry Oliver, not Vaughn. My life had become a mixture of odd circumstances.

"You are beautiful, Miranda, like an angel," Sarah said softly, adjusting my long dark curls lying over my shoulders. "You will have happiness with Oliver. Don't worry so. You're just nervous, as are all brides."

"Sarah, I do love Oliver," I whispered. I couldn't say anymore.

"Yes, I know. Now we have a wedding to begin," she assured.

I stared into those green eyes that knew me so well and nodded my head. My hands gripped the bouquet of pink roses nestled in streams of silky ribbon, and I walked to the church's narthex where Braxton stood waiting for me. He had kindly agreed to walk me down the aisle.

He leaned over, "Miranda, this is right. You'll see," he whispered as he gently caressed my hand.

The church doors opened wide and a hush fell over the sanctuary that was full of pink roses and candles. The wedding march began; Braxton held my arm, and we slowly marched down the aisle.

Oliver stood so handsome and self-assured waiting for me. His long hair combed back from his eyes that were now only on me. I knew our life would be one of fulfillment. Oliver wasn't one to sit and wait for things to happen. He had dreams and had promised me the world!

The service was a whirlwind in my mind. Before I had a chance to think, I was outside being helped into a beautiful coach. We were on our way to the Old Grand Hotel to a reception like Grace and Braxton had. I didn't mind, since Oliver had so many friends and business acquaintances who wanted to be a part of the wedding.

We walked into the beautifully decorated room full of light pink roses. I knew this was going to be my new life, one surrounded by people, dancing, and delight. When Oliver walked into a room, it lit up. He was an extraordinary man, and life would not be dull with him.

Edmond Daniel Wilkerson

year had gone by, Oliver and I celebrated our first anniversary, and I stayed busy working and learning to run the bank. I joined Sister Margret Mary helping her with needy children, and I began to wish for a child of my own. I knew Oliver had always wanted a child.

The day arrived when I learned I was expecting our first child. I rushed into his office and told him the news. He raced around the desk and wrapped his arms around me and declared he was absolutely overjoyed.

I teased him as I gently touched his face. "I do hope this child will have your wonderful deep dimples, but I hope," I smoothed back the hair from his face, "not that wild hair of yours." He smiled showing his dimples.

This child would have everything it could ever want in life including a father who would adore it. My life now would be complete. I had a new family.

Grace, of course, was thrilled. Carlton would have a playmate to grow up with. The news traveled fast, and Sister Margret Mary was delighted. She knew how much I wanted a family.

The months swiftly went by, and I had been busily planning and getting ready. Less than a month before the baby would be born, Grace and I had everything prepared for the new arrival. The nursery was beautifully decorated in pastel green, blue, yellow, and pink colors, and the room contained everything imaginable, as it sat waiting for this special baby.

One night the house seemed warm, and I couldn't sleep. My bulging body was more than a little uncomfortable. I quietly climbed out of bed, not wanting to wake Oliver.

I walked into the parlor to my chair next to the window when all of a sudden the room began to swirl. I tried to grab the side of the chair but knocked over a lamp. Our housekeeper, Nora, rushed into the room and found me on the floor. I could hear screaming and Oliver's voice, but that was the last thing I heard until I woke up in St. Mary's Hospital.

I saw the look on Oliver's tearstained face. I knew something horrible had happened. Sister Margret Mary was standing next to him, her face drained of color.

"Miranda, you will be alright, but we lost our baby son last night," Oliver said stonily staring at me.

He turned away, and Sister Margret Mary rushed to my side. Her arms enveloped me. I couldn't stop crying. This couldn't be happening. My baby had died. Why did I keep losing family? Everyone I love goes away. Why was I being punished? I laid in my stark white room sobbing, believing my heart could explode with pain and feeling as if someone had taken my life.

The next few days seemed a blur. I couldn't think. The doctor allowed me to leave the hospital early. We had a small funeral at Old Saint Mary's and buried little Edmond Daniel Wilkerson in a tiny casket on May 20, 1899.

The pain and loneliness were unbearable. The other losses in my life didn't compare to this. My son, my little baby, who I had carried had been taken from me. The pain of losing a child was indescribable to others. My soul was yanked from me. How could I go on? I thought this was my punishment for killing a man, but Sister Margret Mary put a stop to that thinking.

I didn't have Oliver to help me through this trying time. He was in his own world of agony, and I didn't like what baby Edmond's death was doing to him. He was a man who seemed to be able to conquer anything. Nothing before had stood in his way to accomplish everything he wanted in his life. He didn't have control over the loss of his son, and I could see he blamed me.

Sarah was there for me day and night. She was still the true friend who I had made from the first time we met on the train. She wouldn't leave my side, and said that she understood my loss from her own experience, but she never elaborated. Her pain had been put on a shelf and she didn't want to relive it. I now understood.

I handled this tragedy the same as I had in the past and tried to stay busy. I began to go to the bank since I couldn't stand staying home anymore; it was too lonely. Just as I always had done, I was shocking everyone. I wore my black dress, the horrible color to tell everyone of my loneliness. However, this time, I believed the punishment of black was appropriate.

The months moved on and numbness subsided. My life had the same coldness consuming me day after day. Summer had arrived, and one warm day, I noticed Braxton looking out his window smiling. He had that special look, and I knew something was going on.

"Alright, Braxton, what's happening?" I questioned.

"Good morning, Miranda." He stood from his desk chair and

moved near me, his hand reached out touching my arm. "Grace is expecting another baby this winter. She has been anxious to tell you, but we both would never want to cause you any pain."

"Oh, Braxton, that is great news, and you know I love Carlton and will love this child too. I can't wait until I see Grace. Tell her not to worry and come by and see me soon."

"She'll be so glad to hear that. I'll let her know. Thank you."

I turned and left Braxton and knew the news would be difficult on Oliver. It was challenging on me, but I had to keep going. I didn't know what would happen if I really thought too much about a baby.

I went to Edmond's grave daily to place flowers. I knew I had to stop, but I couldn't let go, not yet. I had to be sure he was taken care of in death as he should have been in life. Oliver wouldn't even visit the grave; he hid from the loss and wouldn't talk about Edmond. It was as if our baby never existed.

My life moved on. We cannot stop time, no matter what the loss or how much we want to. I visited Grace and helped her with the plans for the new baby. I understood how much this baby meant to her. I wanted everything to be special and not overshadowed by my loss.

December was quickly approaching and Christmas would come soon. This was supposed to be the best Christmas for Oliver, me, and our new son, not the saddest time of our lives. Oliver just went through the steps planning Christmas. He had turned cold and uncaring – nothing seemed to help. I had hoped the holiday would bring back good memories from the past. He had loved Christmas from the first Christmas Eve he proposed to me.

The New Year was approaching as days sped past, and we were

welcoming in a new century, 1900. Everyone was planning great parties, so I thought I would plan a wonderful celebration for Oliver at the Old Grand Hotel on New Year's Eve. I was hoping being around his friends would help him understand he would be all right.

I sat in my chair and thought about the last century. So many things had changed in the last few years like the telephone, and the beginning of the horseless carriage. Oliver loved change and new inventions, but nothing could motivate him and make him happy, not now. I blamed myself for a long time for his pain, but Sister Margret Mary helped me understand I wasn't to blame for his unhappiness. It was difficult to look at him and know how the life had sucked out of him.

Sarah helped me plan the most amazing party to welcome the new century. I hoped the New Year would bring joy back to our lives, but Oliver only went through the motions of the party, his charismatic self not there.

January was a busy month with the New Year's Eve party and Grace giving birth to her baby. On January 27, 1900, she had a baby girl that Braxton named Emily Grace. She was perfect and looked just like Grace with light hair and blue eyes. Carlton was thrilled with his new sister.

I could see the hurt in Oliver's eyes, as he looked upon the newborn. His pain was like being stabbed by a knife.

He had never learned what disappointment was in his life. He had grown up with the perfect family. I understood loss, and I never got used to it, but I learned to deal with it. Life does move on. Whether a person joins in or not is a life choice. I knew we had a new century and a new life, Emily Grace, to cherish.

One Lone Red Carnation

Years seemed to go by swiftly, and I was busily working at the bank. Oliver worked from early morning to very late at night, his way of dealing with his loss. My life was not as fulfilled as I had planned, but I wasn't lonely.

A few weeks had gone by and I hadn't heard from Sarah believing she was busy with work and spending time with Albert, who had recently proposed to her. One day I took time off from the bank to catch up on some personal items. I went to the main elevator and up to the men's bar. I walked to the offices but Sarah wasn't around, so I hurried to one of the men working in the back.

"Where can I find Sarah Reed?"

He didn't speak, the papers in his hands slipped to the floor, and he ran out of the room. A man I had not met before came walking into the room.

"Can I help you Ma'am? We don't have guests back here often."

"I'm not a guest, I'm Mrs. Oliver Wilkerson, and I want to speak to Sarah Reed."

"Oh! I'm sorry, Mrs. Wilkerson, but Miss Reed isn't here right now. Maybe you need to talk to Albert Johnson. Please come this way."

I hadn't had the privilege of meeting Albert even though, we were having a dinner next week in the couple's honor to celebrate. I thought it was the greatest news and couldn't wait to plan the most beautiful wedding for Sarah.

Confused, I followed the man through a door in the back of the restaurant. A gentleman with dark, straight hair was sitting in the low-lit room with his face turned to a wall and his head buried in his large hands.

"Albert, this lady. She wants to talk to Sarah."

"Albert," I called out hurrying over to the man, "I'm Miranda Wilkerson, where can I find Sarah? What's going on?"

Albert stood and turned to me. His face drained of color. I became frightened. He reminded me of Poppa on the day I learned about my mother and Jon. I knew something horrible had happen.

"Oh, you're Sarah's Miranda," he looked up with tears rushing down his face. He took a second with a long breath, and wiped tears with the back of his hand. "Sarah's at St. Mary's Hospital, I'm sorry to say."

"What! Why didn't someone tell me? What's going on?" I implored.

He began to cry and his huge hands covered his face. "Miranda, I don't know how to tell you," he gulped for air.

"Please, Albert, tell me what's wrong!"

"Sarah has typhoid fever. One of the women who we hired had it, and Sarah and two others have become infected. The doctor says it ain't good. What are we gonna do?"

"First, I'm going to the hospital and find out what's happening. Don't worry, Sarah is going to get the best care, I promise." I stood for a second and didn't move. I too, as Albert, had to catch my breath.

I turned and quickly ran out of the room. This couldn't be happening all over again. My mind raced; I had to get to Sarah as fast as I could.

I rushed into St. Mary's hospital and straight to the nurse sitting at the desk. "I need to see Sarah Reed," I insisted.

She checked her notes and raised her eyes from the papers, "I'm sorry that's impossible, Ma'am."

"I need to talk to the doctor or a person in charge!" I snapped.

"That'll be a while, but I'll see what I can do," her head turned back to her papers.

"Tell them Mrs. Miranda Curry Wilkerson is here and wants to talk to them."

The nurse's eyes pulled from her work.

It didn't take long for a doctor to come walking up to me. "Mrs. Wilkerson," called out a young man with light hair. He stopped in front of me. "What can I do for you? I'm Dr. Jacobs."

"Is there somewhere we can talk in private, Dr. Jacobs?"

"Yes," he said as he motioned with his hand for me to follow.

I sat in a stiff chair facing the doctor. "Dr. Jacobs, I'm here to find out about Sarah Reed."

"Yes, it's sad. She is so young. We're doing our best, Ma'am."

"I want the best care that she can have," I demanded. "I want her in a private room, and I want to see her."

"Oh, that's expensive, and she doesn't have that kind of money."

"Dr. Jacobs, I do!" I said, as my voice rose. "I want her moved to a private room immediately, and I want to see her."

"Mrs. Wilkerson," he said firmly, "you don't understand she can't have visitors."

"You, Dr. Jacobs, don't understand," I persisted. "I do know about typhoid fever. Here," I added scribbling names on a piece of paper handing him the note, "I want you to contact Dr. Berry in Boston. I've been exposed to typhoid fever, and I'm somehow immune. My mother and brother died from the horrible disease when I was a child. I was with them up until the day they died, and I'm going to stay with Sarah until she's better. Sir, nothing is going to stop me. I'll move her to my home if I have to."

I'd never used my influence, but this time I was getting my way. Sarah was going to get the best care, and I was going to see to it.

"I'll switch her to the private room immediately, and I'll check with your doctor. If he agrees, then I see no problem with visiting Miss Reed. Mrs. Wilkerson, please wait here. I'll see what I can do."

He left. I sat as thoughts flowed through my mind about living this nightmare again. The door opened and Dr. Jacobs walked into the room. "Mrs. Wilkerson, your doctor sent us a telegraph stating that you were somehow immune from typhoid fever, but he hadn't figured out the reason why. He also said to let you know he was sorry you were going through this again." The doctor turned toward the door. "Now, I will let you visit Miss Reed."

He led me to a private room. It was deja vu. Lying in the stark surroundings, Sarah was sleeping quietly, her long hair curled against her face on the white pillow. She so reminded me of my mother.

I moved next to the window and peered out. This room would at least have a view for me to look out onto the city. I just prayed and hoped we wouldn't be here long before Sarah would be going home. I sat in the chair.

Sarah began to wake, and when her tired green eyes peered at me, she smiled, but the expression turned to alarm on her face. "Miranda, you can't be here. You've gotta leave! You'll get sick. Please go," she begged.

I remembered Jon waking up and begging me to leave. I scooted near the bed. I picked up the wet cloth, just as I had done hundreds of times for Jonathon and my mother, and placed it on her flushed face.

"Sarah, I'm fine. I'm staying with you," I assured. "Stop worrying. I've taken care of typhoid patients before."

"Oh, Miranda, your mother and Jonathon had typhoid fever. I remember now. I'm so sorry to make you relive the hard times you had as a child."

That was Sarah, not thinking about herself, only about me.

"I'm fine Sarah, and you'll be getting better soon. They have new treatments that the doctor is going to try. You let me know of anything you want. No matter what it costs, I'll do anything, I promise."

She lay back on the pillow. I could see how tired she was. I wished someone had told me sooner she was sick. She'd been in the hospital for a couple of weeks. I thought she was busy with Albert and wedding details. She didn't have the red rash yet, so I knew she could fight.

I sat quietly next to the bed watching her take deep breaths until she woke again, her eyes opened. "Sarah, I'm going home and get some things, and I'll be back soon."

"Please, Miranda don't wear yourself out," Sarah spoke her voice crackly from the fever. "I'll be fine."

I smiled as I gently touched her arm. "I know you will. With the two of us fighting, nothing will stop us."

Sarah gave me her special smile that could light up a room. I thought back remembering Jonathon smiling after our talks. Smiling had helped him and now I hoped it would also help Sarah.

I hurried home. I quickly packed a bag with a few essentials that I might need. Next, I went through the large door of the hotel to find Oliver. He sat in his huge leather chair with his back to me. I pulled my shoulders back, and clenching my hands in front of me, I cleared my throat. "Oliver, I have some bad news. Sarah is sick and in St. Mary's hospital."

"Yes," he said, his desk chair spun around facing me, and he leaned back against the wall. His eyes squeezed together. "I know."

"You knew and didn't tell me!" I shouted staring at him with fury.

"Yes, Miranda, she has typhoid fever," he replied, resting his elbows on his desk, his hands clasped together, "and you can't help her."

"Yes I can and I will." My foot stomped. "I'm going back to the hospital and stay with her."

"They won't let you in," Oliver said firmly with a stern face, his fingers tapped on his desk.

"I told you about my mother and brother. I've been around typhoid fever, and I didn't get infected," I snapped getting furious with him.

"I won't let you go; I forbid you," he demanded, his hand pounded the desk, "She's just an employee, and you might get sick."

"No! She's my best friend. Oliver, I don't want to argue about this. I'm going, and I'll be going each day." I moved around the desk. "She's going to be taken care of." I bent down, gave him a kiss, and gently touched his face. "I'll see you later." He gave me a hard glare, but he knew he couldn't stop me.

The next few days I stayed with Sarah in the hospital and only went home for short periods. The word had gotten out. Early one morning while sitting by Sarah's bed, the door slowly opened and Sister Margret Mary peeked into the room.

"Are you alright being in there?" she questioned. "It won't help Sarah for you to get sick."

"I'll be fine," I assured, "don't worry."

"Well, if you need anything, let one of the sisters know," Sister Margret Mary said. "I've talked to them, and they'll help you with whatever you need."

"Thank you, and I'll let Sarah know you were here."

"Miranda, will you please give Sarah this note. Let her know how much we're all praying for her at Old St. Mary's, and here are some Rosary beads."

"Certainly, I'll let her know that you and the other sisters are praying for her."

"Goodbye, Miranda, and the Lord be with you."

The door closed. When I turned around Sarah was awake.

"This note is from Sister Margret Mary. She was just here."

"Would you read it to me?" Sarah whispered.

I began to read.

"Luke 6:20

How blessed are you who are poor:
The kingdom of God is yours.
Blessed are you who are hungry now:
You shall have your fill.
Blessed are you who are weeping now:
You shall laugh.
Blessed are you when people hate you,

Drive you out, abuse you,
Denounce your name as criminal,
On account of the Son of man.
Rejoice when that day comes and dance for joy,
Look! your reward will be great in heaven."
"Be not afraid for the Lord is with you, my child."
Sister Margret Mary.

Tears grew in Sarah's eyes, and I knew it wasn't for her sorrow of being sick, but knowing how much she was cared about. Her head snuggled deep in the pillow, and she fell into a relaxed sleep.

I left that afternoon and went to the bank to explain to Braxton why I was going to the hospital each day. He wasn't the one to convince. He understood and cared for Sarah, but Grace didn't. I hoped someday she'd understand.

I opened the door hoping Sarah would have improved, but it was as it had been with Jonathon and my mother.

Each day, Sister Margret Mary sent a verse:

"Peace I bequeath to you,

My own peace I give you,

A peace which the world cannot give,

This is my gift to you.

Do not let your hearts be troubled or afraid."

"Be not afraid for the Lord is with you, my child,"
John 14:27
Sister Margret Mary

The verses came day after day, and I could see Sarah anxiously waiting each day for the reading. The weeks slowly moved on, and Sarah's fever wasn't letting up. I could see the stages just as my mother had gone through. I knew the end was coming, and it was difficult to sit and do nothing. I wanted to scream, but I was going to be strong for Sarah, just as I'd been for my family. I'd cry later.

When I came in the room, the afternoon of June 26th, 1905, Dr. Jacob was standing over Sarah. The fever had taken over, and I knew it was a matter of time.

He left the room, and I picked up the note and began to read.

"So it is with you:

You are sad now,

But I shall see you again,

And your hearts will be full of joy,

And that joy no one shall take from you."

John 16:22

"Be not afraid for the Lord is with you, my child,"

Sister Margret Mary

I saw tears in her dark, emerald eyes, and she was fixed on me. I gently wiped the tears from her face. I knew I was right about my mother, and I was correct about Sarah; they did know what was happening. She sighed and was gone. She was at peace. Now, I could finally cry.

The doctor came into the room. I stood from my chair, the one I had been sitting in for weeks, and left the room. A cool wind hit me in the face when I stepped outside the hospital descended the steps into the bright sun and got in my carriage. It was a beautiful day, a day to enjoy and not a day for sorrow. I hated the day for its brightness believing it should be raining, but I stopped—that wasn't what Sarah would want. My heart was breaking as I slowly marched up the steps through the large doors of Old Saint Mary's Church. I knew what I had to do, just as I had done before, plan a funeral.

Sister Margret Mary was lighting a candle and had somehow known what had happened. She turned to me with tears on her face glistening from the candlelight. "Miranda, she is with the Lord and has found peace."

"I know, but I already miss her," I said sobbing.

Her hands gripped mine. "We will make it through this with the Lord's help. Now we need to pray. Father Brady has prepared for the funeral and I will see to everything else. You go home, child, and get some rest. We will talk tomorrow."

I didn't ride in the carriage but chose to walk back to the hotel since I needed some fresh air. I took the elevator to the men's bar where Albert was working. When he saw me, he dropped his work and ran to me.

"Miranda, I see it in your eyes," he said as his voice got quieter. "She's gone."

"Yes," I said nodding my head, "I'm sorry."

Tears dripped from his face, and I knew he had loved Sarah. The dreams they had were now gone. Her life had been cut short, just as Jonathon and my mother's.

"The service will be tomorrow afternoon at Old Saint Mary's. You take all the time off you need. You don't have to worry about work."

"Thank you, Miranda, and I know how much she cared for you, and how hard this is on you. I also want to thank you for all you did for her."

"Albert, Sarah and I had an understanding. We didn't have to say thank you to each other. We knew how much we cared for one another. I'll see you tomorrow at Old St. Mary's."

I made my way home and into the parlor where Oliver was reading some papers. He was sorry to hear about Sarah. I saw concern for me in his eyes, but he still wouldn't go with me to the service. He, like Grace, believed Sarah wasn't in their social class.

The next morning, I pulled myself out of bed hoping this was all a bad nightmare and Sarah was back at work. There staring at me in the mirror was a face full of sadness. That wouldn't do, not for Sarah. She loved life too much. I began to dress, once more in my black dress, which I despised. I knew it wasn't a nightmare or horrible dream. I had to get to the church to help Sister Margret Mary.

I reluctantly arrived at the church. Down at the front of the sanctuary was the casket with Sarah. *No! This wasn't right* I wanted to scream. We should be planning the most fairytale wedding for her, not saying goodbye. But this was for real, and I was going to have to say goodbye to her. My shoulders slumped. "Lord why?"

I had bought the most beautiful ivory and green embroidery dress for her and she looked, as she had called it, classy with her reddish brown hair curled around her creamy face. I couldn't move. I was waiting for her beautiful, sparkling eyes to open. She should be talking and giggling as telling me her fairytales, just as she had done with delight on the train.

"Miranda," Sister Margret Mary softly called out.

"Yes, Sister," I answered looking up from Sarah. "Is there anything I can do to help you?"

"No, everything is arranged. We will begin soon. Please sit and rest. I can see you haven't had any sleep."

The door opened letting sunshine flow into the church. Albert slowly walked down the aisle and behind him was Braxton. I smiled at them.

Braxton took my arm. "Miranda, how are you doing?"

"As well as I can. Thank you for coming. She did care a lot for you."

"I know, and she was a fine person."

The sisters joined us in the sanctuary; Father Brady began the service and tears flowed down my face. My body convulsed with grief.

When the service was finished, we walked past Sarah, and I had to say my final goodbye.

Braxton had to go back to the bank. This left Albert, the sisters and me to go to the cemetery. The sun shown down and a soft breeze spread the fragrances from all the flowers. A lone bird sat in the large, old tree sang sweetly, like an angel from Heaven.

Once more I was standing by the grave of someone I loved, saying goodbye. I looked at all of the beautiful flowers placed at the gravesite. Oliver had sent the most incredible arrangement. I looked at the casket my heart stopped. A singular, dark red carnation lay on top.

I had not seen that flower earlier in the church. Where did it come from?

"Albert, did you bring the red carnation?" I questioned.

"No, I brought the bunch of flowers in front. Why, does it matter?"

"Did you know what Sarah's favorite flower was?"

Albert's head ducked. "No, she never told me, and I never had the chance to ask," he whispered with his voice trembling.

"Her favorite flower was a dark red carnation and one lone flower means love." I answered.

I didn't move from my spot. Only one other person knew about the red carnation—Vaughn. I looked around, but didn't see him.

The service started and the prayer began.

I slowly walked to the casket, as I did that day for my father with the lone tulip. I lay down my one red carnation beside the other one.

"Good bye, Sarah. I love you and you'll always be in my heart. Peace be with you. God bless you, my true friend forever."

Sister Margret Mary walked over, put her arm around me, and said her goodbye in a prayer.

Leaving Albert alone with Sarah, I walked to my carriage. I searched the cemetery as I walked touching my locket with my fingers. I knew Vaughn had been there; I could still feel his presence. He had cared for Sarah. I had to smile, but it made me miss them both so much.

Oliver Promises the World

The days and weeks moved on, but not a day went by that I didn't miss Sarah. She had that free spirit, like Vaughn. Maybe that was the reason I was drawn to them. I took risks, but not the same as Sarah or Vaughn did. It helped to know that Vaughn had been at the cemetery the day we said goodbye to Sarah. I knew he was a kind and caring man.

On the other hand, my friend Grace was furious chastising me for staying at the hospital and taking a chance of getting sick. She was a good friend, but so different from Sarah. She didn't take risks or worry about others, like Sarah.

A few months after Sarah died, I came home early from the bank. I sat in my chair by the fireplace reading a book trying to hide from the world. The front door flew open, and Oliver rushed into the parlor.

"Miranda, guess what?" he anxiously call out.

I laid my book on the coffee table. "Alright Oliver," I said looking into his eyes, "what's going on? Has something happened?"

"Yes," he excitedly replied, as he paced the room. "I've found the best home." He stopped walking and reached over taking my hand in his pulling me up to him.

"A home," I questioned, my fingers smoothing back the wild hair from his face.

"Yes, a perfect house in Pacific Heights. It's huge and has a mahogany staircase that you'll love. Are you ready to see it?" He was as excited as Poppa had been when he showed us our new home in

Boston so long ago.

"Of course, Oliver. Let's go," I said grabbing my cloak.

He pulled me close leading me outside to our new 1905, red Cadillac Runabout that he had just bought. He helped me inside before getting behind the wheel. The automobile jerked to a stop in front of a marvelous home that was sitting on a landscaped hill with redwood trees and beautiful flowerbeds loaded with colorful California poppies and ice plants.

"Well, what do you think?"

"Oh Oliver! It's perfect," I squealed with delight as he helped me from the vehicle.

The front doors opened wide, and we stepped into a huge vestibule. I spun around staring at the gorgeous mansion. I moved to the parlor, and I stopped moving. I gasped. I couldn't believe my eyes as I beheld the view.

There, in front of me was the bay of the Golden Gate with the bluest water. I would be able to sit in my chair and watch the fog roll into the city. I'd told Oliver about Braxton taking me to see the fog, and he wasn't going to be outdone by Braxton.

I turned around.

Oliver smiled not saying anything. My hands cuddled his face as I kissed him, not ever wanting to let go. He was back to his old self, to the man that I had fallen in love with.

We slowly walked up the long stairs with my hand gently rubbing the mahogany railing.

Oliver turned to me. "Well, when do you want to move?"

"Immediately," I said, throwing myself into his arms.

The next day, I quickly sent a telegram to Marion telling her to ship my furniture and keepsakes to our new house in Pacific Heights.

A few weeks later, Grace found a home on our same street. I thought it was wonderful that our lives were moving forward in a positive way.

One cool, rainy night, Oliver stepped into the vestibule and handed Nora his coat. His hands rubbed together, his body shivered as he hurried to the fireplace. His face twisted with excitement looking at me. He could never hide his emotions.

"Miranda I have a business trip to Boston and New York next April," he avowed. "How would you like to travel with me?"

"Yes!" I screamed leaping from the chair. "You mean, I'm going home for a visit? Oh, I can't wait to see Marion."

"Yes, you're going home," he replied giving me a hug.

The next few months, we both stayed busy planning our trip. Life was thriving, and I wasn't lonely anymore without Sarah, even though a day didn't go by without my missing her. She would always be with me, just as Jonathon was.

One early cool December morning, I went downstairs. Oliver was sitting in his overstuffed chair in his study busily reading some papers.

"How long have you been up?" I asked pouring a glass of orange juice.

"Oh, I've been up a couple of hours," he said excitedly leaning back in his chair. "My dear, we are going to have the most outstanding Christmas party on the evening of the twenty fourth at the Old Grand Hotel. Everything is all planned and you, my darling, only need to buy the most marvelous dress you can from Callot Soeurs of Paris."

I smoothed his wild hair from his face and gave him a kiss. I took in a deep breath. Oliver was back entirely. I couldn't wait to tell Grace about the party. This was going to be the best Christmas ever. I might even talk Grace into our getting Gibson Girl coiffures for the event.

I believe this time my anticipation of waiting for the party was greater than anybody's. Our special Christmas Eve arrived. Oliver wrapped his arm around me and led into the enormous ballroom, the same room where he had proposed to me.

My body shivered seeing a winter wonderland right in front of me. A gorgeous Christmas tree, at least twenty feet tall, stood in one corner and Christmas holly and ivy were draped everywhere around the room. White, crisp, linen tablecloths covered every table with lit candles in the center. The smell of Christmas greenery and cinnamon brought back my memories as a child. Oliver brimmed with excitement as he led me to the colossal Christmas tree decorated with red and green ribbon.

His hand reached deep into the tree and brought out a small present wrapped in bright green paper. A big smile spread across his face showing his dimples, as he handed me the box.

"Merry Christmas, my sweet Miranda."

"Oliver," I whispered, "it isn't Christmas day."

"You know me and how I love Christmas Eve. Open it," he said affectionately, as eager as a child on Christmas morning.

I pulled the elegant, velvet, green bow off the tiny box, and while lifting the lid, my heart started pounding in anticipation. I drew out two tickets to England on the *RMS Baltic*. I thought my heart was going to explode.

"My dear, she is one of the largest passenger ships in the world and is owned by the White Star Line. We will be leaving from New York

City then traveling to Liverpool. I can't wait to see what the ocean-going hotel is like," he added eagerly. "After we arrive, we'll be able to stay a while in Europe."

"Oliver, this can't be real. Is this really true? We're going to England?" I asked breathlessly.

"Yes, my dear, I promised you the world, and I'm going to fulfill my promise. You're going to see England, France, and Italy. Then we'll travel home on the same ship. This is only the beginning." He snuggled close. "I'm going to show you the entire world, like you've dreamed of," he said holding me tighter.

Tears welled in my eyes. I sniffed, "This is my dream to travel and see the world with you."

"Merry Christmas, my love." He smiled and turned around. Some of the guests were beginning to arrive. He gently wiped my tears of joy. "Yes, our dream is going to be fulfilled." He slipped the tickets in his coat pocket. Still glowing with pride, the man I loved held onto me as we walked around the room greeting all of our guests.

He brought me close in his arms as we danced and talked the night away. I just wished Sarah had been present on this special Christmas Eve. Attending the Christmas Ball with the man she loved was one of her fantasies.

The next week, Oliver had planned the ultimate New Year's Eve party to welcome in 1906. This was the year for me to go back to Boston, then to England and on to other European countries. I counted the months and days until we would leave with my enthusiasm building each day. I knew Marion was getting older, and I couldn't wait to see her.

Grace's Mom, who lived in Salt Lake City, was having surgery the first of April, so Grace and the children had decided to visit her parents and help for a while. They would be leaving Saturday, April 14th. We had everything planned so precisely. On our train ride back from Boston, we were going to stop and spend the night in Salt Lake City with Grace's parents, and then we would travel home with Grace and the children. It was a perfect plan.

The first of April finally arrived. I almost had my trunk ready, and Oliver had just finished packing his. I knew Braxton could handle the bank, especially since he was going to be by himself. Oliver had hired a man to help at the hotel, so the grand lady would be taken care of. I had packed my journal to keep track of my entire journey. Marion was beside herself with joy and couldn't wait to see me and meet Oliver.

Saturday morning, April 14th, I woke early, dressed, and went downstairs. I stopped in the parlor looking out the window across my city. I was tingling with anticipation. One more week, and I would be on the train that I loved traveling home to Boston.

Voices were coming from the patio so I hurried outside. Oliver sat at the small table talking to Nora.

He peered up at me with his big smile.

"Good morning," I said giving him a kiss on the cheek and gently smoothing his hair. "You know the weather sure seems warmer than normal, doesn't it?"

"We're having an unusual heat wave for April. I haven't seen anything like this in my entire life," he responded taking a bite of bread covered in jam.

"Today seems even warmer than yesterday," I declared fanning my face with my hands. "It's almost oppressive. It'll be nice to leave town for a while."

"Yes, a change of scene is just what we need," he said standing as he pulled the chair out from under the table for me.

"Well, this is a beautiful day and I'm going to enjoy it. I've about finished packing for the trip, and I have a little time left."

Teasingly, he leaned down giving me a kiss on my forehead. "My dear, there's not much left in the house to pack; you have everything we own in the bags and trunks."

Laughing, I gazed up into his eyes. "I can't help it, I'm so excited. Oh, so very soon, I'm going to be riding the train back to Boston, and I can't wait to see Marion."

"I know," he said kissing me again.

"I also had to prepare for our voyage to England," I assured. "All my dreams of traveling the world are coming true."

"Yes, I know, and soon, my dear. Soon, we'll be on our way. Now sit and eat," he added pouring me a glass of fresh orange juice.

"I think I'll go see Sister Margret Mary this afternoon while you're at your meeting at the hotel. I'm going to miss her."

"That's a good idea, and tonight we'll have a special dinner to celebrate out trip. I'll go and talk to Nora." He pulled me close as my fingers once more swished his wild hair to the side showing his raised eyebrows. "My dear, I really need to get to the hotel," he said, but he didn't move holding me for a few seconds longer gazing into my eyes. Then he sighed and repeated, "I really need to get to the hotel."

I sat at the round metal table and looked at Oliver's lovely flower garden with so many different colors of red, yellow, and even some blue bells; and of course, my special pink roses that Oliver had grown for me. The spectacular morning was enjoyable as I finished my breakfast and watched the bees busily going about their day.

The next couple of days, I stayed as busy as the bees preparing to leave next Saturday. I was unrelenting in checking my list, since everything had to be perfect.

Tuesday afternoon, Oliver called from the hotel to tell me he had become busier than he thought with his final preparations. Tonight, he had one more important meeting, and then he would be done. His meeting would be stretching until late, so he decided to stay at the hotel. I normally would've stayed with him, but decided instead to stay home to finish my preparations, which I did earlier than I thought possible.

Later that afternoon, my checklist was finished and the house was quiet. I laid my book on the end table in the parlor and stared outside. I already missed Oliver, and the house was quiet, so I thought I'd invite Braxton to have dinner with me since he was also alone.

The day's oppressive heat grew, so I sat outside in the flower garden where it was cooler. Nora had lit the lanterns, which gave off a peaceful feeling.

As the old grandfather clock chimed six o'clock, I heard a knock at the front door, and Braxton's voice rang out. "Good evening, Nora. Nice night, but a little warm."

"Yes'm, Mr. Braxton, it shor' is warm. Let me take yer hat. Miss Miranda is sitting out back in the garden."

I leaned over looking inside the house and could see Braxton handing his hat to Nora. "Come out back, Braxton," I called out, "I thought we might enjoy eating in the garden, since it is a little cooler out here. Oh, have you heard from Grace and the children?"

He stepped outside. "Yes, the children are having the time of their lives with their grandfather and Grace's mother is feeling better." He pulled out a chair scooting it around facing me. "I agree; it's nice out here. Oh, I don't want to forget, Emily Grace told me to tell you she has been filling up the diary that you gave her and can't wait to show you."

"I'm glad they enjoyed the train ride, and I can't wait to talk to her. She's the sweetest child," I offered sipping a glass of lemonade.

"Miranda, you are showing partiality. It couldn't be because Emily Grace is so like you," He chuckled. "That's what you get for telling her tales about traveling the world."

"Maybe," I grinned. "She is a special child."

The evening flew by as we sat for hours talking and remembering our train ride from so many years before. We speculated about all the adventures Oliver and I would have on our trips. Braxton was one person who understood me so well. He left around ten o'clock. I was too keyed up to sleep and missed Oliver, so I sat by the window in the parlor. The moon shone intensely glistening on the water of the bay. It was still warm, but a beautiful and tranquil night. It was almost too quiet, except for the strange dogs howling in the distance.

I heard the old grandfather clock strike twelve.

"Miranda you need rest," I said softly, laying my book on the table. I stepped carefully up my beautiful staircase, climbed into my soft feather bed, and quickly drifted off to a peaceful sleep.

The Shaking of the Earth

I woke abruptly. A violent shaking of the house startled me. I sat up in bed adjusting my eyes to the dim light. I could see the small grandmother clock standing in the corner of the bedroom swaying and tilting against the walls. The moonlight showed the pendulum swinging wildly and the hands on the clock had stopped at 5:18. The trembling of the house quit for a second, but that respite didn't last long.

Suddenly, the bed pitched back and forth, and the house swayed from side to side. I screamed, terrified, and my heart raced. I didn't know what to do. Years before, Oliver had told me to get to a doorway if an earthquake occurred. Nonetheless, I couldn't move; I was petrified. The bed's legs danced rocking on the floor. Afraid I would be literally thrown out of the bed, my hands fiercely gripped the headboard. The rose painted china lamp plummeted to the floor smashing into tiny pieces.

Crashing of china and glass breaking downstairs wouldn't stop. Everything seemed to rattle, clink, and groan throughout the house. The furniture in the bedroom continued to slide back and forth as if it were alive. Large items started tumbling to the floor, wood crackled, and the house moaned as if in pain. I let out a scream hearing a loud crash of bricks falling to the ground outside my window. A deep rumbling began causing plaster to fall from the ceiling which produced a cloud of white dust.

Then, as fast as the earthquake had started, it stopped, leaving an alarming host of structural groans behind. It had only been a few minutes, but it had lasted a copious amount of time it seemed to me.

I quickly leaped off the bed and was grateful the entire ceiling hadn't fallen. I shook the plaster from my hair, grabbed my clothes, and immediately dressed in record time. I ran down the stairs, but I slammed to a stop before I made it to the first floor. My mind churned at the sight. Windows were shattered and books, lamps, and crystal vases had fallen. Nothing was sitting where it should be. It was as if someone had shaken my home like a snow globe. I looked into the dining room and my mother's china was in pieces lying on the floor by the table. I walked to the parlor and saw that the main part of the house looked in good shape. I heaved a sigh of relief. The house had made it.

I franticly began shouting, "Nora! Hershel!"

Nora came running into the parlor and slid to a stop in front of me. "Miss Miranda, Miss Miranda! Gawd almighty, Miss Miranda, what do we do?"

"Are you okay, Nora?" I yelled looking around the room.

"Yes'm, I reck'n!" she answered, her entire body trembling.

"How about the others? Is everyone safe?"

"Yes'm, 'n Hershel's checking out the house. Both of the chimneys fell! I don't mind saying I was scared ta death. Miss Miranda, nows what does weez do? Is it gonna start again?" she asked hysterically.

"Nora, you need to calm down. We're fine, the house seems alright, and Hershel will see to it."

I stood frozen trying to focus my mind to think what I had to do, but I knew there was only one thing I had to see to first.

"Nora," I said standing with my body shaking, "I need to go to the hotel and check on Oliver."

"No ma'am, Miss Miranda," she yelled back at me. You needs to stay put! I'm sure Mr. Oliver be fine, ya hear? That's a well-built hotel. He wouldn't want ya ta leave this house. Ya might get hurt. We don't know what kind of damage is out there. Youse can't leave," she screamed in a panicked voice.

Braxton came running into the house. "Miranda, are you okay? Is anyone hurt?"

"We're fine, Braxton," I called back, looking into his terrified eyes. "What about you?"

"I'm fine, and everyone at my house is safe. I left Jackson at home with a gun to protect the house. Nora," he turned around, "where's Hershel?"

"He's in the kitchen. I made some coffee earlier before the earthquake, and it's still warm. That big o' puter urn I puts it in just wobbled around. You wants a cup, Mr. Braxton?"

"Good," he pivoted quickly around in a half circle and ran to the kitchen calling out. "I'd like a cup or maybe something stronger. I need to talk to Hershel."

Braxton and I drank a fast cup of coffee, and I grabbed a piece of apple bread as I paced the room.

"Now Hershel," Braxton began, "I want you to get Mr. Oliver's gun out of the cabinet the one in his study. I want you to use it if someone comes near this house and tries to steal anything. Don't be afraid to shoot. Do you understand me?" Braxton asked. "It's a disaster outside, and people aren't thinking properly."

"Yes'ur, Mr. Braxton," Hershel declared loudly. "I will protect this house. Don't ya worry. I won't let anything happen ta Mr. Oliver's home."

"Okay, Miranda" Braxton said as his voice rose, "I'm going to the hotel to check on Oliver."

"So am I, Braxton, and don't try and stop me," I said firmly.

"No ma'am, Miss Miranda. Youse shouldn't go! It's dangerous. Mr. Braxton, make her stay with me," cried Nora.

"I'll take care of her. She'll be fine," he quickly gulped his coffee. "Let's go!" he exclaimed knowing it was futile to argue with me when I had already set my mind to take action.

As we left, Nora pursed her lips and shook her head no, but she made no further comment.

Braxton ran and I followed him out the door. We jumped into his new 1906 Buick Model F. We didn't get far since the roads were torn up and we had to abandon the automobile. Using a lantern Braxton brought from his home, we started walking as fast as we could.

The morning sun was rising and trying to burn through the fog and dust. My mind couldn't take in what I was witnessing. Big buildings had crumbled to the ground and dust floated in the air. The buildings looked like children's blocks that had been knocked over in a fit. The front wall to most of them were missing. The streets were buckled as if someone had shaken a blanket in the wind and hadn't smoothed it out when they had lain it back down.

Bodies stuck out from underneath the rubble. Blood seeped from under the wreckage as if the buildings were bleeding. My body trembled. I wanted to close my eyes from the scene, but I had to watch where I was stepping. Piercing cries for help came from all directions. I clasped my hands over my ears trying to block out appeals for assistance. People ran past and others walked in circles going nowhere. Women and children walked toward us stunned with their eyes wide open from fear and shock. I couldn't panic, I had to keep going and find Oliver. The closer we got to the hotel, the more the pandemonium grew.

Braxton and I began to run. It had been difficult even to walk, but we had to get to the hotel.

Unexpectedly, I tripped, stumbling over some bricks and flew across a pile of timber from an overhang that was lying on the ground.

Braxton stopped and lifted me up. Blood flowed down my leg from a sharp piece of wood that had pierced my calf. I gripped the piece of wood jerking it free as blood gushed filling my shoes. My leg throbbed with a searing pain. I tore my petticoat and tied a tourniquet around my leg to slow the bleeding. I wasn't stopping. I had to keep going, and Braxton sensed it. I looked up at him. "I'm alright; let's go!"

He wrapped his arm around my waist and I hobbled along. As we got closer to the hotel, the chaos grew. My leg burned with fiery pain. I made a fist, let my nails bite into my palms, and tried to forget the excruciating pain. Nothing was going to prevent me from finding Oliver.

The dust from the buildings floated in the air like a storm cloud hanging over the city. My lungs hurt as I gasped for air, and it was difficult to see. As the sun rose higher in the sky the light tried to filter through, but it only added to the eeriness of the morning.

We turned the last corner to the hotel and slid to a stop. In front of us standing tall was the Old Grand Hotel. She had made it through the disaster. I sighed with relief. Now we needed to find Oliver, and this part of the nightmare would be over.

We raced to the front of the building and saw that some of the columns had fallen and were strewn everywhere, but the main structure was intact.

I started yelling, "Has anyone seen Oliver Wilkerson?"

Mark, the young man who had helped me years ago move to my suite in the hotel, came running to us. "No ma'am, Mrs. Wilkerson," he said, his tall thin body quivering. "I haven't seen him since the earthquake. He must be inside. I know he was in his office this morning. I said good morning to him when I arrived. You know he is always up early. Mrs. Wilkerson, I need to go home. I've gotta find my family. Is it alright for me to leave?"

"Yes, Mark you can leave, but be careful. I hope your family is alright," I yelled to him.

"What time was it when you saw Oliver?" Braxton called out to Mark.

"It was around five o'clock when I got to work," the young man shouted running fast down the chaotic streets. His feet didn't seem to touch the ground.

"Thank you, Mark," I yelled back.

Braxton had already entered the building, and I limped after him. I was like a fish swimming against the current with everyone else trying to get outside.

I eventually stepped into the lobby. I couldn't move. The building gave off a creepy feel, dark and cold. My eyes took everything in around me. My head leaned back staring up at the chandeliers that were hanging only by their wires. The cornices and trim looked as if someone had peeled them from the ceiling. All of the beautiful glasswork had shattered across the floor and the shards made crunching noises under everyone's feet as they ran to the entrance. The elevators hung crooked like a tongue hanging from a hot, tired dog. The hotel guests climbed over debris down the stairs. A woman carrying her large suitcase with clothes sticking out the sides knocked me to the floor. I stood up and climbed over the rubble making my way to Oliver's door.

My body swayed to a stop. I let out a piercing scream. Lying in front of me was a body covered in plaster and bricks. My scream continued and my body trembled. The man's face was hidden and only his arm stuck out of the rubble.

I leaned down wiping the plaster from the man's face. I let out a sigh. It wasn't Oliver. I closed my eyes, "Thank you, Lord." I then said a prayer for the man and his family.

Braxton grabbed me. "That isn't Oliver! Miranda, you need to get out of here. I will search for him. We have to hurry. I was told fires have started and are headed this way. We don't have much time."

"Then let's get to work. I'm not leaving this building without Oliver."

I lifted my dress and stepped over the dead man. My stomach churned, but I was too scared to be sick. I heard the building moaning and the pipes hissing steam that resonated throughout the building.

Braxton struggled but was finally able to pull Oliver's office open. He pushed a chair away from the doorway and ran to the other side of Oliver's desk.

I followed, but he abruptly stopped. My heart hammered in my chest as a voice inside of me whispered, *"Stay strong."* Lying crushed beneath his large credenza was Oliver. I pushed books, lamps, and everything out of the way. Nothing was going to stop me from getting to him. My quivering hand reached down, and I touched Oliver's lifeless face. He moaned and was barely breathing, but he was alive.

"Braxton, we have to free him!" My heart pounded loudly in my ears as I climbed over his desk slipping down on the other side of the credenza. My hands grabbed the edge of the furniture, but it didn't move. The credenza wasn't budging. "Hell's fire!" I yelled, "I'm not strong enough."

Braxton kept trying, tugging on the huge piece of furniture with all his strength, his face purple red, but it was no use.

"Now what do we do?" I screamed panicking. I leaned over and touched Oliver's face. "His breathing is so shallow. We have to get him out of here and fast."

"Mr. Wilkerson, are you here?" came a voice from outside.

I climbed over the desk running to the door. "Albert, I'm in here! Hurry! We need help!"

"Miranda! Is that you?"

"Please, help us! We can't move this piece of furniture. It's too heavy! We have to get Oliver out of here!"

"Miranda, you pull him free when Braxton and I lift the piece of furniture!" Albert yelled, moving to the other side of the credenza.

I cupped my arms under Oliver's shoulders and tugged with all my strength. "He's free!" I screamed, wrapping my arms around him. He moaned. His face was covered in pain, and it made my heart ache.

"We have to hurry, Miranda! When I came into the building I

could see heavy plumes of smoke not far from here. They said the city is burning and no one can stop it!" Albert yelled frantically.

Braxton wrapped his arms around Oliver's shoulders and Albert lifted his legs carrying him outside of the building. They gently lay him on the ground. I knelt down on my knees and lifted his head into my lap. I smoothed his wild hair from his pale face.

I screamed as the ground rumbled! Damaged buildings from the first tremor shook from side to side, crashing with tremendous force to the ground! The screams from people being crushed to their death sliced through me! I leaned over holding Oliver to protect him. I kept my eyes closed. I couldn't witness any more destruction. The tremors stopped, but the screams continued, and I wasn't able to block out the wails.

A loud rumble, then an explosion came from the block adjacent to The Grand Hotel.

"I heard the fire department is blasting some of the buildings trying to stop the fires," Albert shouted. "We don't have much time. I'm going to find ahorse and buckboard if I can."

My eyes finally opened peering up the street. Flames licked the buildings not far from us, teasing us with their strength. Some of the buildings exploded from gas lines. I shuttered from the deafening noise of discharges. Feeling the tremor, not of an earthquake, but from more large buildings crashing to the ground, I hovered near the men. Metal and debris, flew into the air sending up more clouds of dust. The intensity and swiftness of the flames were consuming building after building. The flames created a hellish horizon in the dark sky filled with smoke and ash swirling like ghosts.

I watched and felt the tumble of buildings and bricks crashing to the ground from the fire alone. I saw a massive wall of flame, like a monster eating up everything in its sight, headed straight for us. Fires were blazing in all directions. The water mains broken by the earthquake were useless, so there wasn't any water supply for the fire engines. Everyone was helpless. Ashes and soot floated like black snowflakes covering the once beautiful city. The day had become black.

I began to shout. "Braxton, we need to get Oliver to the hospital and soon, but I don't know how?"

"I know, Miranda, I know," Braxton replied tightening his fists.

I looked up shocked. Albert drove up on a worn wagon with a scared, exhausted horse.

"Were did you get the wagon?" Braxton frantically yelled.

"A man over there gave it to me," Albert shouted with his arm pointing across the street. "Let's get going before someone tries to steal it!"

I saw a tall man leap behind a group of people. My heart raced. No, it couldn't be Vaughn. I shook my head. My mind was playing tricks on me.

Jumping from the wagon Albert helped Braxton pick up Oliver and gently lay him in the wagon bed full of dirt and debris. Leaping into the wagon, Albert reached out his smut-covered hand to me, and I grabbed my skirt lifting it high climbing into the back of the wagon. Modesty was gone along with the burning city. Albert held onto the back of the seat and stood with his eyes fixed.

Braxton took the reins and popped them across the horse's back.

The horse jolted raced down the street, which was in utter confusion. The wagon bounced high above the ground over bricks and mortar. We hung on as Braxton tried to dodge all the debris.

People pawed at the wagon and the horse. The whip would snap, and I would jerk. It wasn't the horse being whipped. There was an endless flow of humanity, shouting and swearing at us.

Braxton pulled out his gun and handed it to Albert. "Use it if you need to!" he yelled gripping the reins.

"Yes, sir!" Albert assured. He held the gun firmly in his hands, and I could see in his eyes that he wasn't afraid to use it.

The roads were like waves on an ocean, but the wagon just leaped into the air with each bump. Oliver's head was secure in my lap with my arms wrapped around him. I gently wiped his pale face with the end of my dress. He moaned and his eyes popped open. His greenish-brown eyes looked up at me.

I leaned over. "Oliver, you're going to be alright. We're taking you to the hospital. Everything is going to be fine now."

"Miranda, are you okay?" he whispered. "The earthquake…I tried to leave to get home. I was so worried about you."

"Yes, I'm fine, and you're going to be alright too. Just hold on to me." I smiled, "Braxton is driving, and you know how he drives."

Oliver tried to smile. I leaned down and kissed him smoothing his hair again.

"My hotel how is she?"

"The hotel is standing tall," I assured. "There wasn't a lot of damage." His face was swelling and the pain growing with each second. I wasn't going to tell him about the fires. I hoped the Old Grand would survive, but first we had to get him to St. Mary's Hospital.

People didn't stop grabbing at the wagon. One man's hand reached over the side and pulled his body off the ground. I let out a scream. Albert leaped to the side of the wagon and punched the man. I watched as the stranger lost his balance and fell with a loud thud onto the road.

Another man grabbed the wagon and lifted his leg over the side allowing him to climb onboard. I screamed, seeing the anger in the man's wild eyes. Albert spun around and landed a blow square in the man's face. The man shook his head with blood flowing from his nose and mouth, but was not deterred. He was acting like a crazed animal, his glazed eyes turning to Braxton. Albert didn't hesitate to fire the gun. The man shifted back and forth with blood oozing out of his chest. He glared at me with dead eyes before his body flipped over the back of the wagon into the crowd of people.

I held onto Oliver trying to concentrate on him and not the dead man. I gasped for breath because the air was thick with smoke and ash. I could make out the hospital in the distance. Not much further—we were almost there. The wagon jerked to a stop.

My eyes peered over the side of the wagon. The hospital building leaned to one side, and some of the walls were partially crumbled. The streets were in pandemonium. The tall flames were flickering through the dense smoke coming at us. People were screaming in pain and bodies were lying on the ground surrounding the hospital. People ran from the hospital and more were running to the hospital. They were like rats jumping off a burning ship with nowhere to run.

"Where's a doctor?" Braxton called out to one of the nuns.

"I don't know sir? We are moving everyone to safety."

At that moment, I spotted Dr. Jacob. I gently lay Oliver's head down in the wagon. I jumped down and limped across the hospital grounds. "Dr. Jacob!" I shouted. "I need help!"

He turned around, "Mrs. Wilkerson, I have my hands full."

"Dr. Jacob, my husband is hurt! A piece of furniture fell on him! Please, help him!"

"Take me to him."

"He's in that wagon," I shouted with my arm flying in the air pointing. "Hurry." The doctor ran to the wagon, and I followed as best I could with my wounded leg.

Dr. Jacob climbed into the wagon and bent down by Oliver, he sighed shaking his head. I saw in his face, the same apologetic look I had seen before with Sarah.

"I'm sorry. There isn't anything I can do for him, Mrs. Wilkerson," he said with sympathy, quickly climbing down from the wagon.

"You have to do something!" yelled Braxton flying from the wagon seat.

"I can't help him, sir. The furniture crushed his ribs and punctured his lungs. He is bleeding inside. Even if I could operate, he wouldn't make it. He doesn't have long. I'm so sorry, but there are a lot of people I need to see to." Dr. Jacob turned and ran toward the crowd of people.

"No!" I yelled. Braxton grabbed hold of my arm. His face said it all. I buried my face in his chest for comfort but none came.

"Please, Miranda, go be with Oliver," Braxton begged. I could see Braxton's pain of losing his friend. I too had to face the realization that Oliver wasn't going to make it.

Albert helped me climb back into the wagon. I gently lifted Oliver's head and placed it on my lap. I leaned over and kissed him one more time. Tears rolled down my face.

Oliver looked up with weary eyes and took some sharp breaths. He whispered, "I love you, and I was going to show you the world, Miranda. You deserve the world."

"Oliver, you're the only world I need. I love you," I sniffed wiping my tears on the sleeve of my dress. "Please hang on." I took in a deep breath, "I can't lose you. I need you so much."

He breathed out his last breath and was gone.

I looked up at the city and shouted, "No! Why Lord!" I could see the fires headed in our direction.

"We need to go, Miranda. Hold on," Braxton said, as he and Albert climbed back onto the wagon. He shook the reins, the wagon lurched, and rolled down the street. Albert fought the crowds of people grabbing the wagon.

Braxton looked back at me. "The fires will be here soon."

I sat cuddling Oliver in my arms as tears dropped onto his body. I knew where Braxton had turned the horse's head.

We pulled in front of the funeral home in Pacific Heights away from the fires. A man was standing out front. "We don't have room for any more bodies, Sir," the man called out. His hand nervously rubbed his head, "Sorry."

Braxton hopped down from the wagon. "Not even for Mr. Oliver Wilkerson."

The man gulped taking in a deep breath, "I'm sorry, sir. Please let me help you if I can. I'll try."

They walked to the back of the wagon, but I couldn't let go of Oliver. I just held him.

This couldn't be real. As black ash flakes continued to fall, I sat in an old worn wagon and held Oliver in my arms. I lifted my weary eyes to the burning city of San Francisco and asked aloud, "How will we go on?"

"Please, Miranda," Braxton begged, "say good bye and leave Oliver in the care of the undertaker. Oliver would understand."

I remembered Poppa telling me the same thing about Jonathon. I did as I had done that day. "Oliver," I whispered, "I love you, and this is not goodbye. You will always be in my heart. You're my world, and I'll love you always." I smoothed his curly brown hair from his face. I smiled. That wild hair was always getting in the way. I leaned in kissing him goodbye.

I let go. Albert and the undertaker lifted Oliver out of the wagon and carried him into the funeral home. I sat numbly.

Braxton climbed back up on the wagon. His body was bathed in sweat. I could see the pain in his eyes as we headed home to Pacific Heights. I turned and looked back at the city. The fire was spreading mercilessly, like a huge monster taking anything and everything in its path. I knew in my heart that the Old Grand Hotel was gone as well.

I looked up at our house as the old wagon jostled us to a stop. Braxton leaped out and lifted me down from the wagon seat. Nora opened the front door and came running outside.

"Did ya find Mr. Oliver?" she shouted.

"Yes," Braxton replied. "Nora, I'm sorry, he died a little while ago."

Nora's large body bent over and wept.

Braxton turned to face Albert, "You stay here with Miranda, and I'll be back in a little while. I need to check on my house."

"No, you can't leave, Braxton," I grabbed his arm. "Please stay," I begged. "I don't want to be alone."

"I'll be back, Miranda. Albert and Nora will be with you," he assured, leading me into the parlor. "Albert," Braxton gestured pointing to Oliver's study, "fix her a strong glass of bourbon. Get her to drink a little, I'll be back soon."

"Yes, Sir." Albert said, as he turned and followed Nora, her apron held tight to her nose sniffling.

I sat in my favorite chair by the window and looked out at the bay. The waters seemed so calm like nothing had occurred, but it had. All of it had happened. My hands gripped the arms of the chair. I could feel the stabbing pain in my heart as weariness was sweeping over me. If we had just left last week with Grace, Oliver would still be here. I sighed, why did this have to happen?

Albert brought me the liquor, but I pushed the glass away. "Miranda, you have to drink some. It'll relax you."

I sipped some of the bourbon and then set the glass down on the table by the chair. My eyes stayed glued to the window.

Braxton returned and walked into the parlor. He lifted the glass; his head nodded, "Miranda, another sip…please." I brought the strong liquid to my lips sipping it as it ran down my throat burning my insides.

Nora put down a plate of some cold bread, jam, and butter for us to eat.

"We can't use the stove. The gas is off, but ya do need ta eats something, Miss Miranda."

"I can't eat Nora, but thank you."

"Miss Miranda, ya need ta eat a few bites. Mr. Oliver would be upset at me if I didn't take care of ya," she said red-eyed and weary herself. "It's a sad day, a sad, sad day fer me."

I picked up a piece of bread again refused it. How could I go on? I had lost too many loved ones, and I didn't know how much more I could take. I fell limp in my chair; the life was gone from me.

Nora squatted by me. "Here, Miss Miranda, let me see ta yer leg. That's a nasty cut." She lifted my leg, gently lay it on the ottoman, and untied my shoe sliding it off. It was full of dried blood and dirt. Nora tenderly washed the deep cut causing more blood to ooze out. Once she got the bleeding to stop, Nora covered the gash in salve and swathed my leg. The pain in my heart took the pain away from my leg.

I sat in the chair the rest of the afternoon and finally fell asleep. Braxton lifted me in his arms. My eyes slowly opened as he gently put me on the sofa and placed a blanket over me. "Miranda, just rest."

I woke startled the next morning. A gray dim light had crept into the room, and I believed I was having a nightmare, but soon realized that it was a real nightmare. My clothes were torn and frayed, and they reeked of smoke. My leg throbbed.

I scanned the room. Braxton was sitting in the chair by the window softly rubbing his eyes.

He felt my stare and asked, "Miranda, how are you doing?"

"Oh, Braxton, is it true?" I cried out, sitting up. "Oliver is gone?" I began to weep uncontrollably.

"Yes, Miranda it is," Braxton said sadly, weariness showed on his face as he stood from the chair and sat down by me.

"How will I go on?" I questioned.

"Just as you always do. Take a day at a time. Don't give up now. We need to go back to the funeral home and prepare for Oliver's funeral."

My head bent downward.

"I'm so sorry, Miranda, there is still chaos everywhere, but we'll give Oliver the exceptional funeral that he deserves. Now you go upstairs and get cleaned up, as well as you can," he patted my arm. "There isn't much water."

I stood shakily and my feet shuffled to the stairs. My leg pulsed with pain from each movement. My hand gripped the mahogany railing, and I looked up at the majestic staircase. It was so like the one in my home in Boston. That was one reason that Oliver had bought the house. It reminded me of my home when I was young. My body shook and tears began to fall as I slid down and sat on a step. I couldn't move.

Albert walked over and sat next to me. He took my hand in his large hands. "Life's not fair, is it, Miranda? I understand how you feel." He lightly caressed my hands. "I wish Sarah was here every day, and I've been so angry that God took her away from me. We had so many plans. It's been hard to go on, but I know I'd have disappointed her so much if I'd given up." He took a deep breath. "Sarah would be telling you to hold your head high. Don't let death beat you. She wasn't a quitter and neither are you. Miranda, I'll help you get through this."

I looked at him and my head nodded yes. I wasn't a quitter, and I had to go on, just as I had done for my family. I had to stand up and put one foot in front of the other.

"I will go on, Albert, for Oliver and Sarah." I stood and walked up the magnificent staircase, one slow step at a time.

I opened the door of my room. Nora had come in and straightened things up. I walked over to the bureau and picked up the photo of Oliver; tears fell onto the photo. I would plan the best funeral I could, one that Oliver deserved.

I lay my clean clothes on the bed and squeezed the rag from the bowl of water. My eyes turned to the mirror. I gasped touching my chest.

"No!" I cried out, grabbing my throat. My locket was gone! I must have broken the chain in the hotel trying to move the furniture. I wanted to sit and cry, to give up, but I didn't have time right now for feeling sorry for myself. That would have to be another day. I didn't think my heart could break any more, but the loss of my locket was like completely losing Vaughn. I had lost both the men I loved, and I had nothing left. Everything was gone, all of my hopes and dreams.

I looked into the mirror; the woman looking back had a blank and fatigued look. I didn't even recognize her with her bitter eyes of pain.

I finished dressing. I unlocked and opened Oliver's trunk. I lifted out one of his new suits, the one he had bought to wear on the train home. I lay it over my arm and made my way downstairs.

I left with Albert and Braxton in the wagon early that morning. The air was heavy with lingering smoke and fog hovering as we slowly rode to Old Saint Mary's church. I gripped the side of the wagon because my eyes couldn't take in what I was seeing. The church was in ruins still smoldering from the fire. My life and my beloved city were gone.

Braxton dashed over to a man who was sitting on the ground near the burned church. The man's eyes stared out into space not seeing anyone or anything.

"Sir," Braxton interrupted, "can you tell me where the sisters and Father Brady are?"

The man looked up at Braxton with a glazed exasperated face. Braxton put his hands on the man's shoulders. "Sir," Braxton shook the man as he repeated, "can you tell me where the sisters and Father Brady are," he questioned again. The man just sat not moving staring out into space.

Braxton turned to leave.

"They left to go to St. Brigid at Van Ness and Broadway," the man finally spoke. "That church has survived. Sir, they were all fine." His glazed swollen eyes looked up at Braxton, "My family is gone," he whimpered. "I can't find them, I don't know what to do."

Albert stood in the back of the wagon. "Sir," he called out, "a shelter is set up down the street not far from here. Maybe your family is nearby. We'll be going right past. Climb on and we can drop you off."

Albert leaned his hand down. The man grabbed hold climbing into the back of the wagon.

Skeletons of structures lined the roads that once sat as magnificent homes and businesses. Braxton pulled up on the reins and the rickety old wagon wobbled to a stop in front of a loan building. The solemn man jumped down. He bowed his head to us and speedily walked off disappearing into a crowd of people.

My brain wasn't working and time wasn't making sense, but it didn't take us long to make it to St. Brigid Church. Braxton hopped from the wagon and hurried to find Sister Margret Mary.

I watched as Sister Margret Mary ran to me. Her once crisp clean clothes covered in smut, dirt, and blood. "Miranda, I've been worried about you," she called out taking my hand, "I am sorry about Oliver. Braxton has explained that you are planning his funeral. Father Brady said it was fine to have the funeral here, this afternoon. Don't worry, my child. I will see to everything."

She clutched my hand in her blackened hands. I couldn't say anything, but "Thank you." My brain was muddled, numb, and uncertain. My capabilities had died along with Oliver and the city. I didn't believe that I could go on. I was like Poppa, a shell of the person I once was. All my dreams were gone just as all of my loved ones. My voice wouldn't work; I couldn't seem to get my lips to move. "Is all hope lost?" I finally whispered.

"Miranda, you will make it," Sister confirmed, "just as you have always done." She paused for a second, "There is always hope. God does have a purpose for you." She turned to Braxton. "You and Albert take good care of her."

My head swung around and I looked at her. I couldn't believe what she had said. It was as if Poppa was speaking to me through her, just as he did so long ago after Jonathon and my momma had died.

"Yes, Sister, we will," Braxton assured. "We'll see you later today," he called out climbing back into the wagon.

The wagon slowly moved along the battle torn street. Braxton took his time to miss as much of the debris as possible. The old worn horse was as tired and numb as I was. His head dipped to the ground as if he didn't want to see the destruction. I sat staring into the dark clouds of smoke covering my glorious city. Unwillingly, we arrived at the funeral home. If only we could keep riding, maybe this nightmare would disappear.

Albert leaped from the wagon and lifted me from the seat to the ground. We walked inside the building. I cringed seeing bodies lying everywhere. I had seen so many dead on the road yesterday, and I never wanted to see death again, not in my lifetime. The undertaker who had helped us yesterday with Oliver came out from a back room hurrying over to me. He began to tell me how sorry he was for my loss. I didn't speak and just handed him Oliver's clothes as Braxton finished the plans. The man promised he would move Oliver to the church later that morning.

I walked outside the cold, dismal building. Watching as people brought loved ones up to the funeral home and lay their bodies on the cold ground was arduous. But, there was no alternative. It was still unbelievable how many people had died.

We rode home in silence to dress and prepare for Oliver's funeral. Nora and Hershel couldn't leave to go to the funeral since someone needed to stay and protect the house from looters. Braxton wanted Albert to go with us in case of trouble and, of course, Albert had known Oliver for many years. Looting and stealing were going on everywhere in this great old city and we had to be careful. At least the dead did not have to experience the fall of San Francisco.

One Lone Red Rose

When we arrived home, I plodded upstairs to my bedroom to don myself in mourning attire. I was going through the motions, not feeling anything. I went to my armoire. My beautiful dresses hung so clean and fresh, but I didn't have anything black, so I picked a dark navy dress. I was almost happy not to be wearing the loneliness of black and knew Oliver would approve of the navy dress. My dress slipped over my head, and I pulled my hair into an old fashion bun on the back of my head. I looked into the mirror. How could I have lost Oliver and Sarah so close together?

I could hear Jonathon and Sarah talking; it was as if they were standing in my bedroom.

Jonathon's voice was crisp, "You have always been headstrong and determined, Miranda. Life is for the living. Let the dead bury the dead. Miranda, we will have no more tears."

I smiled staring at my reflection in the mirror hearing Poppa's voice. "Miranda, God has a purpose for you."

I didn't know what purpose God could have for me now, but I wasn't going to give up. The words from Mr. Clemons flowed in my mind. "Remember, keep your faithfulness for life no matter what tragedies life sends swirling at you."

I had to smile thinking about Jonathon, and I could see Sarah with those green eyes and her big smile. Then in the quiet Sarah's sweet voice resonated. "Miranda, you are a fighter, and nothing has ever stood in your way. I hope you never give up."

I had made it through losing my baby Edmond, Jon, Momma, Poppa, and Sarah. I could get through this as well. I had to remember the good times with Oliver and Sarah and write down all I could remember. Life would go on. Time does not stop for anyone. I was a fighter, but I wondered why I was always the survivor.

I went downstairs. Albert and Braxton were waiting in the vestibule. Nora gave me a hug. "Ya tell Mr. Oliver I said good bye, 'n I'm sorry I couldn't be at the funeral." Tears were falling down her exhausted, dark face. I looked over at Herschel seeing tears in his old eyes. They had been with Oliver for many years.

Nora handed me a bouquet of flowers that she had picked from Oliver's garden. Oliver loved his flowers. He was a very busy man, but not too busy for his garden. He loved tending to it in the mornings before he would leave to go to the hotel.

"Yes, Nora, I will tell him. The flowers are perfect, just as Oliver would want. Thank you."

The three of us climbed into the old wagon. I could still see smoke coming from the buildings downtown. The fires were burning relentlessly.

The church was in the distance. Braxton pulled the wagon to a stop and helped me out. We went into the sanctuary while Albert hid the wagon and horse in the back of the church. Sister Margret Mary walked up and hugged me.

"How are you doing, Miranda?"

"I am going to be alright. With your help and my friends, I will get through this. Oliver wouldn't want me to give up. He was a man of dreams."

Braxton and I sat down. Albert joined us. I had to smile thinking we were the same ones that were at Sarah's funeral. Life can have an odd twist sometimes.

Father Brady began the service, and the sisters from both churches came into the sanctuary. I sat listening as he spoke about Oliver's accomplishments and the improvements he had made to the city.

"Oliver Edmond Wilkerson was a good, loyal man and very generous to the church. His wife, friends, and the city of San Francisco will dearly miss him. When a young man dies such a tragic death, it is indescribable. However, we hold God's promise of hope close. This man and the great city of San Francisco will be reborn."

I thought about how alike Oliver and Poppa were. Poppa would have liked Oliver. They both died too young, before seeing the world.

When the service ended, each of us walked down to the casket. I stood looking at Oliver in his new suit. He looked so handsome lying as if he were asleep, and I wished with all my heart he would wake up and tell me everything would be all right. I had to smile seeing his hair —that wavy, wild hair was sticking up. I reached over and smoothed it down, just as I had done hundreds of times before.

Braxton walked up and took hold of my arm. "Miranda, it is time to go to the cemetery."

I unwillingly turned to leave but would always remember how peaceful Oliver looked.

Braxton led me out of the church with Albert following. We made our way back to Old St. Mary's cemetery.

Our small trio slowly walked over to the gravesite, and Father Brady began once more.

"Christ our eternal King and God,
You have destroyed death and the devil
By Your Cross and have restored man to life
By your Resurrection'
Give rest, Lord, to the soul of Your servant
Oliver Edmond Wilkerson
Who has fallen asleep,
In Your Kingdom,
Where there is no pain, sorrow or suffering.
We then shall rejoice in Your mercy,
And exalt and praise
Your Holy Name,
O Father, Son and Holy Spirit,
Both now and forever
And to the ages of ages.
Amen."

"We are saying goodbye, this April 19th to Oliver Edmond Wilkerson who died on Wednesday, April 18th, 1906, in the most catastrophic earthquake in history."

I gasped thinking I might faint feeling lightheaded. This couldn't be real. I hadn't even realized what day it was, Thursday, April 19, I was standing in the cemetery again saying goodbye to someone I loved.

We finished with a prayer, and Albert walked up to say his goodbyes to Oliver. I could see the pain in his eyes for all of his losses.

Next, Braxton slowly walked up. He didn't want to say goodbye to his longtime friend. He stood and wiped the tears from his eyes.

Sister Margret Mary walked up and said a prayer.

I looked at the beautiful flowers that Nora had picked. In all of this destruction and death, there was hope.

Everyone walked away so I could talk to Oliver. I had saved one lone red rose for him, to place upon his casket.

"Well Oliver, this isn't goodbye. I will never say goodbye to you because you'll be with me the rest of my life. We didn't get to see the world together, but I'll think of you anytime I travel. I also promise to rebuild the Old Grand Hotel in the style you loved. You will be proud of her, and she'll stand tall among the other buildings. I hope you have found peace and the most beautiful gardens. God bless. I will love you forever."

I turned and walked to the small grave next to Oliver. I had saved one small red rose bud and lay it upon baby Edmond's grave. I looked back over to Oliver's casket. "You take care of Edmond. I love you both."

I turned and walked hesitantly to the three waiting for me. I was leaving my world and the life I had known, just as I had done before so long ago in Boston. I was trying to be strong, but it was so difficult. I wasn't sure at that moment if I would make it.

"Miranda, the Lord is with you and will never leave you," Sister Margret Mary assured me wrapping her arms around me.

"Thank you, Sister."

"I have to get back to the church since many people need help. Braxton and Albert will take good care of you. I will talk to you in a few days, but if you need me, send for me. The Lord be with you and keep you safe, my child."

The other sisters had stayed at the church to help the wounded, the homeless, and the grieving. The wonderful city of San Francisco had turned into and infirmary and orphanage, and downtown, an inferno. People were sleeping on the streets and anywhere they could find. Everyone was afraid of another tremor, but most were numb like I was.

Hershel had fixed a makeshift stove out back that used wood, and Nora was able to cook us something to eat. I sat at the table but couldn't eat. She started in on me, as Marion had done so long ago, so I ate a few bites.

Braxton stood from the table after he finished eating. "I need to go home and check on things. I'm so glad Grace and the children are safe and not here in this chaos. I'll be back soon, Miranda."

Albert stood. "Well, it's time for me to be going too. You take care, Miranda, and if you need anything, let me know."

I rose from my chair facing Albert. "Where are you going Albert? Didn't you live in the hotel like Sarah?"

"Yes, but I'll find somewhere to live."

"Where are you going to live? Aren't all of your things gone?"

"I'll make it. Don't worry Miranda."

"Albert, I have this huge house and plenty of room for you to stay. You are welcome to live here until we rebuild the hotel. I could also use your help. Making repairs here and rebuilding downtown will be quite a load. You knew the Old Grand Hotel as well as anyone."

"Thank you, Miranda. That is kind of you."

"Remember, Albert. Friends don't have to say thank you." I finally smiled.

"We will build the most impressive hotel in the world. I'll do everything I can to help you, I promise. This will be for Sarah and Oliver," he said proudly.

"Go upstairs with Nora and pick a room. Between Oliver's and Braxton's clothes I'm sure we can outfit you."

"I'll pick some clothes out and bring them back with me," Braxton added turning to Albert. "I'm glad you're staying here. This house does need to be protected at least for a few more days."

I left the two men standing in the kitchen. I went upstairs to my room. I opened my satchel and slid out my journal. I wouldn't be writing about the exciting times on the train with Oliver, or visiting the cities along the way, but I needed to write about what was happening now. I sat in the chair by the bedroom window that overlooked the bay and began to write.

A knock at my door startled me. "Miss Miranda, are ya alright," Nora, shouted. "We're all worried."

The grandmother clock sitting in the corner of the room chimed. I hadn't realized how long I had been sitting. "Yes, Nora, you may come in. I was writing and had lost track of time."

The door opened and she began busily to straighten things around the room. "Well, I've fixed a little something ta eat 'n ya need ta take a break 'n come downstairs."

"Yes, Nora, I'll be right down."

She smiled and turned going out the door.

I stopped on the staircase. I could see Braxton and Albert sitting in the parlor having a glass of bourbon.

"Gentlemen are you ready to eat?" I announced.

"Yes, I'm hungry," Braxton admitted. His hand reached over taking my arm, and we walked into the dining room. I was happy to see three place settings and not one on the dining room table.

Rising from the Ashes

After dinner, I excused myself, went back to my room, and hoped I would be able to sleep. I climbed into bed and looked up at the ceiling with its plaster missing reminding me of the earthquake. I pulled the cover over my head and tried to hide from the world.

I slept that night from fatigue and woke with the sun coming in through the window. I unwillingly dragged myself out of bed and dressed in a normal dress. There would be no more black for me. I hurried downstairs.

Albert and Hershel sat in the kitchen talking. They had heard from some of the men in the neighborhood that the fires were still burning, and it would be a few days before we could go to the hotel.

I walked outside, and Nora was cooking breakfast. I sat at our special table. Oliver's flowers were full of new blooms, so I couldn't tell where Nora had cut them. He'd be proud. My life was like the flowers. I'd see that the Old Grand Hotel would rise up again and bloom just like the flowers. It was nice to see beauty in all of the turmoil. Oliver had planted light pink roses for me along with his favorite red. I picked a pink rose and one red rose. I found a small vase to put them in and set it on the table to remind me that Oliver still lived through his garden and through my pleasant memories of him.

I finished my breakfast and sat in the chair by the front window in the parlor. It gave me a peace that I needed.

"Miranda, I've talked to some of the business men, and the city is already planning on rebuilding," Braxton called out coming in the front door. "They're having a meeting in the morning. I think that you, Albert, and I should attend. I checked on the bank and it is gone. As soon as the vault cools down, we will be able to open the door and get back to business. We can't open it now, as it would be too dangerous. It might explode. We'll begin our plans soon to build a better bank and hotel for Oliver."

"I can't believe that they're planning on rebuilding so soon. Then we do need to prepare too," I added.

"Yes, they want everything back as quickly as possible. It's going to be a lot of work, but we can get it done. They're saying the city is going to rise up out of the ashes," Braxton proudly announced.

"I agree, the Old Grand Hotel is going to be as the Phoenix. It's going to be resurrected from the ashes," I said victoriously. "We will win over the earthquake." I had a mission now to build the Old Grand Hotel back, and I wasn't going to let Oliver down.

The next morning, we were up early for our meeting with all of the businessmen, and it was as Braxton said. The city officials wanted the city to be rebuilt soon, just as I did. The fires were away from the hotel and bank, and we could go see them.

The old wagon creaked as we slowly made our way down the streets of San Francisco. The wagon slowed to a stop. Braxton sat quietly staring.

In the distance stood what was left of the grand old lady. I clutched my hands together tightly, remembering when we found Oliver, the building was standing tall and proud. Tears fell from my face. I knew this would have broken Oliver's heart to see her like this. She was his pride and joy.

The grand lady's outside walls were still partially standing, but the inside was gone and looked like the inside of a fireplace with only ashes. I had a big job ahead of me, but I'd succeed and the old girl would stand just as majestically as she had before.

Albert helped me from the wagon. I saw the sadness in his face as he looked at the Old Grand Hotel. He'd lost everything he and Sarah owned in the fire and had to start over from scratch with only his memories.

I knew my locket was gone forever. There was no way for it to have survived. Life would go on, and the once imposing grand lady would be rebuilt along with our memories.

I stood and remembered the first day we had arrived with Braxton, Vaughn, and Sarah. That was the happiest day of my life. I was in San Francisco at the Old Grand Hotel. That was the first time I met Oliver. That wonderful, glorious spring day, so long ago would be forever in my heart.

I turned to Braxton, "I've seen enough. Let's go and check on the bank."

The oppressive silence was deafening to me—so dreadfully quiet. The city also had a horrible stench from the fires, mortar, bricks, and of course, the dead buried beneath the buildings. The life was being pulled right out of me, just as the buildings were only charred and full of ashes.

"That'll be fine," Braxton said, helping me onto the wagon, as Albert jumped in.

When we stopped in front of the bank, we saw it was like the hotel, only the red brick walls stood. Braxton had hired some men to guard the building. The ashes were still smoldering. Sooner or later, we would have to get the vault open. Braxton was hoping for sooner, wanting to get his life back as soon as possible.

We left the bank and silently rode to our houses. We were grateful to have homes. I had heard our old house in Nob Hill was gone. Oliver's buying our new home in Pacific Heights had saved us, and he'd be proud that our home was still standing.

Saturday, March 19, 1910

The next few weeks were difficult. We were getting a better picture of the devastation of the city. This was going to be some campaign. Some streets were being cleared enough to make it through, but others were impassable because so many walls had collapsed, dumping rubble into the roads. The city had a quietness that gave off an unnatural feel. I tried not to visit the hotel often. I'd wait until the rebuilding began.

Many of the government buildings downtown had escaped total damage and were quickly repaired, and *The Fishing Shack* on the waterfront had made it better than we expected.

Braxton found out that the depot was saved and the tracks had been repaired. The train was running again. Grace and the children would be coming home soon. He hated that his family would see the city in ruins, but didn't want to live without them any longer. Our houses were safe for now. The military was patrolling the streets keeping looters under control.

One amazing enterprise was that, Sunday morning after the earthquake, the United Railroads began the first streetcar service on Fillmore and 16th Street line. The news traveled, and it gave people a feeling of normality and that the city was coming alive after all the death and destruction.

The morning of May 31st, Braxton brought his family home. It was tough for me because Oliver and I were supposed to be riding the train back with Grace and the children from our trip to Boston. That was to have been a joyful occasion. Then we were to leave on our voyage in a few weeks to Europe. We had so many dreams and plans that would never be.

I was watching out the bay window for Braxton to arrive. His automobile pulled to a stop, and I hurried and flung the front door open wide. The children ran to me, and I wrapped my arms around them not wanting to let go. I looked up and Grace was standing there in tears.

I let go of the children and hugged her. Seeing the city in ruins and knowing that Oliver was gone was devastating for her. She had worked for him for years. He had been more than her boss. He was her good friend. We went into the house. Nora came into the parlor and took the children back with her to the kitchen.

"Miranda, I'm so sorry. I wished I could've been here for you."

"I know, but I am so glad you and the children weren't in the city that horrible day."

"How are you doing? Is there anything I can do to help you? I can't believe that Oliver is gone," she said overwhelmed, sobbing.

"Yes Grace, you can do one important thing for me; take care of Braxton. The last few weeks have been hard on him, too. He's been strong for me. Now, he needs to lean on someone else. He needs you even more than I do. I'm rebuilding the Old Grand Hotel and I'll be busy and distracted with that project for a long time. Grace, life does go on, and we'll all come through this."

I knew she couldn't or wouldn't understand what I was saying. This was shocking to her. I had stunned many people over the years. She didn't comprehend how I was making it without Oliver. Grace would never understand me, but that was all right.

"You and the children need to go home and take care of Braxton; he needs you. I will talk to you later. We'll be all right, you'll see."

I called for Nora to bring the children. I gave them hugs and wiped Grace's tears. "We will have no more tears. You have a family to see to."

I led them to the door, and Braxton sat waiting outside for them. I smiled and he smiled back; he had his family home. I closed the beautiful wooden front door, went to the parlor window, and watched the bay for a few minutes. Then I went back to work on plans for the hotel's decor.

Albert came home that evening and reported on the progress of the Old Grand. Each day the old hotel was being reborn.

The next few months, I was able to watch the construction of the massive hotel and the bank. The city was coming to life. I spent my days planning and working to get the old girl finished. I had to furnish the hotel as elegantly as Oliver had. He had a way with things, and I had to remember and not forget any detail, not even the smallest ones. The hotel was going to open with style and grace, just as it did at its beginning.

The bank was soon up and running, and Braxton was busy daily at the bank. He cherished being home at night with the children and Grace.

I spent my nights writing and describing in my journal how the building process was proceeding. I also helped Sister Margret Mary at the church. One day, I asked her if she had heard from Sharkie. I learned the tavern had been spared from the fire, but did have some damage. All of his family was safe, and that was what mattered.

I was so glad to hear that they were alright. I didn't want to hear any more heartbreak. I also visited the cemetery often and kept Oliver informed about the rebuilding.

Albert and I stayed busy. The months turned into years and the years zoomed by faster than I would have believed, but the end of the rebuilding was nearing.

The year of 1909 was ending. It had taken three long years to accomplish my goal. I stood out front of the grand lady in awe as I looked up at her. Albert and I had decided to change the entrance to the hotel. The striking carriage entrance was now a fabulous courtyard inside full of fresh flowers growing all around. Oliver would have his garden along with the grand lady, something I knew he'd love. Of course, we had plenty of red and pink roses and special red carnations for Sarah.

I filled the hotel with the best furnishings that I could find from around the world. We were nearing the end of rebuilding and the grand opening day was approaching, March 19, 1910. The majestic ball that Saturday evening was to be the most elaborate and astonishing party that the city of San Francisco had ever seen. It was what the Old Grand Hotel and Oliver deserved.

I invited everyone worldwide who had attended when the Old Grand Hotel was first built. Grace helped me with the invitations. She had written the original ones with Oliver, and they were designed the same. This was going to be a glorious day for the city of San Francisco.

Albert had become more valuable than I could have ever hoped. He was a diamond in the rough, and I knew why Sarah had been drawn to him. He was caring and had an incredible business sense. I hired him to be the manager of the hotel. He couldn't believe that I offered him the job. He had put his love and everything he had into making the wonderful hotel come to life. It was his dream too. It was how we both were dealing with losing Sarah and Oliver. He was as unwavering as I was, and the Old Grand Hotel was coming alive right in front of our eyes. It was one loss we could fix.

I'd given him the choice of any suite in the hotel. He picked his old room, the one that had been next to Sarah's. He could have chosen anywhere he wanted, but he chose a simple place. I hoped Sarah was watching him. He did love her and would've made her dreams come true.

I went back to the same spot, to my suite that Oliver gave me. I was like Albert, I couldn't change rooms. I had added larger windows to most of the rooms that overlooked the city. I wanted everyone to see the glorious sights.

The day arrived. I was excited and so sad at the same time. I quickly dressed that morning and hurried to greet each guest who was staying in the hotel, just as Oliver would have done. It was a celebration, and I wasn't going to have it any other way.

That evening came swiftly. I went upstairs to my suite and dressed in the most marvelous, dark maroon gown. Before I left for the party, I walked to the mirror.

"Miranda, you can do this. Remember, this is for Oliver."

I wished so much that Oliver could be here. He thrived on parties like this, and I knew he was with me, so I could pull this off. I walked out the door and to the new elevator.

I took a deep breath and walked into the magnificent room—it was amazing! I stood panning the room for a brief second and knew Oliver would be proud. I remembered the last party he'd given here, the Christmas Eve of 1905. The time he gave me my present of traveling to see the world.

Braxton and Grace walked into the ballroom and brought my thoughts back to the present. Grace was as lovely as ever and was as much at ease as Oliver at these events.

Braxton smiled, "Miranda, you did it. You pulled it off, and the Old Grand Lady is perfect. Oliver would approve." He gave me a hug.

Albert followed them into the room, and I saw the look on his face. He too wished Sarah could have been here, remembering how she loved fairytale balls. I hurried to him taking his hands in mine. "Albert, we did it. Sarah and Oliver are with us tonight. This is for them." He smiled and nodded, "Yes, Miranda, I believe they are."

The celebration began. So many important men and women from all over the world had arrived. I was fascinated to talk to each of them and hoped someday to travel and see them again.

The evening was as wonderful as I'd dreamed. It ended as Braxton stood and raised a toast to Oliver and his Old Grand Hotel. I couldn't stop the tears from falling, but these were tears of happiness that the old grand lady was reborn.

My Lost Locket

Many years have gone by since the night I toasted Oliver and his Old Grand Hotel.

I liked sitting in my hotel suite looking out the window. I stay there most nights. It was too lonely at the house to stay very often. That was what was difficult for me, being alone. I kept my beloved home, and I'd visit when I needed to look out at the bay, but my suite was my sanctuary.

This April 19, 1916, I thought about the good and bad times that had happened to me at this time of the year. My life had many tragedies, but it was exceptional too, and I wouldn't trade it for anything.

I remembered meeting my longtime friends for the first time on the train, the sorrow and loss of many of them, and the loss of a city. But as the city was rebuilt, so were the memories in my mind of each of my loved ones. Life did go on, and I made it.

I also had my letter from Samuel Clemens that I'd cherished all of these years. I had read about his sorrows of losing his wife and all of his children, except one. His family was his life, not his writings. I knew his brother Orion had died the year after we met. I was sad when I learned of Samuel's death on April 21, 1910. He was a man of unbelievable knowledge and his passing was a lost to all humankind. I was disappointed that I wasn't able to travel to Connecticut and meet his family.

I thought about the first part of the letter that he gave me. *Keep your faithfulness for life no matter what tragedies life sends swirling at you.*

I flipped to the beginning of my journal and read what Poppa had told me when momma and Jonathon had died. "Miranda, life is full of things we don't have a say in. God has a purpose for you." Poppa was correct, God did, and I have met many people that have touched my life.

Marion's been gone for many years, but before she died, she sent me the letters that I had mailed to her. The letters told of my happiness and sorrow. I'd always remember the great joys of my life and would treasure the envelopes postmarked from across this great country.

A knocking at my door brought me back from my thoughts. When I opened the door, standing in front of me was a delivery boy holding a long white flower box. I took the box and closed the door. I held it in my arms and my hands carefully opened the lid. Lying in a bed of white crinkled paper were two entwined long, stemmed, beautiful pink roses. My heart raced. Lying on top of the flowers was my necklace that I'd lost in the earthquake. My fingers lifted the locket and opened it. I couldn't breathe. Inside was the same picture of Vaughn and me taken so many years ago.

I held the necklace and the flowers close as tears began to fall. Two entwined roses meant would you marry me? This could only be from one person.

I raced to the door and swung it open. Standing in front of me was a man with wavy gray hair, the bluest eyes, and the warmest grin, holding one light pink rose.

Emily Grace closed Miranda's journal, bringing it to her chest. Silent tears dropped on the book as she lifted the golden pendant from the jewelry box that was sitting on the bureau.

She left the bedroom, made her way slowly down the long staircase and opened the front door letting it swing wide. She didn't move as her fingers caressed the necklace with the picture of Miranda and Vaughn inside, the other symbol of an everlasting love. A soft sweet breeze touched her face. She smiled as she shut the door.

She walked into the yard and carefully picked one red and one pink rose from the flowerbed full of weeds. With one final look at the home, Emily Grace softly whispered, "Goodbye, Miranda."

About the Author

Diann Shaddox is a Native American Indian and a member of the Wyandotte Nation of Oklahoma and she has Essential Tremors. She's the author of *A Faded Cottage,* a SC love story about a man with Essential Tremors, a Mom's Choice Honoree; *Whispering Fog* a time travel romance; and *Miranda,* a love story, a journal of a young girl living in the late 1800's.

Diann Shaddox is the Founder of Diann Shaddox Foundation for Essential Tremor, a Non-Profit 501c(3) public organization committed to help people struggling with Essential Tremor.

Diann was born on December 18th in a small southern town of Nashville, Arkansas, the youngest and only daughter of William and Mary Ann Shaddox. But, fate stepped in and William, a crop-duster, at the age of 25, died in a plane crash on November 20th, a month before she was born, therefore, Diann was never able to meet her father. Mary Ann, who grew up in Miami, Oklahoma, moved back to Miami after William's death, where Diann lived until her mother died when she was only 3 years old. Diann then moved to Nashville, Arkansas to live with her grandparents. At the age of 10, Diann's Granddad Holt died of a stroke, leaving her grandmother alone to see to her.

Diann learned from an early age about death and how life should not be squandered. Her Mamow Holt, who had lost her right hand in an accident at a factory in Nashville, Arkansas, taught her, you never give up. Her grandmother never let anything stand in her way. She taught herself to write, cook, and even how to sew and make quilts with her left hand, without any prosthetics. Being handicapped was a word she never used.

Growing up in a small town was wonderful, learning to fish, growing a garden and the most important thing, patience of a grandmother. Stories from the past evolved of family bringing many stories to life. Sitting out late at night on cool summer evenings, swinging on an old swing staring up at the stars helped Diann's vivid imagination grow.

On May 20, 2014, Diann's son Richard died of a brain tumor.

She has an enthusiasm for travel and living life to its fullest. You have only one life and shouldn't waste it. The zest for meeting and getting to know people is a very important component in her life. She is a believer of herbs, natural and organic foods, and a big supporter of Bio-identical Hormones and keeping our planet green.

Diann has lived in eight great states, Arkansas, Oklahoma, Kentucky, New Jersey, Virginia, Texas, and Florida. South Carolina is now her home with her husband, Randy, her greatest supporter. www. diannshaddox.com

Diann Shaddox Foundation for Essential Tremor

The Diann Shaddox Foundation for Essential Tremor is a Non-Profit 501 c(3) public organization committed to find a cause and cure for Essential Tremor, the largest and most common movement disorder. Diann Shaddox Foundation is dedicated to educate and increase awareness to the world about people living every day with Essential Tremor and to donate research grants to doctors to find a cure.

Essential Tremor (ET) is the largest movement disorder and is a progressive neurological condition that causes a rhythmic trembling of the hands, head, voice, legs, or body. About 10 million Americans have Essential Tremor, including children and babies, and millions more people worldwide. That's about 5% of all people in the United States. For comparison sake, 7.8% of the population have some type of diabetes. Most people though haven't heard about Essential Tremor and Diann Shaddox Foundation is adamant to bring attention to the world.

Quality of life is a big issue for people with Neurological conditions. Daily activities such as feeding, drinking, grooming and writing become difficult if not impossible. Many people with movement disorders are too embarrassed to go into public and depression sets in. Children and teens are bullied and teased in school. With awareness, people with Essential Tremor can come out of hiding; live normal lives as anyone with a disability. Diann Shaddox Foundation is working with people of all ages, all genders, all ethnic groups, and all movement disorders.

Please join Diann Shaddox Foundation to make a difference for millions of people around the world with Essential Tremor and donate. Diann Shaddox Foundation for Essential Tremor.

www.diannshaddoxfoundation.org

Essential Tremor

Also known as Familial Tremor or Hereditary Tremor, Essential Tremor (ET) is a progressive neurological condition that causes a rhythmic trembling of the hands, head, voice, legs, or body. It is often confused with Parkinson's disease and Dystonia.

An estimated 10 million Americans have Essential Tremor, the largest movement disorder. People with Essential Tremor are often stereotyped as being nervous, withdrawn, anxious, and elderly. Essential Tremor is not confined to the elderly. Children and middle-aged people can also have Essential Tremor. In fact, newborns have been diagnosed with the condition.

There is evidence that Essential Tremor is genetic. Each child of a parent who has Essential Tremor have a 50% chance of inheriting a gene that causes the condition. However, sometimes people with no family history of tremors develop Essential Tremor. Many people who have Essential Tremor become disabled at worst and feel frustrated or embarrassed at best.

Quality of life is a big issue for people with Essential Tremor. Daily activities such as feeding, drinking, grooming and writing become difficult if not impossible. Many people with Essential Tremor are too embarrassed to go into public and so remain isolated in their homes. Stereotypes shape the way we think about people and situations.

With awareness, people with Essential Tremor can come out of hiding; live normal lives as anyone with a disability.

For more information on Essential Tremor (ET), please visit the Diann Shaddox Foundation.

www.diannshaddoxfoundation.org

Kim Poovey

K im Poovey is an author, storyteller, and living historian. Having travelled the Southeast for more than 18 years, she performs in period attire as noted historic characters such as Jane Austen and Scarlett O'Hara as well as the main character from her novel, *Truer Words*. In addition, Kim presents on period fashion, mourning practices, and other Victorian era topics.

In 2011 she portrayed Mrs. Stanton, wife of Secretary of War Stanton (Kevin Kline), in the Robert Redford film, *The Conspirator*. Additional film projects include portraying the wife of a villainous husband in the Book version of Jude Devereaux' novella "Promises" and the Fireball Run fundraising series 2012 *Southern Excursion* at Frampton Plantation.

Her novel, *Truer Words*, was published and released by Tate Publishing in May 2012. This work of historic fiction transports the reader to the Victorian era on a wealthy plantation in the Lowcountry of SC. Readers experience the joys, sorrows, and civil war experience of Emma Victoria Brown as she faces the daily challenges of 19th century life as well as a dangerous family secret.

When not writing or performing, Kim works as a school psychologist. She lives in Beaufort with her husband Darryl, three dogs, and a cat.